PRAISE FOR *THE L*

BEAUT

"*The Last Bathing Beauty* is a pitch-perfect summer read, starring Betty 'Boop' Stern, a plucky heroine with a tackle box full of secrets and enough regret for a lifetime. Using dual timelines, Nathan expertly unravels the events that derailed Betty's sparkling future in 1951 and continue to haunt her even as an eighty-four-year-old woman. Full of characters that shine and told with compassion and humor, this is women's fiction at its best."

—Sonja Yoerg, *Washington Post* bestselling author of *True Places*

"Amy Sue Nathan is a true storyteller, and *The Last Bathing Beauty* is her best book. It's an epic tale of family, secrets, loss, marriage, betrayal, friendships, laughter, and regrets."

—Cathy Lamb, author of *Julia's Chocolates* and *All About Evie*

"*The Last Bathing Beauty* is a gorgeous story about how life doesn't always work out the way we want it to, but if we're willing, we can still make it a great life. This book ripped at my heart in the best possible way, and I won't forget it. Told across three generations of smart, determined, compassionate women, *The Last Bathing Beauty* is the loveliest of stories about the sacrifices and triumphs that come from being a daughter, wife, mother, and friend."

—Juliet McDaniel, author of *Mr. & Mrs. American Pie*

"For those who believe in happily ever after, Amy Sue Nathan's *The Last Bathing Beauty* is a real winner. She has spun a heartfelt tale about romance, heartbreaks, friendship, and the wisdom that comes from living a life with no regrets. Told with tenderness and humor, readers will love this journey back in time with Boop and the girls."

—Renée Rosen, bestselling author of *Park Avenue Summer*

"In this reimagining of *Dirty Dancing*, Nathan demonstrates expert storytelling when we meet the charismatic Betty 'Boop' Stern as a young woman, and also as an eighty-four-year-old as she looks back on a difficult choice that altered the path of her glittering future. Told with empathy and lyrical prose, *The Last Bathing Beauty* is a winning tale of friendship, regret, and second chances with a ring of endearing and spirited women at its heart."

—Heather Webb, *USA Today* bestselling coauthor of
Meet Me in Monaco

"A thoroughly enjoyable, past-and-present tale of a life-changing summer and its echoes decades later. This story has it all—great characters, sensory-rich settings, and a sweet salute to believing in second chances. The finale will have you cheering."

—Susan Meissner, bestselling author of *The Last Year of the War*

"*The Last Bathing Beauty* is an emotionally gripping story that captivated me from page one. Amy Sue Nathan knows how to thread the past and present together in a way that readers won't soon forget. A moving tale about second chances and the fathomless depths of true love."

—Tina Ann Forkner, author of *Waking Up Joy*

the LAST BATHING BEAUTY

ALSO BY AMY SUE NATHAN

The Good Neighbor
Left to Chance
The Glass Wives

the LAST
BATHING
BEAUTY

AMY SUE NATHAN

Published by Lake Union Publishing, Seattle

www.apub.com

Amazon, the Amazon logo, and Lake Union Publishing are trademarks of Amazon.com, Inc., or its affiliates.

ISBN-13: 9781542007092
ISBN-10: 1542007097

Cover design by Faceout Studio, Lindy Martin

Printed in the United States of America

Dedicated to
Elaine Bookbinder
and
Charlene Klein

It is *not* the Atlantic City of the west, as has been erroneously stated by ambitious writers. There is no comparison and probably never will be. It is simply the same old South Haven that has charmed so many thousands in the past and hopes to charm as many thousands in the future. Do not come to South Haven with the idea of finding a Coney Island or an Atlantic City, for you will be disappointed. If you are looking for an ideal place to spend a week, a month or a year in a rational sane way then come to South Haven and you will find it.

Picturesque Michigan, pamphlet, 1913, author unknown

SOUTH HAVEN, MICHIGAN

PROLOGUE

BETTY

September 1951

Any other bride might have gazed into the mirror, stepped away, and then glanced back over her shoulder for another peek. Not Betty. She hadn't looked at herself once today, and in fact she'd avoided her reflection all week. She knew the person looking back from the mirror would not be her. Betty Claire Stern no longer existed. She wanted to say *she died*, but Betty was mindful of her reputation for melodrama.

Perched gingerly on the window seat with a layer of crinoline crunching beneath her thighs, Betty studied her bedroom. Pink and floral, it had been perfect for growing up, for playing with her friends, and for private times. Her slice of North Beach and Lake Michigan was also perfect. She turned, glanced out the window to the west, and sighed.

As of tomorrow, Lake Michigan would be to her east, and her bedroom—one she had never seen, but that likely wouldn't have pink posies—wouldn't boast a view of anything besides a patch of grass or a front stoop. Betty was moving from Michigan to Illinois, from South Haven on the lake to Skokie in the suburbs.

It wasn't really that far. Just a few hours' drive.

Would she have a car?

Betty lifted the curl cluster at the nape of her neck with one hand and fanned herself with the other. She inhaled through her nose, puckered her lips, and exhaled so hard it sounded more like the wind than the sigh she'd intended. Perspiration gathered on her brow. If she blotted or wiped, the pancake makeup would lift, so she leaned toward the sill and a light breeze brushed over her face, refreshing her as it dried the dampness. The air chilled Betty's skin, giving her a cold forehead to go along with her cold feet.

Pre-wedding jitters, that's all it was. According to *Ladies' Home Journal*, it was normal. And hadn't Betty longed for normalcy?

Nerves were not the same as doubt.

A man strolled at the lake's edge; his shirt hung loose over his shorts; his arms swung wide. Betty's heart pattered for a hopeful second, and then regained its steady beat. There would be no unexpected visitor today. No impromptu drive, hike, or ice-cream cone. The day had been perfectly planned from her dress to the guests, flowers, and food. She needed to stop daydreaming about what-ifs. The fellow on the beach seemed capricious—without a care, a schedule, or a mandate. He was likely looking for dropped coins. No, he was probably collecting bits of beach glass for his sweetheart, the way visitors had done all summer.

Her whole life had included treasures for the taking right outside her door. Sometimes she'd grabbed them. Sometimes she'd overlooked them. But they'd been within reach. Betty flinched, about to abandon her room in search of riches, forgetting, for one sliver of a moment, that she was getting married today.

That beach glass might as well have been on the moon.

Turning away from the window, Betty pressed her hands against her thumping chest. No matter where she lived or traveled, South Haven would always be home to her heart. She had always counted sunsets as a way to mark time, tracked the migration of birds and the level of rain. She'd peeled carrots in the kitchen of her family's resort at age eight and learned to use the rotary iron when she was twelve.

Betty was accustomed to the unconventional calendar, composed only of summer and the off-season. She had always loved how, from Memorial Day until Labor Day, the town's population swelled from six thousand to thirty thousand. Summer transformed her unassuming lakeside town into the "Catskills of the Midwest." She was proud when that slogan was printed in big sunny yellow letters on the brochure for Stern's Summer Resort, "the premier family destination in South Haven." But she also loved the off-season—the serenity of autumn and the isolation of winter—when she had her grandparents' full attention. The peculiarities of South Haven were as much a part of her as her blue eyes.

Betty scanned the sparse pearls Nannie had sewn onto the tulle overlay on her tea-length wedding dress. They caught the sunlight and glinted, just like the sand. Her dress was perfectly fitted and flattering. Still, this wasn't what her grandparents had had in mind for their only granddaughter.

No matter, Nannie had ordered the finest material from a friend in Chicago who was a dressmaker, and then in record time had created the dress without a pattern. Had Betty been afforded the luxury of time or circumstance, it was the dress she would have chosen. She could almost picture herself poring over the latest bridal fashion magazines with Georgia and Doris, and then pointing to this very dress as "the one." She'd already decided that would be the wedding dress story she would tell.

The real story was that for three weeks Nannie had done little more than sew and bead, neglecting her duties at the resort until the end of the summer. And with pins between her teeth, she'd mumbled through it all in a mix of Yiddish and English about her troubles, her *tsuris*.

Betty had told her not to go to the trouble of making a dress. She'd buy a pretty one at Lemon's department store. But Nannie wouldn't have her granddaughter married in a *shmata* off a rack. What would people say?

Betty traced her hips with her hands and felt how her body curved like an hourglass beneath the gathered, full skirt that ended just below her knees. The dress was long enough to be modest but short enough to show off her calves, muscular from a summer of leading calisthenics, carrying piles of laundry, and dancing with her friends on the beach after dark. She clamped her lips at other thoughts and swept them from her mind like cake crumbs. She touched the neckline that scooped just below the gold locket at her throat, a present from her grandfather and a quiet gesture of hope for her future "to shine like this," he'd said. Betty knew the gift was due to relief, but pragmatic Zaide would never say anything negative and tempt fate any more than Betty already had. She considered whether the locket could be her "something new."

"Knock, knock." The door opened and Georgia entered as if walking onstage for a one-woman show. Her hair had been curled and teased into a fashionable bouffant—something Georgia loathed. Betty loved a good bouffant, and she'd never forget this effort of fashion and friendship.

"I can't believe you're here," Betty said.

"Wild horses couldn't keep me away." She shrugged. "Plus, it's Sunday. No classes. I came up yesterday and got this." Georgia spun once and stopped, like a weary jewelry-box ballerina.

Her dress was a sophisticated, sleeveless, corn-on-the-cob-yellow sheath that skimmed her curves and stopped just below her knees. The color accentuated her gold and copper hair and highlighted the amber flecks in her green eyes. Even Georgia's freckles seemed to sparkle atop her nose. That the dress was more meant for summer than fall didn't matter. She could have worn a romper or her tennis whites, Betty wouldn't have cared.

"You look beautiful. You're not supposed to show up the bride, you know."

"Oh, Betty, don't be ridiculous! You're beyond stunning." Georgia grabbed Betty's hand and twirled her around like a dance partner until Betty stopped. "You're going to have a wonderful life. I know it," Georgia said. "Doris thinks so too, and she knows these things. She's beside herself that she couldn't get the day off."

Betty coughed, and then burst into tears. Her throat felt as if she had swallowed sand, and she imagined her mascara dripping and scattering like polka dots onto the dress. She tapped at the tears with her fingers, but then Georgia reached into her ivory satin clutch and handed Betty a folded handkerchief. Betty dabbed beneath her eyes, and then Georgia yanked her to sit on one of the matching twin beds they'd used for sleepovers. "You'll see Doris soon; you won't be far from her at all once you're in Skokie."

Betty shook her head.

"That's not why you're upset, is it?" Georgia reached her arm around Betty's shoulder. "You're going to be fine. You made the right decision."

"Did I?" Betty gasped. "Maybe it's not too late for me to go to college. I could say there's been a change of plans, defer my admission. Do you think they'd still take me? I could go forward with my original plan." Or at least a version of her original plan.

"Is that really what you want? Guests are starting to arrive."

Even Georgia didn't want to hear her misgivings. Betty kept her truths inside, where they disquieted only her. She fiddled with the one-carat-diamond engagement ring, not yet accustomed to its weight on her finger, or the intensity with which it sparkled.

Footsteps echoed down the hall. Nannie stepped into the doorframe. Four feet eleven never looked so tall.

Georgia stood and blew Betty a kiss.

The doorbell rang.

"Everyone should be going around back to the patio. It was right on the invitations," Nannie said. "Georgia, would you answer the door and redirect the guests? I know it's only a dozen or so, but I don't want everyone traipsing through the house."

"Of course, Mrs. Stern." She leaned down to Betty's ear. "You'll be fine. Better than fine. You always are."

The closeness should have comforted her, but her best friend's confidence was unsettling. "Fine," Betty realized, was subjective. Georgia sauntered away in her ivory satin slingbacks, her calf muscles still defined from a summer of tennis. She left the door open.

"Let me see you." Nannie waved her hands so that Betty would stand. "Turn around."

Betty didn't turn. Instead she stood tall, with her back straight and her shoulders square. Her three-inch satin pumps meant she towered over Nannie, and it was Betty's only advantage, even if imagined.

Nannie would have none of Betty's resistance. Dressed in a royal-blue dress she'd made herself, along with a matching felt pillbox hat that had small white feathers on one side—the same ensemble she'd worn for Betty's high school graduation back in May—Nannie tugged her in a swift but gentle motion away from the window, in front of the oval gilded mirror that hung above the dresser. Betty, Georgia, and Doris had always pretended it was the magical mirror from *Snow White*, even when they were too short to see into it.

"You're beautiful." Nannie sighed as she smoothed the front of Betty's hair, which was unnecessary considering the can of Aqua Net that had already been sprayed on it. But the soft touch of her grandmother's hands forced Betty to close her eyes and wish that when she opened them it would be June again, when she could relive the summer. A silly thought, a girlish whim really, but one more couldn't hurt.

Nannie withdrew a small red ribbon from her pocket, tied it into a bow no bigger than the tip of her little finger, and then pulled a straight pin out of her hat. In one quick motion she pushed aside the neckline of Betty's wedding dress and pinned the red ribbon to her brassiere strap.

"I don't think you need to protect me from the evil eye," Betty said.

"*Kinehora, kinehora,* poo-poo-poo." Nannie sputtered the Yiddish words and spit the sounds that would ward off evil spirits coming to siphon Betty's good fortune. "You know if you think things are going well and we forget to say 'kinehora' then something bad will happen."

"I know."

"Every bride wears a red ribbon. This way you look imperfect to the evil spirits. It's extra protection."

"Nannie . . ."

"All people will see today is a beautiful girl in a beautiful dress marrying a handsome boy."

Betty rolled her eyes.

"Fine, he's not so handsome. But handsome isn't always so good."

Betty turned away, the summer nipping at her heels, urging her to run. "I'm not so sure about this anymore."

"I'll tell you a secret. I had the jitters before I married Zaide."

"No!"

"Yes. I was moving away from my parents. From everything I knew. Marriage is a whole new way of living, and I had no idea if I'd be any good at it. Or if I'd like it," she whispered. "But if you tell Zaide, I'll deny it."

Betty smiled, the lump in her throat receding.

"The jitters will go away, and you'll have a husband you can build a life with." Nannie placed her index finger beneath Betty's chin. "You are a very lucky girl." She cleared her throat, and her low, firm voice cleared as well. "And do you know what else?"

"What?"

"He's lucky too."

Betty swallowed, blinking as fast as a hummingbird flaps its wings. But even with Nannie's hand on her arm, and her grandmother's attempt to soothe her, the distance between them had already grown to miles.

Nannie affixed Betty's cap-style headpiece and pushed bobby pins against Betty's scalp. The veil skimmed the back of her shoulders. "There. All finished. Now, look in the mirror." She prodded Betty toward the rest of her life.

"You're getting married. For heaven's sake, smile."

Betty did as she was told.

Chapter 1

BOOP

Summer 2017

Boop Peck had looked everywhere for her favorite lipstick. It wasn't in the bathroom, or in her purse, bedroom, or pocket. She shuddered at the injustice: Boop remembered her first telephone number—359J—but not the whereabouts of the lipstick she'd worn the day before. Or was it the day before that? She peeked around and patted herself again. Nothing. A lost lipstick wasn't the end of the world. Unless it was Sly Pink, her discontinued color of choice, which it was.

Enough with the lipstick.

The girls would arrive soon. No, the *ladies* would arrive soon. Boop chuckled. *Ladies* sounded stuffy, boring, and inaccurate. Even at eighty-four, Boop and her friends would always be girls—and they'd never be boring.

In the bathroom mirror, her reflection was framed by the floral shower curtain behind her. The hair she'd allowed to go white under the watchful eye and skillful hand of her Chicago hairdresser had lost most of its bounce but retained a bit of its wave. A year earlier she'd had it cut into a chin-length bob. She tucked it behind her ears. Boop looked nothing like the girl who grew up here, back when everyone still called her Betty. Back when she *was* Betty.

Boop turned her head from side to side. In the old days her hair would have brushed against her cheeks. Marvin wouldn't have liked this 'do, but he'd never minded the lines on her forehead or the ones on her cheeks where the rouge liked to settle.

She'd been a widow for three years now; would she ever stop wondering what Marvin would think of her?

Boop believed her stylishness was like wine and had improved with age. Over the years she had taken bohemian *bubbe* and mixed it with beach chic. When her granddaughters Hannah and Emma were teenagers, they'd dubbed her flair "Boop-tastic."

The woman before her had panache.

When the girls arrived, she'd also have purpose.

Boop dressed in a soft yellow rayon shift with bracelet-length sleeves and decorated her wrists with silver bangles. Then something unlatched in her brain—maybe the tinkling of the metal jewelry had an effect on her memory—and the location of Sly Pink tumbled forward, as if it'd been awaiting an invitation. Boop's lipstick rested in her grandmother's small white Lenox bowl among pennies.

Downstairs by the front window with lipstick applied, Boop tugged down her sleeves to guard against the late-May chill. She bobbed her head in time to watch the day's flock of gulls resting on the shimmering surface of Lake Michigan. *My lake.* It looked like someone had called a meeting to order. Did the birds grow bored or did they know that the summer people would arrive with Memorial Day weekend, and with them an abundance of crusts and crumbs?

Boop rubbed her hands together, which didn't work to warm them. There was a time she would have ignored the chill and slipped out of her sweater, allowing it to puddle on the floor behind her as she pushed through the door, which she'd let swing and slam even though she hadn't been raised in a barn. She'd have abandoned her shoes, if she'd been wearing any, and then run onto the beach, kicking sand so high it would have landed in her hair.

Boop couldn't recall the last time she'd walked on the beach, let alone kicked up anything, and that had nothing to do with her memory. Canes were a bitch in the sand.

The shrill of Boop's landline reverberated from the kitchen. By the time she reached the only receiver, where it had been attached to the wall since the 1960s, it had stopped ringing. They'd call back.

She sat at the kitchen table, then looked at her watch. The bedrooms were prepared with fresh linens, new towels, and bunches of dried lavender tied with purple ribbon. She'd raised the windows so the breeze would refresh anything she'd missed. Still, there was no time for lollygagging. She figured she had fifteen or twenty minutes before the girls arrived, just enough time to brew a pot of decaf and set out a late-afternoon snack. Boop filled a vase with daisies, Doris's favorite flower, and broke out the embroidered cloth napkins she usually saved for holidays, as this was as close to a celebration as she'd felt like having in a long time. She'd defrosted some blueberry muffins and set out the chocolate bridge mix that Georgia loved.

Then the front door squeaked, and Boop gathered her thoughts as she left the half-readied feast and hurried to greet her friends, glad they'd coordinated flights and would arrive together for a double homecoming. Boop's pulse quickened with girlish giddiness. What would they do first? Eat? Chat? Unpack? All of the above! Years had passed since it had been the three of them in South Haven—alone together, which meant not alone at all.

"I'm coming," Boop called. "You're early!"

"Boop?"

That was not Georgia's voice. Or Doris's.

After having only seconds to revise her expectations, Boop watched her granddaughter Hannah walk through the living room. She held a gray duffel bag in one hand, and in the other a bouquet of purple alstroemeria in a plastic sleeve. A smile tugged at Boop's lips. She loved purple flowers and Hannah knew it.

But with Hannah here—a duffel bag didn't signal a quick visit—all plans would change. Boop couldn't ask Hannah to leave. She'd adapt. That's what she'd always done.

"Hey!" Hannah hugged her with the force of undeniable love. Boop wrapped her arms around her granddaughter, and Hannah laid her head on Boop's shoulder and sank in. Tears welled in Boop's eyes. She hadn't seen Hannah in a month or two. This was what she missed—regular hugs. The realization closed in around her with a hug of its own.

"This *is* a surprise, right?" Boop said. "I didn't know you were coming, did I?"

"No, I wanted to surprise you. I hope that's okay."

Hannah stepped back. Her jeans hung low on her hips, and the fly was unbuttoned in an intentional way. The knees of her pants were torn, a fashion trend Boop tried to neither understand nor emulate. Hannah's hair draped over one shoulder as if in a side ponytail without the rubber band. Not a stitch of makeup on the girl's face, yet she was beautiful—big brown eyes, flawless skin.

Hannah rested her arm over Boop's shoulder and guided her through the house to sit at the kitchen table. Then Hannah opened the correct cabinet for a vase, filled it with water, and arranged the blooms. She set it on the table and sat across from Boop, leaned on her elbows, and smiled.

How Boop loved this girl, all grown-up at twenty-six, yet with her whole life still ahead of her—a life that she was mapping out for herself as a high school English teacher, with a master's degree, no less. Maybe she'd go on to get a PhD. Maybe she'd write a book. Or a screenplay. For her, limitations were nonexistent.

Her youngest granddaughter had always been Boop's sidekick, content to watch the lake and count the colors in the sky at dusk, while her sister, Emma, wanted to be swimming in the lake and hadn't the same notion of sunsets. Sometimes Boop wished Hannah were less like her. Less reflective. More carefree.

Hannah drummed her hands on the table. "Why haven't you been answering your phone? Dad said his calls went to voicemail two nights in a row."

"Oh, that. I was busy. Your other bubbes will be here soon." Hannah and Emma had spent summers in South Haven with Georgia and Doris as their intermittent bonus Jewish grandmothers.

"I know, and I can't wait to see them, but can we talk about you not answering the phone? That's why you have a cell phone. So we can reach you. Make sure you're okay. He worries about you. So do I."

"Oh, Hannahleh, you're sweet. Do you want a muffin or some chocolate? I was just setting out a snack."

Hannah shook her head. "Boop, are you listening to me? You have to answer your phone."

"Yes, yes. I was busy, that's all."

She didn't want to worry Hannah, who called regularly and lived just fifty minutes away in Kalamazoo, close enough for a short visit and far enough to maintain her privacy—not that Boop was dropping in on her and her boyfriend, Clark, the "artist."

Emma, two years older than Hannah, lived in Highland Park, Illinois, with her husband, Grant, and their three-year-old twins, Oliver and Holden. Emma didn't call on a schedule, but she did call every week or so. Boop was proud and at peace with her presence in her granddaughters' lives.

She and Hannah settled onto the ticking striped couch in the living room. Boop sat at one end with her feet on the floor, and Hannah rested at the other end, her legs stretched out across the cushions and her now-bare feet resting on Boop's lap. The arrangement reminded Boop of when her granddaughters were little girls, when a tickle and a kiss cured all ills, when her own troubles were of no consequence to them. But Hannah was an adult now.

"Your dad thinks I should move to San Diego," Boop said. "I wanted to tell you myself. That's why the girls are finally coming. It's our last chance to be here together."

Hannah lurched forward, grabbing her shins. "You can't move away."

Boop patted Hannah's legs, and she eased herself back upright. "We can still talk on the phone. And your visits to California will be twofers with me *and* your dad there."

"I didn't mean you can't. I guess I mean—why would you? You always said you'd leave this house—"

"Feet first," Boop said. "I know."

"You grew up here. You married Pop here. We spent summers here with you two and Dad. What will I do if you're not here? Don't do it, Boop. Please stay! Some of my best memories are in this house, and I don't want that to end." Hannah's voice quivered. The tears were next.

Boop's heart thumped. This was out of character. Something was wrong. "I know, dear," Boop whispered in a singsong manner, and rocked side to side. She hoped her tone and demeanor would ease Hannah's worries, whatever they were. "I love that you love it here, I do. But it's a big old house, and it's only me most of the time. I'm not getting any younger. Don't you dare tell Georgia I said that. And no matter where I go, South Haven will still be here; it's not like you can't come back."

Hannah smiled, her lips together, so it wasn't a real smile. It was an okay-whatever-you-say smile. "It wouldn't be the same without you. To me and Emma, you *are* South Haven."

Boop understood. The wonder of South Haven was more than the colors of the sunsets and the silkiness of the sand, the blueberry farms, or even the lighthouse—though Boop wouldn't trade those away. When she had been a girl growing up in the shadow of her family's business, Stern's Summer Resort, or a young mother bringing Stuart here for summers, or a grandmother doting on Emma and Hannah, the people here had been her family. Her friends, the resort guests, the neighbors. They were part of her life, and she theirs. But times had changed. People her age had died or moved to assisted living. Homeowners rented out their houses now. Her neighbors weren't her neighbors for more than a week. In the resort days, families stayed for two to four weeks and returned every summer.

Stern's Summer Resort had been lavish in a welcoming way— *hamish* yet elegant. Offering guests a cozy and sophisticated escape had been Yetta and Ira Stern's trademark—along with the abundance of food. The closest Boop had ever come to experiencing the same gourmet gluttony of her grandparents' resort was on her and Marvin's one Caribbean cruise vacation.

But this house had always been her true home, even though resort guests had believed that Betty and her grandparents lived in the main house of the resort, despite it having no bedrooms. With the resort's grandiose dining and activity rooms, in addition to the massive kosher kitchen that housed two of everything—one for milk, one for meat— where would they have slept? Boop smiled at the magnificent innocence of that era, when even the adults believed teachers lived at school. Nannie and Zaide needed to escape at the end of summer days that lasted from before breakfast until after dinner. And that's where home came in. It had been their safe haven from the staff's requests and the guests' demands, at least for the hours they slept.

For Boop, "home" had served as a respite from the public life of being the Stern granddaughter, and later from the private pressures of marriage and motherhood. And it had always been the gathering place for her friends.

It was moments like this when Boop agreed with Hannah. How could she leave? But she knew the bigger question was, How could she stay? The house had more bedrooms than they'd ever needed and a hardwood staircase. The winters were long and frozen. Stuart lived in California, Georgia in Florida, Doris in Arizona. Boop had moved back to South Haven from Skokie after Marvin died. She had thought the house and the surroundings would be enough to sustain her, but she'd been wrong.

Hannah sniffled, and tears dripped down her cheeks.

No one loved South Haven more than Boop, and it seemed like this was a bit of an overreaction from Hannah. It wasn't like Boop was leaving tomorrow. They'd have this one last summer.

"What's really wrong?" Boop asked.

Outside, a horn beeped twice. Then a third time.

"That must be the girls," Boop said. "We'll talk later?"

"Of course." Hannah stood. "Go! I'll be right out."

"Are you sure?"

Hannah nodded, and then Boop stood, steadied herself, and walked outside onto the porch as Doris and Georgia were shutting the back doors of their cab and retrieving their suitcases from the driver. He shooed them away and carried their bags to the porch.

Doris waved both hands over her head. "Yoo-hoo!"

Even from a distance, Boop could see Doris's natural silver hair was tinted lavender—more like the color left behind after attempting to wash a blueberry stain from a white tablecloth than the vibrant shades she'd favored as a younger woman. Her makeup was light, as she had never needed much more than a little pink lipstick to accentuate her turquoise eyes that had not faded or changed over the years. Her petite frame, though, had softened as the result of natural padding. She walked up the three steps to the porch. In that moment Boop imagined the short sandy-haired, curvier version of the woman with an undetectable waistline who stepped toward her, smiling wide.

Doris had married Saul recently—her fifth husband after two divorces and two funerals. That much loss was unimaginable, as was Doris's romantic resilience. Her motto? You're never too old to find love and throw a good party. What skin was it off Boop's nose? Doris should live and be well.

Georgia walked around the cab from the passenger's side. She strode toward the house, regal with her still-auburn hair skimming her shoulders against her white linen blazer. She had neither a slouch nor a stoop belying her five feet, nine inches. Her face appeared a smidgen slimmer than last November, when Boop had visited Boca Raton, likely the result of all that tennis and early-bird kale salad. She placed one hand on her head as if holding down a wig—though it wasn't a wig at all. She turned toward the beach and tipped back her head before pivoting around to Boop, her arms wide. "We're back!"

Boop met the girls in the center of the porch, a lump lodged at the base of her throat. She had so much to say yet couldn't speak. She grasped Georgia's left hand and Doris's right, and then they clasped hands as well. Georgia and Doris squeezed her hands, their touch familiar and restorative. Boop gripped their hands more tightly in return as the lake breeze seemed to swirl around the trio like a playful older brother, mussing their hair and scattering sand on their feet. It had missed having them here together.

Maybe Hannah was just missing South Haven—and missing Boop—before she needed to. But that wouldn't explain the duffel bag.

With her attention back on the girls, thoughts of Hannah faded, and Boop smiled. Then her heart stirred up the perfect words: "Welcome home."

Chapter 2

BOOP

"Can an outsider break into this circle?"

Hannah's voice reminded Boop of her worry about her granddaughter, and Doris and Georgia flinched. It seemed none of them had heard her step outside. Nostalgia was like that—blocking the present the way a cloud blocked the sun.

Doris pulled her hands away from Georgia and Boop, and held out her arms. "Hannah! We didn't know you were here!" She turned to Georgia. "Did you know?" Georgia shook her head, and Doris nodded once and returned her gaze to Hannah. Then she hugged her as only a bonus bubbe could. "You look wonderful."

Hannah's eyes were red and swollen from crying, but through Doris's bubbe lens—and Boop's—she still looked lovely.

"How long has it been? How long are you staying?" Georgia asked.

Boop hadn't thought to ask. Her granddaughter rarely stayed more than one night, but it was a big duffel bag. Boop needed to know what troubles were packed inside. Good thing she and the girls were expert listeners and problem solvers.

Hannah pulled back and scurried a few feet to Georgia and kissed her cheek. "It's been years since I've seen both of you. Or the three of you together!"

"It's been years since the three of us have been in South Haven," Boop said.

Georgia removed her sunglasses with a flourish, even though the sun was shining down. "That's why we're here."

Boop pulled open the door, and Hannah grabbed the suitcases and followed everyone inside.

They all walked to the kitchen and sat at the Formica table, the refurbished one that had belonged to Boop's grandparents. Years back, Hannah had told her that old was new. She'd called it retro.

Sitting there, Boop could almost taste Nannie's blueberry doughnuts and hear Doris and Georgia shouting, "Go fish!" She'd played checkers with Stuart at this table, and one summer served grilled cheese with the crusts cut off every evening for dinner. Tea parties with Hannah and Emma were some of her fondest memories. Having two granddaughters around had felt like hitting the family jackpot, and their dress-up clothes and dolls had sparked Boop's girlie-girlishness.

"You must be starving." Boop rose from her chair and collected the blueberry muffins and chocolate bridge mix and set it all in the center of the table instead of on elaborate serving platters no one cared about. Georgia opened the box of chocolates and plucked out the chocolate-covered peanuts. She had a lifetime of practice and a sixth sense about this, and always ate the peanuts first. Boop didn't know whether that meant the peanuts were Georgia's most or least favorite.

Doris placed a muffin onto a napkin. "Do you have any—"

Boop raised her index finger, and Doris said nothing more until Boop retrieved the butter and a knife and arranged them in front of her. "Thank you."

Hannah tittered and shook her head. "You knew what Doris wanted and she didn't say anything. That's amazing."

"Not really," Boop said. But she knew it was.

"We know everything about one another," Doris said. "From butter to big things."

"Big things like Boop moving to San Diego?" Hannah asked.

"You finally told her," Georgia said.

"I was just waiting for the right time."

"You didn't know I was coming. If I hadn't shown up, would you have left without telling me?"

"Don't be ridiculous," Boop said.

Georgia raised and lowered her eyebrows. She knew Boop didn't want to talk about leaving South Haven.

"Try to understand," Doris said. "Your grandmother wants a fresh start. We've done it." She motioned to Georgia and then back to herself.

"I'm not leaving until after Labor Day," Boop said. "Hannah, visit as much as you can this summer. We'll talk about this another time— can we change the subject?"

Without missing a beat, the conversation turned to Georgia's tennis game, Doris's most recent Vegas wedding, Hannah's favorite students, and Boop's square-dancing class, each of them filling in details omitted on the phone or too lengthy for email. Even repetition was welcome in person.

Hannah's demeanor softened. No more urgency, no more tears. Instead, laughing and lively conversation. How quickly Boop, the girls, and Hannah had eased into joyful repartee, but sorrow didn't dissolve that quickly. This was a temporary remedy for Hannah, which would do for now. It reminded Boop that what mattered was how much she and the girls cared about one another and how that could be a tonic for any ailment.

Even Dr. Georgia Lemon agreed.

Georgia had always been a little different from Boop and Doris— science- and math-minded, she'd earned her MD in 1959 from Chicago Medical School, the same year Boop had been voted president of the PTA and Doris had followed her first husband, the doctor, to Indianapolis. In addition, Georgia had been the only one of their group who'd never married, and also the only gentile.

Georgia and Boop had become friends because of Nannie, at a time in Boop's life when her grandmother could do no wrong. "A new family bought the big store on Phoenix Street," Nannie had said. "So be nice to the new little *shiksa* in your class, Betty."

Nannie had always used slurs for non-Jews, so as a girl, Betty thought nothing of this descriptor. Now, Boop cringed at the thought of Nannie's easy insult.

Of course, Bitty Betty Stern had done as she was told. Georgia had also been told to be nice to Betty, since her grandparents would order their resort staff's embroidered shirts through the store.

The little girls hadn't cared about that, only that they both liked hopscotch and collecting beach glass.

Boop and Doris had met in kindergarten, as evidenced in a packed-away sepia class photograph. Neither of them remembered a time when they didn't know one another. And then, by extension, Doris and Georgia became friends.

Why had she waited so long to insist the girls come back? Better late than never, she supposed. Still, the passage of time and the subsequent limits on possible future gatherings struck Boop like a cold shower. She swallowed a bite of a blueberry muffin that pushed down regret and kept it inside like a cork. Like Hannah.

Boop's heart and head wouldn't settle until she knew what made Hannah cry. Her own disquiet, her craving for time alone with the girls, would have to wait.

The animated banter around her trickled into Boop's head and heart, scattering her troublesome thoughts like cake crumbs. Unaware of Boop's subconscious wandering, Hannah, Georgia, and Doris chit-chatted about the dry heat of Scottsdale and how Georgia's doubles partners were twenty years younger.

Boop nodded at no one in particular and at all of them, mentally catching up on the conversation and silently swearing to stay alert and involved and to remain rooted in the wonder around her.

At sunset, Boop watched as Hannah sat sideways on the low concrete divider that separated the porch from Lakeshore Drive, the narrow one-way street separating her house from the beach. She faced south. They all faced south.

A crowd gathered at the pier and stood witness as a resplendent wash of marigold and honey crept over the blue-gray dusk. Neither the girls nor Hannah spoke, their collective breathing as deep as a sleeping baby's. Boop flicked on the porch lights, then stepped inside the house, as her well of sunsets was filled for the moment.

Besides clicking on the lamp in the screened porch, she clapped on the light in the TV room. Both would illuminate the porch. She grabbed four cotton throws from the living room and hurried back outside. The sun was gone, and it had taken the May warmth with it.

Boop handed Doris and Georgia their coverlets, and they draped them over their legs. She wrapped a rose-colored throw around Hannah's back and shoulders like a shawl.

Hannah slid off the divider and into a blue Adirondack chair. Boop sat in her old wicker rocker, the caning ripe for repair, worn from many seasons of sunset gazing. She laid her blanket over her. How lucky she was to have a full house and a full heart.

"Can I tell you all something?" Hannah asked.

"Of course you can," Boop said. Hannah had been waiting hours to say whatever was next.

"You have to swear not to tell anyone."

"Who are we going to tell?" Doris asked.

"That's not the point. Do you swear?"

Boop would never betray a confidence, but a prickle traveled down her neck and across her shoulders, her personal three-alarm warning.

"We are the best secret keepers on the planet," Georgia said.

"Troubles are better out than in," Boop said. "You know that." She trembled. *Oh Hannah, what is going on?*

"Clark proposed," Hannah said.

"Clark proposed what?" Boop knew, but she wanted to hear Hannah say it.

"He wants to get married?" Doris clasped her hands with glee. "How wonderful. *Mazel tov*, dear."

Hannah stared at Boop. "I said I'd think about it."

Boop hadn't been shy about her opinion of Clark. He'd gone to law school and now he was a hippie artist or something.

"You didn't say yes?" Doris asked.

"Thank God," Boop and Georgia said in unison.

Hannah was young. Twenty-six. She didn't need to settle down to something so official, so permanent; she should explore the world and her own dreams before committing to marriage.

"Maybe Clark isn't the one," Boop said.

Hannah leaned forward. "Is there such a thing?"

"Absolutely," Doris said.

"How can you say that?" Georgia asked. "You've been married five times."

"And each time he was the one."

"How did you know?" Hannah asked.

"I have a sixth sense," Doris said.

"You're being logical, Hannah," Boop said. "Good for you." She knew deep inside that logic was not the preferred method of handling one's heart. She also knew sometimes it was best. "Doris is a hopeless romantic."

"I am nothing of the kind," Doris said. "I'm a hope*ful* romantic."

Hannah reached out to Boop. "I need your advice." She glanced at Georgia and Doris. "And yours too."

25

"If you have doubts, that speaks volumes," Boop said.

"And maybe not," Georgia said. "Sometimes a leap of faith is warranted."

"A marriage shouldn't be a leap of faith," Boop said.

Georgia opened her eyes wide. "Is that so?"

"I have a list of pros and cons," Hannah said. She tugged a paper out of her back pocket and unfolded it four times.

Boop stood slowly and held out her hand. "May I?" Boop asked. At least she knew now what was bothering Hannah. Yes or no, this was the decision of a lifetime. But it was a choice, and it was Hannah's choice alone.

She handed Boop the paper.

"Why I Should Marry Clark." Boop glanced at her granddaughter. "Catchy title."

"Just read it," Georgia said.

Boop resisted the urge to yell that if you're in love, you don't need a list. If you're in love, you don't run away to your grandmother's house. Boop now knew that Hannah would have shown up that day even if Stuart hadn't tattled about having to leave voicemails.

Hannah had needed South Haven. Hannah had needed Boop.

"'Number one: he's kind to animals. Number two: he's polite to waiters. Number three: he puts the toilet seat down.' Hannah! Is this a joke?"

Hannah grabbed the paper. "No, it's not a joke. These are fundamental character strengths. Well, maybe not the toilet seat, but it's thoughtful." She looked at her list. "He's a talented artist. He likes independent films. He's ambitious."

"I don't think he's ambitious, dear," Boop said.

"Oh right, he quit law school," Doris said.

"No, it's worse," Boop said. "He graduated law school and quit a job at a law firm. That's not very responsible."

"What's he doing now?" Georgia asked.

"He's an artist," Hannah said. "He's following his dream."

"There's nothing wrong with dreaming, but don't think he's going to suddenly work a nine-to-five job and bring home a steady paycheck when he stopped doing that after just a year," Boop said.

"He's very passionate about building his sculptures. And the weekend craft fairs. A friend even commissioned him to build something for his backyard."

Boop wanted her granddaughters to have security—the kind that she'd had with Marvin. But she also wanted them to have undeniable love—the kind where you don't say "maybe" to a proposal.

"Are you in love with him, Hannah?" Doris asked. "I was deeply in love with each of my husbands."

"With all due respect, Doris," Georgia said, "Clark or no Clark, I think you'd agree five marriages is not the goal."

"Of course it's not," Doris said. "But it has been a blessing."

Boop crossed her arms. The choices she made long ago chilled her to the bone. "Are you in love with him, Hannah? Can you imagine yourself with anyone else for the next sixty years?"

"We've been together since freshman year of college. I love him."

"That's not what I asked you."

Hannah folded her hands in her lap, something Boop's grade school teachers would have asked of a class full of rowdy children to quiet them and command attention. Boop mimicked Hannah and set her hands in her lap.

"I'm not denying the value of friendship, or of loyalty, but those aren't good enough reasons to marry someone," Boop said.

"How about this?" Hannah coughed. "I am pregnant." She enunciated each word as if Boop would be wont to understand. "Is that a good enough reason?"

"*Oy vey,*" Georgia said.

"Might be," Doris said.

"This is awful!" Boop blurted out, though that wasn't what she meant. Babies were wonderful, but Hannah wasn't ready. Her life wasn't ready. Boop wheezed and inhaled but couldn't fill her lungs. Shallow breaths would make her dizzy but what choice did she have? She couldn't hold her breath. The girls grabbed her hands.

"Breathe," they both said.

Boop blew a slow stream of air. She inhaled through her nose and didn't look at Hannah. This couldn't be happening again.

In that moment everything changed. Moving away didn't matter. Even Georgia and Doris didn't matter. She wanted to scoop Hannah into her lap, brush the flyaway hair from her face, and tell her everything would be okay. Because it would be okay, and it would be fine, in time. Then Boop's thoughts flipped to practical.

"Is the baby Clark's? Have you been to a doctor?"

Hannah sat in the yellow chair, closest to Boop. "Yes, I've been to the doctor and of course the baby is Clark's!"

"What do you mean 'of course'? It happens."

"It certainly does," Georgia said.

Hannah gasped. "Well, it didn't happen to me."

The worry that Boop had collected inside her dispersed like grains of sand, pouring over her, prickling her limbs, and dissipating. "And you're sure you want to have the baby? *Keep* the baby?"

"I'm sure. And so is Clark." Hannah broke out into a smile. "We heard the heartbeat."

Boop placed her right hand over her own heart, connecting her somehow to this new heartbeat. "So why didn't you say yes?"

The girls stayed quiet and still, allowing grandmother and granddaughter privacy within their presence.

Hannah shrugged, looking like the wide-eyed girl who'd been caught so long ago eating blueberries on a farm outing instead of adding them to her basket, her purple tongue, teeth, and fingers betraying her.

Boop cleared her throat. "Can you be happy enough if you marry someone you're not sure about? Maybe. Is a baby a blessing? Absolutely.

But you asked—and my answer is no. Being pregnant is not a good enough reason to get married. Not anymore."

"I can't believe you're saying this," Hannah said.

"I believe it," Georgia said. "Boop is a thoroughly modern grandmother."

Boop nodded at Georgia. How times had changed.

"It's the twenty-first century," Boop said. "You're a twenty-six-year-old college graduate with a full-time teaching job. Don't tell me you haven't thought about doing this on your own."

"I want the baby to have two parents."

"Oh, Hannah," Doris said. "Maybe it will all work out. The baby will have two parents. Even if you're not married, nontraditional families can work wonderfully if you do it right." Doris had children, grandchildren, great-grandchildren, and so many steps and halves that Boop couldn't keep track.

"No one is cutting Clark out of the picture," Boop said. *Or pushing him off a pier.* Maybe Clark would be an unlikely provider and protector—those were a blessing as well.

She knew that type of man existed because of Marvin. He'd excelled at the family-man thing most of the time. Fatherhood became him, a relief and joy when Stuart was born. Conversely, Boop's father, Joe Stern, couldn't have been bothered. Intrinsic nurturing had skipped a generation in her family. Nannie and Zaide cherished three generations of resort guests and a granddaughter, yet their character traits had whizzed right by Joe. Perhaps that was why he'd been attracted to her mother, the stunning yet non-maternal Tillie Feldman Stern—the two people responsible for her mostly wonderful childhood but only because they'd abandoned her. The summer Boop was four, her parents had dropped her off in South Haven for the weekend—a weekend that lasted until she was eighteen.

Sometimes Boop couldn't even bring herself to mutter, "May they rest in peace."

Hannah tipped her head to one side and smiled. Her eyes filled, glassy with emotion and memories. "I just wonder if I'm the marrying type. Because if I was, I have always wanted a marriage like yours and Pop's."

Doris stroked the fringe on her blanket and Georgia stared at her hands. Hannah's statement provided a fork in Boop's road.

"Things aren't always what they seem," she said.

"And sometimes they are," Hannah said. "You and Pop were such good role models. I just want to do you proud."

"You'll make me proud if your marriage doesn't start like mine and Pop's," Boop said.

Besides Boop, there were eight people in the world who knew why Boop would say that. Two of them were sitting on the porch pretending not to hear her, and the other six had died. She'd assumed her untold story would accompany her to the grave, sheltered in a broken corner of her heart.

But like so many times before when her heart was involved, Boop was wrong.

"I don't need perfect," Hannah cried. "I just need to know Clark is the one. Like you did with Pop."

"I didn't know," Boop whispered.

"What?"

"I didn't know that your grandfather was the one. I took a leap of faith—like Georgia said. And luckily it worked out. But I want you to be sure. Times are different."

"Why would you say that?" Hannah's voice squeaked.

"Because it's true," Georgia said.

Doris nodded.

Boop gathered all the courage that had forsaken her throughout her lifetime, as if it had been waiting right here for her on her forever porch. "I wasn't in love with Pop when we got married." Blasphemy! The words had been thick and heavy on her tongue, yet at the same time, they'd been easy to say, as if she'd pushed a boulder to the top of a hill and had finally let it roll down the other side.

Hannah deflated, then roared up with laughter and smacked her knee as if a toddler had told her a knock-knock joke. "Yes, you were totally in love. You got married right here on the patio after Labor Day, months after you graduated from high school. You picked out your dress from a bridal magazine and Nannie went to Chicago to buy it. I've heard the story my whole life. I've seen the pictures. You were glowing."

Boop inhaled, tasting the lake, maybe a speckle of sand, surely a droplet of sadness at remembering how her grown-up life had begun.

Antiquated yet still ample in Boop's mind, Nannie and Zaide's expectations, fears, and stereotypes popped to the surface and bobbed like a buoy, threatening her current feminist sensibilities. Still, she didn't want to dispel the myth of her and Marvin's love story.

"Why would you say you didn't love Pop?" Hannah asked. "She's lying, right?"

Georgia shook her head.

"Then why did you get married?"

Boop looked at Doris, then at Georgia, not for permission, but for confirmation. They nodded. Their expressions were neither happy nor sad. Hints of smiles documented their acceptance. As always.

It was time.

Boop was faced with saying things her granddaughter did not want to hear, words she would remember forever. Memories shrouded her resolve, but Boop shooed those thoughts away. She was *not* Nannie. Hannah was *not* eighteen. It was *not* 1951.

Boop filled her lungs with enough night air to expel a hidden truth. "I was pregnant."

Hannah walked around the porch. Boop stopped counting after twenty laps.

"You're making me dizzy," Georgia said. "Sit down."

"You both knew?" Hannah looked at Doris and then Georgia. They nodded.

"My family, the doctor, the girls," Boop said. "That's all. Others probably suspected, but it wasn't something you talked about."

"It was something you lied about," Doris said.

"Did your grandparents force Pop to marry you?"

"Not exactly."

"Then what exactly?"

"Oh, Hannah, it's a long story. All you really need to know is that your pop was a *mensch*." Boop had always known this, and she'd been grateful. But had she been grateful enough?

Hannah gulped. "You did it for the baby. For my dad. I can't believe I'm saying this, but maybe that's enough."

"Just because it worked out for us doesn't mean you don't deserve more than that uncertainty now," Boop said.

"If you didn't love him, why did you stay?" Hannah's voice cracked.

"I did fall in love with him. It just took time." But there was more to it. While there had been many things Boop had wanted to become, a leaver was not among them. Unlike her parents, every time Boop had escaped back to South Haven to recharge, whether for a weekend or for months in the summers, she'd returned home on the day she'd promised to do so, sometimes ahead of schedule.

She'd never forgotten that she was a lucky girl.

"I will always come back," she'd said to Marvin when she was nineteen and had been Mrs. Peck for less than a year. "I'm going to help my grandparents with the blueberry festival. I'll be back on Tuesday before dinner." She hadn't ever asked permission. She'd simply share her intention, which Marvin would accept because she always returned as promised.

True, he hadn't been a child then, but a psyche could easily be bruised at any age. Boop had made sure her husband never had to sneak downstairs and unlock the door, rationalizing that she might have forgotten her key. He'd never tapped strangers on the shoulder because they had Boop's hair, walk, or mannerisms. Marvin never had to make up a story about where his wife was or why she was gone. She'd kept the promises she'd made to Marvin before God and their families as well as the one she'd made to herself.

But these promises were also her penance for needing to get married.

Hannah shouldn't have worries or what-ifs when it came to marriage. Enough of those would come along with motherhood.

"If you're not in love with Clark anymore, or if you never were, you'll fall in love with someone else one day, and you'll see. And that's what you deserve. That's even what your baby deserves. Heck, it's what Clark deserves, don't you think? Even if that means waiting."

"You didn't wait," Hannah said.

"She's right," Doris said.

"I didn't have any other acceptable options," Boop said. "They called it 'getting in trouble' and that's exactly what it was. Trouble."

"And marrying Pop got you out of trouble?"

"You bet it did." In more ways than one. "And Pop got something in addition to a pregnant bride. Your great-grandpa Stan wasn't going to give Pop the business until he had a nice Jewish wife—one that he approved of—a healthy Jewish baby, and a brick bungalow in Skokie."

Hannah flinched. "That's awful!"

"Your grandmother has had a wonderful life," Georgia said.

"I did, but yours can be better. Learn from my experience. Pop and I both got what we needed—but was it what we wanted?" Boop shrugged. "Eventually, yes, but I don't want you to wait for eventually."

Boop wanted Hannah to have what she'd lost.

Smothered memories gasped for air through unguarded cracks in Boop's consciousness. She'd once had drive and ambition. Dreams and naivete. And a figure to die for.

Far-off big-band music, Zaide's laughter, and the roar of roadsters resounded inside her. The clean scent of hair cream tickled her nose. The bite of peppermint toothpaste coated her tongue. Was it all in her imagination? Or could the girls and Hannah hear it and smell it and taste it too?

Hannah studied her. "You have a lot of thoughts about love for someone who says she wasn't in it."

Boop diverted her gaze and gathered her thoughts, then looked back at Hannah. "I've had a lifetime to consider it."

Hannah nodded, her curiosity momentarily muted. "What would you have done if you hadn't gotten pregnant? What were your dreams? Did you have plans?"

The questions chipped away at Boop's resolve to keep that summer veiled within the personal story she'd created—how she'd been a young woman who wanted nothing more than to be Mrs. Marvin Peck, housewife and mother. She looked at her friends.

Doris shrugged.

"It's up to you," Georgia said.

After all this time, Boop remained unsure of how to explain the unexplainable. "It was another lifetime, Hannah. It doesn't matter anymore."

"It matters to me." Hannah placed her hand on her stomach. "It matters to us."

Boop had so wanted it all to matter.

Time tumbled forward and back. People and actions overlapped and crisscrossed through the years. Would it be possible for Boop's experiences at eighteen to benefit her granddaughter now? Could Boop's pain be Hannah's gain?

She was not a frivolous old woman, yet Boop recalled a frivolous girl—one who'd been charging toward a limitless future until she'd crashed.

"You must remember *something*," Hannah said.

Against her heart's better judgment, Boop remembered everything. After all, it had been the best and worst summer of her life.

Chapter 3

BETTY

Summer 1951

Betty needed to pick up her pace or she'd miss what she'd been waiting for since forever. It was almost noon and the summer staff would arrive in South Haven in about three hours. And now that she was eighteen, she would no longer be "Bitty Betty Stern"; she'd be part of the gang.

She was old enough to join in on the secret bonfires that weren't so secret; enjoy a day off, playing cards in the staff cabins; or drive to a nearby beach in Benton Harbor or St. Joseph, where no one knew them. Most of the kids caravanned from the University of Michigan, about one hundred fifty miles away. Ann Arbor had seemed so far away when Betty was a little girl, but ever since she'd seen her first fashion magazine at about age ten—a copy of *Harper's Bazaar* left behind by her mother—she'd wanted to leave Michigan for New York City. That's where magazines were made. Nannie had said so when Betty asked.

She hadn't read the articles at first but had lost her thoughts among the images of women in swimsuits on a windy beach—a beach not unlike her own, aside from the palm trees. Later that day, she'd read the articles, so she had a reason to keep the magazine open and on her lap. Nannie would never ask her to stop reading. Betty was a good reader, above her grade level. Someone had written those words about the fashions and fabrics and styles—of course they had: words didn't appear by magic. The idea that this was someone's *job* had ignited her imagination. Betty had wanted to be that person, have that job, from that day forward. And now in a few months she'd be headed to Barnard College in New York City. She stopped short of attributing her aspirations to her mother and credited Diana Vreeland and *Harper's Bazaar*.

The only things she thanked her mother for were her hair and her figure, and Tillie had had no say in bequeathing either one.

On one of their visits, Betty's parents had chosen to give her a Sally-kins doll, the kind with a soft body and hard, molded head and hair. Betty had already gravitated away from dolls and toward books and puzzles—but how would they have known?

Betty turned the pages of the latest *Seventeen* but gazed out the laundry room window. A few clouds floated by, though not enough to dim the sky or her excitement. She balanced the open magazine on top of a box of borax, flipped one more page, and read the headline: "Your Future: Where Is It?" She dog-eared the article for later. Then she dipped her hands into the pocket of her apron, knowing she'd find bobby pins and rubber bands from the summer before. Bits of lint collected beneath her nails. With the bobby pins pinched between her lips, she swept her hair off her neck, securing it into a ponytail, then off her face with pushes and twists.

Work could not be put off any longer. She fluffed the pile of blue embroidered curtains that would hang in the guest cottages once she ironed them. It was the same blue her grandfather had mimicked in all of Stern's Summer Resort's tablecloths, napkins, and bedspreads. Even the matchbooks and ashtrays were the same shade, a color that was "easy on the eyes and just right for a vacation," Zaide had said. He'd dubbed it "Stern Blue." Betty was never sure if he realized the irony.

The iron hissed its willingness to begin, and Betty laid a linen and lace panel flat on the board at her waist. The back and forth sliding motions were hypnotic. For the past three summers, Betty had been the lone ironer until the laundry girls' shifts began.

The air grew damp with steam and crisp with the smell of warm starch. Betty closed her eyes and pretended it was the lingering scent of an extinguished bonfire. She'd been awakened by that smell throughout her childhood, as well as by laughter on the beach outside her bedroom window. When she was twelve, her curiosity and a preteen crush on a waiter named Gerald had compelled her to the window, and she realized it likely wasn't boring grown-ups outside. She padded over and watched as shadows danced at the lake's edge without music—at least, she couldn't hear any—their arms in the air or around each other. Others lay close together atop blankets spread out on the sand. From that moment on Betty had wanted to be the girl a handsome boy teasingly chased across the beach, laughing with that knowing kind of smile that said, *I dare you to catch me.* The girl who was still dancing a slow dance in the arms of a dashing prelaw major as the sun came up, and whose evening ended at daybreak with a perfect kiss. Just like in the movies.

By her junior year of high school and after a month of milkshakes and movies with Robert Smith, Betty was secretly thrilled when Robert had carried a blanket during their usual after-dusk walk on the beach. It was so romantic, even more so because it was fall and she knew he'd put his arm around her. He'd unfolded the blanket and swung it out like a red tartan sail, and the fabric had floated down to the sand. He'd chosen a spot far from the light of her house or that of her neighbors. Soon his arm around her led to kissing, which led Robert to press his body against Betty's so that she'd had to lie back on the blanket. She hadn't stopped kissing him, though the wool had itched her calves, back, and shoulders as if an army of ants was running rampant on her skin. She'd squirmed, which somehow had prompted Robert to skim his hands over her blouse and unbutton it. It had been an odd sequence of sensations, but not entirely unpleasant.

Betty had later told Georgia that she'd allowed Robert to go to second base because she was sixteen and it was time. What she hadn't told Georgia was that she'd kind of liked it.

A week later she'd set her limits with Robert when he unzipped her pedal pushers. Flustered and curious, she'd allowed him to do so; then, despite her haze, she'd lifted Robert's hand and placed it above her waist.

"Can't blame a guy for tryin'," he'd said.

With a sizzling jolt, Betty opened her eyes wide. "Criminy!" She'd jammed the front end of the iron into the underside of her forearm. The summer hadn't even officially begun! Betty would need to be more conscientious during her daydreams.

In the kitchen, Nannie held Betty's arm firmly but gently, and patted butter on the burn, tsk-tsking with each circular motion. She wiped her greasy fingers on her apron in even strokes. Even Nannie's messes were meticulous.

"Betty, how many times do I have to tell you not to iron with your eyes closed?"

"I only closed them for a second." It hadn't been much more than that. "I was thinking."

Betty didn't want Nannie to know she was thinking about necking when she should have been thinking about creases and pleats. Plus, Robert had dumped her for Joan Kepler, who had a bigger bosom and fewer morals.

"This is quite the burn," Nannie said. "What on earth were you thinking about? Boys, perhaps?"

"No! I was wondering if the Bloomfields were coming back this year."

Nannie narrowed her eyes. "Why wouldn't they be coming back? Everyone comes back. Did you hear something?"

"No. I just liked my nights babysitting for them. That's all." Betty had enjoyed those evenings because the Bloomfields were a handsome couple who deserved a night away from their three girls. Or maybe because the Bloomfields had tipped her even though it wasn't required.

"I'll make sure you're first on the list." Nannie examined Betty's arm again, then wrapped it with a cotton bandage she kept on hand for kitchen burns. "You'll meet a nice Jewish boy at Columbia when you're at Barnard. You'll see. Someone with ambitions. Brains. Have patience."

Betty had plans other than patience.

Nannie set the butter into the commercial Frigidaire marked with an M for *milchig*—for dairy products only. Then Nannie followed Betty to the laundry room. Betty lifted the half stack of pressed curtains from the bottom. The weight against her makeshift bandage sent a wave of prickling pain through her, so she placed the curtains onto Nannie's arms with care. She did not want to iron them again.

Nannie stood on her tiptoes and kissed Betty's forehead, then twirled one finger in the still, humid air. "I'll finish these," she said. "You go home and freshen up. It wouldn't look right if you were late."

An hour later, Betty returned. She wasn't wearing the pink checkered shirtwaist Nannie had laid on her bed, but Nannie wouldn't reprimand Betty in public. That afternoon she would see some of the staff who'd known her since they were college freshmen and she was fourteen. Betty needed to look grown-up to be taken seriously. She wasn't in high school anymore, and her appearance should say "college girl." She shuffled her feet and stared at her new summer loafers as she pressed the damp grass one way, then the other. No saddle shoes, even though they were in style.

Nannie and Zaide sat on the wrought-iron bench under the biggest maple tree on the property, on the center lawn. They sat there every year waiting for the staff to arrive before Memorial Day weekend.

She blew her grandmother a kiss. Later, Betty would explain that she hadn't really disobeyed her grandmother by wearing a different outfit; she was simply saving the dress for another occasion and didn't want to soil it. Nannie would, of course, see through Betty as if she were a piece of glass, but summer meant her grandmother would be distracted by the guests, the kitchen, and her image as the *balabusta*—the best hostess and homemaker—of South Haven. She might not even realize that Betty was wearing a gift she'd received from Tillie.

During one of her parents' visits, Betty realized Nannie called them "Tillie" and "Joe," so she had started calling them by their first names too. Everyone had thought it was so cute that a six-year-old with light-brown, sun-streaked ringlets and wearing a dress inspired by Shirley Temple would call her parents by their first names.

Or at least that's how it played in Betty's memory, since no one would ever refute or confirm her recollection. Ostensibly this served to safeguard her feelings, but not knowing where her parents had gone, or why, had been fertile ground for a little girl's imagination. When the adults in her life had decided to be honest with her, she was ten, and more than a little disappointed that her parents weren't spies or special agents or that they hadn't been kidnapped by pirates. The truth: Tillie was a singer, and Joe her manager and piano player. They had kept their daughter with them until she was ready to attend kindergarten and then handed her off to her father's parents.

Betty remembered most of the times her parents had visited. She'd straighten her room and theirs, wear her best dress, wait by the door after days, weeks, months of seeing them in every childless couple, hearing phantom voices, dreaming outlandish dreams of a normal family. When they arrived, Tillie and Joe behaved like distant relatives—polite and interested but detached. It was as if she had no bearing on their life. She knew she did not.

Betty always waved at the window and pretended their leaving didn't hurt. She'd feared that seeing her hurt would wound her grandparents, who only wanted her to be happy. She owed them everything.

That's why Betty usually packed away Tillie's infrequent and feckless gifts, but this one was hard to ignore—a yellow sleeveless blouse with a stand-up collar, like the one Betty had seen in *Seventeen*, a full chambray skirt, and—the best part—a narrow red patent-leather belt. Tillie knew it would be just right, since Betty looked so much like her with peachy skin, blue eyes with flecks of green, and toffee-brown hair. Did Tillie know how the blouse and belt would show off Betty's curves? Did she care?

Betty never wanted to give Nannie and Zaide a reason to be sorry they'd raised her. Most girls didn't have mothers, let alone grandmothers, who were as encouraging as Nannie. She *kvelled* at Betty's grades and ambition as much as (or maybe more than) she acknowledged Betty's beauty, even if she'd inherited that from "the other side" of the family. The side she didn't know. In her grandparents' hearts and eyes, Betty could do no wrong.

One outfit choice wouldn't change that, no matter who sent it.

Betty's best friends walked out of the main house behind her. It wasn't a house in the ordinary sense, because no one lived there. Zaide had bought it in the twenties when it was a hotel. It stood two stories tall with white wood siding and a green pitched roof, green shutters to match, each showcasing a window box that would overflow with impatiens and honeysuckles as soon as there was no longer the fear of frost. A stoop led to the oversize front door with a brass knocker no one used. Once inside the lobby, the vast dining room was off to the left, with its chandeliers and brocade wallpaper and windows overlooking the beach and resort grounds. The social hall and smaller activity rooms sat to the right. The kitchen lived behind it all, sizzling and buzzing and transmitting mouthwatering aromas about eighteen hours a day. The upstairs rooms once housed guests in luxury, but now were used for storage.

Georgia and Doris bopped down the green painted steps, skittered and skipped toward Betty, and stood by her like sentry guards.

"Your grandmother asked us to make sure everything was set in the dining room," Georgia said. "Since you were late. And I see why."

"I wasn't late," Betty said. "I had to get ready." She turned to Georgia. "Zaide said he hired a few new rising seniors. I just couldn't wear a dress from high school."

"Heavens no!" Doris laughed. She wore a madras shirtwaist Betty had seen a hundred times. It didn't matter, though. Doris didn't have plans for her summer other than a sensible suntan.

"You already look like a fashion writer, Betty!" Doris said.

"Fashion *editor*," Betty said.

"Here, Miss Editor." Doris handed Betty a paper name tag and a straight pin. Betty attached the name tag over her heart, as did the other girls. It was true. Her heart belonged to South Haven, at least for one more summer.

"This is going to be a blast," Betty said.

Georgia laughed. "You say that every year. And working here every year is pretty much the same."

Doris raised her arms over her head, faking jumping jacks. "And a-one, and a-two . . ."

"This year is going to be different," Betty said.

"How so?" Doris asked. She was the little sister neither of the other girls had, even though she was the same age. Doris was four foot eleven and effervescent and a little naive, always finding the bright side of things and people. She was friends with everyone, and she truly liked everyone. Betty found Doris darling, but exhausting, with her romantic notions of Prince Charmings and happily-ever-afters. Betty liked boys—she really liked boys—but she was a little more practical.

"Boy-crazy Betty is looking for her summer love." Georgia drew out the last word in a breathy voice.

"I'm sure you'll have your pick," Doris said.

"I am not looking for love. I just know a handsome boy when I see one. And I want to have fun." What Betty wanted was to head to New York and not stick out like a country bumpkin.

"I don't know why you're thinking about the boys here anyhow," Doris said. "You're going to meet a boy when you go to Barnard. A Columbia student. Maybe someone studying to be a doctor or a dentist. Or a lawyer."

"You sound like Nannie," Betty said. She shook her head. "I just want to have a marvelous summer, and what could be more marvelous than a summer romance?" Betty asked. She turned to Georgia. "I'd say I'm looking for a fling, but it sounds so crude," Betty whispered.

Georgia nodded, and Betty shivered from the breeze. Or anticipation.

"I'll meet my husband in Chicago," Doris said. She had a job lined up as a salesgirl at Marshall Field's and was going to live in a rooming house in September. "It doesn't matter that you'll be in New York. We'll still be each other's bridesmaids, of course."

"Life isn't all about boys and marriage," Georgia said.

Doris dropped open her mouth, and if Betty had had a peach, she could have popped one in.

Georgia was right, of course. She was heading to Northwestern University as a premed. She wanted to be a doctor, and Betty knew she would be. That's why Georgia understood Betty's dream of working at a glossy fashion magazine the way her other friends did not. Doris wanted an office job and an engagement ring, like most of the girls Betty knew.

Betty's life would be about first earning her English degree and then landing a job as a fashion writer at one of the magazines she'd read until she'd worn out the pages. *Seventeen. Mademoiselle. Vanity Fair. Compact.* Then she'd work her way up to editor. That's when she'd have a say about fashion and beauty trends and what women read about them. It would be her way of having an impact.

Secondary to that was the idea of meeting boys. Men, really, and to be fair, it was a *close* second.

Nannie and Zaide wanted "their girl" to be educated and to achieve, even if that meant leaving South Haven. Betty couldn't have asked for kinder and more generous grandparents.

Georgia stood taller, checked her watch, and smiled at Betty, who felt small in a protected sort of way. Georgia was five foot nine and her presence commanded attention. Her ginger hair tumbled halfway down her back and a genuine tortoiseshell headband held it off her face. Freckles swept from one cheek to the other, and her eyes were emerald green, not a murky hazel. She wore tennis whites because she was the resort's only tennis coach and she didn't want any of the coeds to think they were taking her place.

Betty had tried to coax Georgia into wearing red lipstick today since she wouldn't really be *playing* tennis. Max Factor's Clear Red would have set her features ablaze against the all-white ensemble, but Georgia stuck with Dorothy Gray's Sea Coral. Betty had to admit Georgia looked sophisticated, and for a moment she stung with jealousy. Then she remembered *she'd* worn the red lipstick. If it was good enough for Elizabeth Taylor, it was good enough for Betty Stern.

Betty wasn't as glamorous as Liz, but she was all right. She'd heard it all her life. She stood five foot four, but little else about her was average. Her hair hung in soft curls without needing a hairdresser, though today she'd maneuvered it all into a red scarf and tied it like a bomb girl, with the knot at the top, pulling a few strands of curls forward to drift across her forehead. Betty's curvaceous figure had sprung to life, so to speak, during tenth grade. The thing about Betty was that she was also a brain who'd earned all As and perfect attendance awards for her four years at South Haven High. She worked hard for her grades and was grateful for the peer recognition. Her classmates had voted her senior girl most likely to succeed *and* prettiest senior girl. That had clinched it. She had always thought she'd enter the Miss South Haven contest when she was eighteen, and her grandparents had encouraged it. With that confidence, coupled with the fact that the hands-down favorite, Nancy Green, was traveling in Europe, she might actually have a chance at winning.

Zaide thought she'd be a shoo-in.

"Win or lose, you're my bathing beauty," Nannie said.

Betty believed her, and she stood a little straighter thinking about the legacy of Miss South Haven, as well as the bragging rights and free publicity for her grandparents.

Three cars rounded the corner to the east, music blaring from the open windows. Summer was just a block away.

"How do I look?" Betty whispered.

"You look swell," Doris said. "Like a real college girl. I wish I did." Doris flicked at her short sandy-brown bangs, then dropped her hand to her side. Her plaid skirt was meant more for winter than spring, but Betty said nothing.

Instead of worrying about Doris's clothes, Betty fretted about her own. Maybe she was a tad overdressed. Would the older girls mock her? Would the boys turn away? She'd brought shorts and tennis shoes to change into later. She didn't have to unload cars and unpack steamer trunks, but she did want to blend in during the staff dinner in the dining room that evening.

Five cars pulled onto the resort's circular drive, and three more turned the corner, all looking shinier and sounding noisier than ever—or Betty watched and listened more closely than she had before. Maybe next summer she'd take classes, or get a job at a magazine in New York. This could be the last summer she'd have the notoriety of her last name, with all its benefits and drawbacks.

The chrome and glass sparkled and danced like the lake at sunset, and exhaust fumes filled the air and held on to the music that blared from the radio.

When the cars were parked, the kids tumbled out. The wet, woodsy scent of aftershave mixed with the medicinal aroma of hair spray smelled as much like summer as Coppertone. Though she was dazed and over-loaded, Betty didn't want the spectacle to end. When the group started toward her grandparents, it broke her trance. In the Stern family, Betty would take second place to the staff and guests for the next few months.

She glanced across the lawn toward her grandparents but couldn't see them anymore in the crowd. What Betty could see was that none of the other girls wore scarves. She'd felt grown-up and slightly scandalous when she'd opted for it over the pearl barrette Nannie had hoped she'd wear, but now she wasn't so sure. Was she old-fashioned or fashionable?

Goose bumps scattered up her arms and across her shoulders even though it was seventy-five degrees. Michigan May could bring any kind of weather. At least there was no more snow.

It was then, the instant Betty thought about snow in May, that she saw a boy who made her heart shudder. Even from a distance, he was movie-star handsome—clean cut like all the boys but with a bit of a natural swagger that drew her attention the way a magnet draws nails. He wore tan trousers, a short-sleeved white shirt, and a tie. He had to be new. She would not have forgotten that face. Those shoulders. But she hadn't seen him step out of a car. Was he an apparition? A manifestation of her dreams? He was bold in his fashion choice. None of the others wore ties. Now she recognized him! He looked like a young William Holden, dimples and all.

Betty unpinned her name tag and tore away her heritage, becoming "Betty S" instead of the more identifiable "Betty Stern."

"Does my lipstick look okay?" She sent a silent prayer to Max Factor that it looked better than okay.

Georgia smirked. "Yes. It's fine."

Betty crumpled the half of the name tag she had removed and shoved it behind her belt buckle. Georgia watched.

"What? I just want to have a fun summer before college," Betty said.

Georgia raised and lowered her sculpted brows. "He's too old for you."

"Who are you talking about?" Betty asked, her heart pounding with possibilities.

"The one with the dimple in his chin, smarty-pants." Georgia pointed toward him with a tip of her head. "I know you, Betty. You're going to get into trouble with that one."

"Betty knows better," Doris said. Sweet Doris. "What are you going to say if your grandparents see that?" Doris pointed to Betty's name tag. "Do you want me to get you a new one? It'll just take a sec."

"They won't notice," Betty said. She looked at her William Holden talking to the other boys, but not standing in their circle. He smiled and nodded but kept a few yards between himself and the others.

Betty's calves warmed as the sun stroked them, making her more conscious of her legs than she'd ever been and shifting her attention away from the burn on her arm. Then she turned her right heel toward the arch of her left foot.

"This isn't a beauty contest, Betty." Georgia pointed to Betty's feet.

"I'm just practicing for Miss South Haven. You know I'm entering this year."

Doris giggled. "You've told us a hundred times."

Betty circled her hands and clasped them behind her back and stood straight, shoulders back. She knew what good posture did for her bustline, even when she was all buttoned up.

"You're blushing!" Doris said. "Your grandmother is not going to be happy you're flirting with staff."

"Get over yourself, Doris," Georgia said. "Betty's just having fun. He's not even looking this way."

And then he was, but just as quickly he turned back toward the street and to the girls who weren't Betty. He stood close enough for the girls to look, but not touch. Betty's shoulders relaxed, and she dragged her arms around front, skimming the bandage covering her burn against her hip, which sent a shock wave not nearly as painful as being ignored. Or worse, not even noticed.

Turn around, turn around, turn around.

Nothing happened.

Turn around, turn around, turn around.

Then he did just that. Not only did he turn around, he saw her, and he smiled so wide that the girls nearby turned to see what, or who, he was looking at.

Goose bumps started at Betty's neck and shot down her body like ice pellets.

"He's looking at you," Georgia said.

"He's not even pretending that he's *not* looking at you, you lucky duck," Doris said.

Betty looked right back at him, or as right at him as she could from the other side of the lawn. Then she reached up with both hands and untied the knot in her scarf, releasing the fabric down her neck. It brushed across her shoulders, and Betty shook with shivers she didn't even try to hide. She tipped her neck from side to side, releasing her cascade of curls in slow motion.

Georgia grabbed the scarf and pounded it into a ball, tucking it as much inside her hands as she could. "Don't be a drama queen, Betty. Everyone knows who you are."

"Not everyone," she said.

Chapter 4

BETTY

The first weekend of summer passed in a frenzy of welcome activities. The resort had filled to capacity, of course, and Betty resumed her summer routine as if it had never ended.

Late Tuesday afternoon, she closed the front door of her family's home and skipped down the patio's cement steps, the skirt of her white broadcloth dress bouncing against her shins. The sun kissed the apples of her cheeks, already rosy from a dab of rouge. It was going to be a great night.

Georgia and Doris waited by the curb, both gussied up like Betty, wearing dresses they'd once saved for a high school dance. Georgia's two-piece lavender-and-purple number with its modest V-neck and a princess waist, cinched tight with a thin white patent-leather belt, made her look as if she'd stepped out of a *Seventeen* magazine spread. Doris's blue eyes sparkled, whether from the sun or her yellow taffeta dress, Betty didn't know. The girls had taken her advice and worn lipsticks in shades that complemented their dresses, Georgia a deep russet, and Doris a bubblegum pink. Betty just had to know the colors and brands! Her friends looked so grown-up. Is that how she looked to them with her pink lips and her dress with its matching sweater that she'd buttoned just at her neck to show off her décolletage?

"No one will recognize us," Georgia said.

"I think that's the point," Doris said. "These boys and their families will be the upper crust. We don't want them to see us as part of the staff, but as possibilities."

Georgia tapped Doris's shoulder. "You mean as potential wives."

"So what if I do?"

Betty set her hands on her hips. Nannie had asked Betty and her friends to act as hostesses for the first cocktail party of the summer and that's where they were headed. The girls had done this before, chatting with the guests, talking up the resort activities and upcoming entertainment, listening for any special requests. The event was a delicious combination of socializing and spying.

"You'll have to limit the flirting tonight, girls; we have to talk to everyone." Betty sashayed ahead and looked back at her friends. "That means husbands, wives, and the children. Not just the boys our age."

Her grandparents threw this cocktail party every Tuesday at five-thirty and then served dinner to the guests at six-thirty, as usual. The kitchen prepared the expected four-course meal. Soup, salad, a choice of four entrées—have as many as you wish—each with two sides, and the dessert plate for sharing at the table. And this was all before the midnight buffet, composed of breads, cakes, and fruit salads piled into watermelon boats, for the women who pretended to be watching their waistlines. This late-night indulgence was set out by the kitchen staff for guests to serve to themselves, many of them wrapping sweets in linen napkins and tucking the parcels into their handbags for the trip back to their cabins.

Stern's serves three meals plus. Emphasis on the *plus*.

As they stepped onto the lawn, Betty stopped. "Before we get there, let's make a pact. If one of us likes a boy, he's off-limits, just like always."

"You're just calling dibs on the one with the dimple," Doris said. "What if I like him too?"

"I keep seeing him in the dining room, but I haven't met him yet. Not really. I can't ask my grandparents to introduce me, or ask anything about him, or they'll want to know why. According to them, this summer is about pitching in around the resort and getting to know my Barnard roommate. I got the assignment last week. She's Italian. From New Jersey."

"Ooh, exotic," Doris said.

"Forget about exotic roommates," Georgia said. "I've met your William Holden."

Betty clasped her hands.

"His name is Abe Barsky and he's an architecture major at Michigan. And he's on the ice hockey team. Apparently your grandfather hired him last-minute."

"Does he have a girlfriend?"

"He left that out of our ten-second conversation. I was walking to the tennis court. He passed by and introduced himself. I assumed he was heading to the Palace. It was after lunch."

The Palace was the largest cabin on the property, but also the most run-down. It housed twenty boys, dormitory-style, and it was more like a barracks—with bunk beds, running water, toilets, showers, and sinks—than the typical Stern's cabins, which were more like the hotel rooms Betty had seen in movies. The Castle was the almost-as-barebones dormitory for the female staff, and was separated from the Palace by the staff mess hall. The boys were forbidden from visiting the Castle, the girls banned from the Palace, but with the buildings out of sight from the main house (meaning Nannie) and set apart from the guest cabins, Betty suspected that was an unenforceable rule.

"So, we have a deal?"

"If it goes for all of us," Georgia said.

"Of course! Let's cross our hearts." Betty drew an invisible X across her chest with her finger. They'd been crossing their hearts since grade school. It was the most serious promise they could make.

"Girls!" a voice yelled from across the lawn. It was Chef Gavin, who'd worked at Stern's since as far back as Betty could remember. A tall man with broad shoulders, Chef Gavin boasted a belly that suggested he liked his own cooking. Nannie never trusted skinny cooks. Even Mabel, who worked in the kitchen (and helped Nannie with everything), was round like Mother Goose in Betty's favorite childhood book. Chef Gavin traveled to South Haven each summer from the Miami Beach hotel he worked in during winter, while Mabel had grown up in South Haven like most of the kitchen and housekeeping staff. Nannie set the menu, including family favorites and recipes from well-loved cookbooks. She managed everything alongside Chef Gavin, but she also counted on him to add his Miami flair to her Michigan menu. Nannie claimed it set Stern's far apart from—and above—the other resorts.

"What are you doing standing there? Hurry! I need your help!" Chef Gavin flailed his hands in the air.

The girls ran to the kitchen, Betty's heart pounding. Had something happened to her grandmother?

"Come inside! It's a disaster! Look!"

Betty held her breath and stepped into the kitchen's prep area, a rectangular space lined with stainless-steel counters, which now were covered with dozens of silver trays filled with an impressive array of canapés. She glared at Chef Gavin. "You scared me! I thought my grandmother was dead on the floor!"

"We'll all be dead if these canapés aren't garnished in the next twenty-five minutes. Katherine and Hazel didn't show up tonight. Get your aprons, girls."

"Not tonight," Betty said, stepping back. "We're hostesses. That's what my grandmother wants. She did not want us working in the kitchen. Look at our clothes!"

"You can do this stark naked for all I care; it just has to get done," Chef Gavin said.

"There's at least a thousand of them," Georgia whispered.

Betty did not need to be reminded. She had spent several summers with carrot-stained fingers from peeling curls for gefilte-fish nuggets. Many times she'd stabbed herself with plastic mini swords meant for the garlic-stuffed olives or with multicolored toothpicks as she pierced hundreds of cocktail franks and sweet-and-sour meatballs, not to mention the skewers she'd poked through the cocktail lilies: slices of bologna wrapped in a cone shape with a pickle spear sticking out of the middle.

Tonight, Betty had thought she and the girls would be noshing and chatting, not stabbing and stuffing.

"I have brisket, carrot *tzimmes*, and baked mackerel to finish, and your grandmother will be here any minute. I will not be the one who disappoints her, Betty. Will you?"

Betty jolted from her daydream and slammed into her birthright.

"No," she said.

Chef Gavin nodded once and walked to the far side of the kitchen.

Betty would never let Nannie down. If she had been there, Nannie would have been the first to pull on an apron over a fancy dress and decorate a thousand canapés. They all knew it.

Betty lifted three clean Stern Blue aprons from the hooks beside the door and handed one to each of her friends.

"I'll never look at parsley the same way again," Doris sighed. She squeezed onto the bench outside the kitchen and leaned on Betty. Then Georgia, on the other side of Betty, also leaned in. If one of them stood, the others would fall.

"We did a good job," Doris said.

"Not too good, I hope," Georgia said. "Remind me to stay the heck home next Tuesday."

"I'm sorry," Betty said. "You both look so pretty, and now our hands smell like garlic and we're in here instead of out meeting boys."

"Do you ever think about anything besides boys?" Georgia asked.

"Yes, you know I do. I have plans. But this summer, well, that *is* the plan. Oh, and to win Miss South Haven." Betty laid her head atop Georgia's, which rested on her shoulder. "I'll make it up to you, I promise."

"Just don't make it up to us with canapés," Doris said.

An unfamiliar deep voice drifted out from the kitchen window. "Good job tonight, girls."

They turned around, but no one was there. "Wouldn't it be swell if that was Abe?" Doris whispered to Betty.

She crossed her fingers.

The next morning, when Betty heard Nannie's light footsteps outside her bedroom door, she pulled the blanket over her head. The door opened.

"It's time to get up."

Betty nodded and knew the blanket around her wiggled enough for her grandmother to feel acknowledged. The door didn't click closed, but Betty heard Nannie walk downstairs. Zaide's voice permeated the soggy morning air.

After the front door closed, Betty sprang out of bed. She looked out the window and spotted Nannie and Zaide walking away from the house. All she really saw were umbrellas, two black circles, one slightly ahead of the other, because Nannie overcompensated for her stature by walking faster than Zaide, who never seemed to mind. He was proud of and delighted by his successful wife. Betty knew most men were not like Zaide.

Betty made up her bed, dressed, then darted downstairs. She dialed the operator. Betty's and Georgia's families were lucky not to use a party line. Betty could not have made this call if they had. South Haven was too small a town to have people knowing her business, or, rather, more of her business than they already knew. Georgia would be awake and ready to unpack new merchandise in her family's store before heading to the resort to teach tennis, assuming it stopped raining.

The gray sky dampened more than the beach. It put Betty's plans in check. She'd wanted to wait at the tennis court to "accidentally" officially meet Abe. Now she'd have to devise a new plan while contending with the varying foul-weather moods of the guests, which would range from delightfully carefree to downright cranky.

If it rained all day, Betty and the other girls would play go fish and war with the children, teach them cat's cradle, organize games of pick-up sticks, and spark impromptu puppet shows—anything to keep the ankle biters out of their mothers' hair and off their laps while the ladies played canasta, bingo, or mah-jongg, smoked cigarettes, and ate bridge mix faster than Mabel could pour it into crystal bowls.

The familiar *brrinngg-brrinngg* echoed through the receiver.

"Lemon residence," Georgia said.

Betty waited until she heard the click of the operator cutting out of the call. "I need your help."

"Where are you?" Georgia asked.

"I'm at home."

"Your grandmother isn't going to be happy you're late for breakfast."

"She's not thinking about anything besides the weather. Rain changes the plan for the entire day, you know that. They're too busy to care. She barely tried to wake me."

"I don't know why anyone fusses; it's a day of parlor games and endless snacks for the guests. Plus, we keep the children out of their hair even more than usual." Georgia never minced words. "What do you need? As if I have to ask."

Betty spit out her words before she could change her mind. "I want you to introduce me to Abe before tonight's bonfire. I want to meet him officially."

"Just walk up and introduce yourself. You are his boss's granddaughter."

"Don't remind me. I want it to be casual but planned. But it can't look planned. Most of the staff will be in the main house during the rain, so it'll be perfect. I don't have to find a reason to wait on the tennis courts. Just keep your eye out . . ."

"Betty?"

"Don't be a stick-in-the-mud, Georgia. Please."

"It's not me. Blame Mother Nature."

Betty spun around. A giant sunbeam split the gray sky, revealing the blue above it. Rain no longer tap-danced on the windowsills or patio. Two children wearing shorts, shirts, and rubber boots jumped and splashed in puddles on the street. Betty turned away from the window and twisted herself in the telephone cord, disappointment stinging her eyes with the threat of tears. The telephone slid across the Parsons table, almost knocking off Nannie's little Lenox bowl with the gold rim. Betty dropped the receiver, which boomeranged around her.

Untangled and undeterred, Betty lifted the receiver and nestled it between her shoulder and her ear. "Fine then," she said. "I'll have to do this myself."

Betty skipped leftover puddles on her way to the dining room, then slowed her pace, maneuvered her wraparound navy dress into place, and smoothed her hair, which she'd already pulled into a ponytail.

She smiled as she sauntered past the guests. The warmth she felt reminded her they were more than visitors. These people had watched her grow up—not only watched her but participated in her childhood. She'd played, eaten, and cavorted with her peers, even once she started working through the summers. Sure, the husbands paid for their well-appointed cabins and days full of food and activities, but her grandparents showered them with time and attention in addition to activities and food. In turn, a genuine closeness draped the property, just as Nannie's hand-embroidered tablecloth covered their elongated dining room table each Passover. It was something unique and special, and it belonged only to them.

Her chest tightened as a trio of wives walked by, heads together, tittering, smiling. One of the ladies pulled out a compact and reapplied her lipstick as she walked. Betty chuckled, knowing she'd have done the same thing. They reminded Betty of herself with Georgia and Doris, though she knew at least she and Georgia weren't headed down the "lady of the house" path anytime soon. Still, she loved seeing these women together, a mirror to Betty and her friends' future selves.

"Calisthenics on the veranda this morning, ladies," Betty said. "The lawn's too wet. See you later."

They turned toward Betty and nodded, and then folded back into themselves.

As breakfast service neared its end, Nannie and Zaide would be chatting with the families who lingered over coffee. The guests would be filled with either bagels and lox, scrambled eggs, pancakes, coffee cake, or all of the above. Even the women who ordered cantaloupe and cottage cheese had likely stashed a Danish or two in their handbags. The busboys would begin removing the coffee-stained, butter-splattered white linen tablecloths, and the guests would send their children to the counselors for a morning of games, art projects, and sing-alongs before they were escorted to lunch with their families.

Betty walked toward the table where her grandfather was talking loudly and gesturing grandly. Zaide told boisterous stories about the local farmers, as he *kvetched* about the price of produce and bragged about the quality of the kosher food they purchased. He was also keen on telling stories about how he and Nannie built Stern's "from the ground up." Some of the longtime guests rolled their eyes, having heard it so many times, but always in a kindhearted way. Everyone listened because everyone loved Zaide. He remembered everyone and everything—from birthdays and anniversaries to pillow preferences and allergies. If someone preferred two sugars or three in their tea, Zaide knew. This was both a sideshow trick and a perk for Stern's guests, though not always for his granddaughter. To the irritation of some, he also recalled invoice balances and intestinal problems.

Betty noticed someone standing at the table with Zaide. Tall and slim, hair combed back with a sheen, hands in his pockets. She knew that profile. She should have been happy to see a childhood summer playmate, but two years ago Marv Peck had been sweet on her, or that had been the gossip. She hadn't been interested. Awkwardness hung in the air and eclipsed any remnants of hide-and-seek nostalgia.

Nannie smiled and waved her over.

"Good morning," Betty said. She kissed Zaide on the cheek and then Nannie. "Hello, Mrs. Peck. It's nice to have you back at Stern's."

"It's nice to be back, Betty. I told Stanley, 'I am not spending another summer *shvitzing* in Skokie.' So my Marvin offered to come along to keep me company." Mrs. Peck winked. Her makeup was a little heavy for morning, but that was probably because she had been known to indulge in pink squirrels (with extra maraschino cherries) from the bar at night.

"Hi, Marv. I thought you were working in your father's shoe stores now." Marv was twenty and had gone right into the family business without a college degree.

"Managing actually, but Father didn't want Mother to be alone," he said.

With a hundred guests at the peak of the summer, and half as many staff, Bertha Peck would never have been alone.

"In the fall I'll start at our new Chicago store," Marv went on.

"If everything goes well," Mrs. Peck whispered.

Betty didn't know if that was a warning or a wish. No matter. She and Marv had played together as children. He was a guest.

"Why don't you sit with us?" Marv asked. "Your grandparents tell us you were admitted to Barnard." He pulled back the empty chair to his right, but Betty patted Zaide's shoulder and he looked up at her and held her hand. Her grandfather usually spent his summers distracted, so this gesture made her feel like she'd won a million bucks.

"I'm *going* to Barnard," Betty said.

"Your grandparents are so generous. And modern," Mrs. Peck said.

"That's right," Betty said. She hoped the offense that simmered inside her wasn't coming out in her voice.

"Betty?" Marv had sat, his arm now around the back of the chair next to him, patting it. She wished she felt the wistfulness of nostalgia, but she did not. Betty wanted her summer romance with a college boy, not with Marv Peck. She had tried to like him that way two summers ago, she really had. It hadn't worked.

"Thank you, but I can't. Almost time for calisthenics. Have to get ready. Can't be late." Betty looked at her grandmother.

"Let's go for a walk tonight, Betty." Marv stood at his place, as if this made the offer more enticing.

Betty flinched and hoped no one noticed. "I was planning on going to the staff bonfire with the girls."

"Great, we can join them and then take a walk on the beach."

"It really is just for the staff."

"Betty!"

She hated even a subtle scolding from Zaide. *Give the guests what they want.* That was his motto.

"I'll meet you at nine then?" Betty looked at Zaide, who nodded.

"Isn't that kind of late?" Mrs. Peck asked.

"I'd like to finish dinner with my grandparents first, escort some of the children to their evening activities, and go home to change clothes."

"Always a good girl, my Betty," Zaide said.

"That's swell," Marv said. "See you at nine."

Swell.

Chapter 5

BETTY

Flames stretched and flickered in the night air. Orange-tipped sparks drifted upward toward the blue-black sky and disappeared as if they were shooting stars. Laughter swirled around Betty. She'd seen these bonfires from her bedroom window, she'd sat on her porch aching for inclusion, but never had she felt their pulse. At first she thought it was the music—Nat King Cole, Patti Page, Tony Bennett—wafting out of the portable radio set atop a red metal cooler. No, it was more like a collective heartbeat thumping with anticipation, flirtation, and carefree joy. Betty's skin hummed.

The heat from the fire toasted the early-June air, which could still be brisk after dark. Betty removed her sweater and draped it over her arm. Marv stood next to her and stared at the fire. Did he regret coming along when no one paid him any attention? Betty looked from face to face. She didn't see Abe. Maybe that was better. She could finish her walk with Marv and come back on her own. Surely Abe would be here later.

Couples were already wrapped together in beach blankets, facing the lake, some facing each other. Doris slow-danced with one of the waiters. Georgia stood in a circle with some of the other girls, chattering away, likely about the boys standing in a cluster nearby.

Marv placed his hand on Betty's arm. "Let's take a walk."

Betty moved her arm. She wanted to stay there, bearing witness and savoring the thrill of everything around her. "I'd like to stay."

"Your grandparents think you're taking a walk with me."

"You're right." The last thing Betty wanted was for Marv to tattle to his mother that she wasn't a proper "date." Betty lifted her hand to wave but no one was looking at her. She turned to the girl next to her. "This was fun."

"It'll get crazy later." The girl bit her bottom lip and quickened her speech. "I don't mean crazy, really. Just more fun. But, well . . ."

Of course she knew who Betty was, likely afraid she was part of the fun police, or her grandparents' spy.

"It's fab," Betty said. "I'm not going to squeal." She realized her grandparents must already know what went on at the beach. They didn't just want the guests happy; they wanted the staff happy as well. "Happy help" was part of Zaide's motto too.

The girl squeezed Betty's elbow. "You're a doll. I'm Barbara. And I know you're Betty. Who's your honey?"

"Oh, he's not—"

"Marv Peck, nice to meet you, Barbara. C'mon, Betty, we should be going." He tapped her elbow. Marv lifted her powder-blue cardigan from her arm and swung it over her shoulders as they walked away from the fire and toward the lighthouse. How dared he behave like they were an item. She yanked the sweater and slung it back over her arm.

Despite her irritation, Betty jump-started the chitchat—the new beach chairs and umbrellas on the beach, the musical talent of the staff who sang after dinner, their favorite desserts (Marv's was apple cake and Betty's was blueberry pie). She remained polite, though she grew bored, aching for the moment they'd turn back to the crackling blaze and all that surrounded it.

Betty had changed out of a peach cotton sateen number and into green pedal pushers with a madras plaid blouse tied at her waist. Marv no longer wore a suit but casual tan slacks and a button-down shirt.

Two years earlier Betty *had* believed she and Marv might share interests beyond their memories of childhood games. Peck's Popular Shoes was, for all intents and purposes, a fashion-oriented business. And if there was one thing Betty loved and respected aside from her grandparents, it was fashion. Betty had attempted to describe the latest spring and summer styles, but Marv had refused to talk about business.

"Why do you care so much about the shoe business?" Marv had asked.

"I know a lot about fashion and cosmetics," she'd said. "And not just how to wear them. I'm going to be a fashion magazine writer and editor someday." She'd been sure of this since the ninth grade, when she'd written a beauty column for her school paper: "Popular Looks for Today's Girls."

Marv had smirked. "Is that so?"

Betty had wanted to slap him. "It is!"

"By the time you graduate you'll be twenty-two. All your friends will be married."

"Good for them."

"Don't you want that? A husband, a house, children? All girls do."

"Sure," Betty had said. "Someday. I want an education. A career. A bank account. Independence. Then I'll have more to offer my husband than just a pretty smile and a trousseau."

"Just for the record, I think that's all a fella wants."

Not any fella of mine. Betty had turned around. "I'd like to go home."

When Marv had asked Betty for a second "walk" the next day, she'd declined.

Yet here she was now, walking with Marv Peck.

"You're a real beauty, Betty."

Betty looked at Marv. She really *looked* at this young man who seemed to like her, though his actions and words were misguided. He stood about five-eleven. She knew this because he was just a trifle taller than Georgia. His shoulders were narrow and his shirt loose. In that moment she hoped he'd fill out. That'd help him look more manly, more mature, take up more space. She wondered how much authority he commanded at his father's shoe stores. She liked to think he had another side to him, one that would attract the kind of girl he wanted, one with a smile and a trousseau, but without brains or ambition.

"I'd like us to remain friends this summer," Betty said.

"Ouch. You really know how to hurt a guy."

"I'm going to New York in September; there really isn't a point to more than that."

"For now."

"No, Marv, not 'for now.' I'm going off to Barnard and I plan to stay in New York. I'm not coming back to South Haven." No magazine jobs in Michigan. No Michigan for Betty. "My grandparents support me." She would have stomped her foot but knew that was childish and would refute her point.

He smirked the way he had before. "Okay."

Betty quickened her step, not easy to do in the sand. Marv caught up to her.

"I'm just teasing you, Betty. Don't be so sensitive."

"I don't think it's very nice to tease someone about her hopes and dreams. Do you know how hard I worked to be accepted to Barnard? How much my grandparents are sacrificing to send me away? You were rude. I said I wanted to be friends when I could have said 'bug off.'" She was at once angry at Marv's dismissal, yet horrified that he might be right, that she had no right to leave the cocoon of her family, to want anything more than she could find right here on the beach or back at home.

No. He was wrong. She could have it all. This is what she had been raised to believe, and Nannie and Zaide didn't lie. Even her absent parents supported the decision, which, up until now, had been the only thing to make her question it.

In the distance Betty saw the glow of the bonfire.

"Actually, Marv, I'm going back, but you don't need to walk with me. I'm quite capable on my own."

Back with the group, Betty saw a few couples were wrapped around each other, slow-dancing in a way that would have made Betty blush, had she not been envious that they'd already found their summer sweethearts. They swayed side to side, even though the radio was gone. Other couples lay on beach blankets the way she once had with Robert Smith, except no one here seemed to be putting a stop to anything. They had wrapped the blankets up and over themselves, but still.

Marv had been a half pace behind her, and now stepped to her side. "Betty, wait," he said.

He'd followed her. They were just a few feet from the safety of the group that was not necking or dancing.

Darn. She stopped and turned toward him, clasped her hands in front of her the way she did when she thought she might fidget inappropriately.

"Before you say anything," Betty said, "I won't tell my grandparents what you said. They like you, and I'm not going to be the one to change that."

Marv tugged gently on her hands. "We can just be friends for now."

"You're not paying attention," Betty said.

"I thought it was a woman's prerogative to change her mind."

"It is. But I won't."

Marv sank into the sand—or he somehow just looked smaller. "All righty then. Shall we roast marshmallows? As friends?"

A cloud lifted from Betty's spirit, though it all seemed too easy. "Sure." She wanted to tell him *heck no*, but she had to think of her standing as the Stern granddaughter.

Three girls held sticks over the embers, their marshmallows slowly browning. Marv and Betty faced them from the other side of the firepit.

"There's two left," a deep voice said from behind, and an open blue and white box of Campfire marshmallows was thrust between Betty and Marv.

Betty turned around to thank this bearer of marshmallows and spun back toward the fire. *Holy moly.* It was him. Abe.

"Thanks," Marv said. He reached into the box, then turned to Betty. "I'll go grab a couple of sticks." He stepped away. What was Betty to do now? She wasn't supposed to meet this boy when she was on a date with someone else. But there was nothing wrong with being polite. "Being polite is always right," Nannie would say.

Betty turned to express her gratitude for the last two marshmallows and stared straight into a square chin covered in fine blond stubble and accented by a dimple. He'd stepped closer. She should have stepped back but did not, so his body occupied all the space that should have existed between them. Betty inhaled the menthol tang of aftershave and wanted to hold her breath and keep it inside. Instead she exhaled deeply.

"Thank you," she said. She glanced up and was so close that even in the dark she saw his blue eyes were flecked with gold. Or maybe it was the reflection of the fire.

"You're welcome."

A chill scurried across Betty's neck, although his voice sounded like it had been warmed by the fire. It sounded deeper and smoother than she'd remembered from the kitchen window, as if that had been an off-the-cuff remark and these two words were deliberate and thoughtful. The tone rolled over her and calmed her, while at the same time shivers traveled her arms. He smiled, and the dimples in his cheeks appeared as if she'd asked them to come out and play. He wore a button-down shirt, open in a casual beachy way and showing off an undershirt, as if he'd just thrown it on after a swim. The shirt hung loose outside his khaki shorts but did not disguise the shoulders that were as broad as any football player's she'd seen. The warm, woodsy scent of the fire wafted into their imaginary lair. Betty couldn't do anything except smile back at him.

"I wondered if I'd see you again," he whispered. The lowered volume of his voice didn't change its resonance. "And not just from across the dining room." Betty's cheeks flushed, but she couldn't blame the fire. He had noticed her. He had wondered about her. "You seem to have recovered nicely from your ordeal with the canapés."

Doris had been right—this voice matched the one they'd heard at the kitchen window. If it was anyone else, it might have seemed creepy, but that's what she'd wanted. For him to notice her. Betty glanced around the firepit for Marv, who was holding marshmallows over the heat, and talking to Eleanor Rosen, back at Stern's for her second year as a children's counselor. Eleanor was popular with the waiters, though Betty knew she shouldn't believe kitchen gossip.

"Your boyfriend looks busy," Abe said.

"He's not my boyfriend. Why does everyone think he's my boyfriend?"

"In case you haven't noticed, people don't usually come to these things alone. And if they do, they don't leave alone." He lifted his eyebrows and Betty turned away, clamping her lips. She was flabbergasted. He was so forward! She should have been outraged that he spoke so plainly before they'd even properly met, yet her heart pounded, and her skin zinged with the thrill of being near enough to touch him. And to hear him talk about the romance around them? Betty's face warmed again, and the flush traveled. *Get ahold of yourself!*

"I guess I didn't realize." Betty turned back. Oh, she'd realized. She'd been realizing for years. That's why she shouldn't have asked Marv to bring her here. She'd misled him, perhaps, but if she hadn't, she wouldn't have met her bonfire man. Yes, that was more apropos than "marshmallow man." He was not a marshmallow at all.

Marv returned with one stick, two marshmallows stuck onto its end. He held it out to Betty.

"Thank you," Betty said.

Betty had tasted marshmallows floating in hot cocoa at Georgia's house, but she'd never tasted one that had been roasted over a fire. After all, marshmallows were *treif*—and her grandparents couldn't serve anything at the resort that wasn't kosher and wouldn't have them at home either. Betty hadn't believed it when she'd learned that marshmallows contained gelatin, and that gelatin was made of pigs' bones.

But forbidden bites were often the sweetest.

"Who's your friend, Betty?" Marv asked, pulling marshmallow strings from the stick, and jutting his chin toward her bonfire man.

"Abe Barsky." He held out his hand. "I'm a new waiter, among other things."

Marv fumbled the stick and shook Abe's hand. "Marv Peck. I'm an old friend of Betty's, among other things." He slid his nonsticky hand around Betty's waist and she slipped to the left, away from his grasp. Marv stuck his hand in his trouser pocket. He looked small next to Abe, whose arms looked like the boxers' arms she'd once seen at an exhibition match she'd been to on a date. It was a bad date, but there were some good-looking boxers (before the match, that is).

"Let me walk you home, Betty," Marv said.

"For Pete's sake, she lives right there!" Eleanor said, as she sauntered up behind Marv wearing a floral halter bathing suit covered only by a towel she'd wrapped around her waist. It was much too late and too cold for a swim, but it was always the right time for Eleanor to show off her curves and her cleavage. Betty should have been discomfited by Eleanor's bold bluster but was mesmerized by her confidence.

Eleanor tapped Marv's leg with her hip. "She's not Bitty Betty Stern anymore, is she? Our little girl's all grown-up. Or that's what I hear."

Betty was not so mesmerized by Eleanor's harsh words.

Marv and Eleanor chuckled. Betty scowled. Abe shook his head, not so much in disapproval but as if assessing the situation and the involved parties.

"I'm not leaving yet," Betty said.

"You can walk *me* home, Marv." Eleanor, her brown hair styled to flip like Myrna Loy's, stared at Betty, daring her to object. Eleanor shifted her gaze to Marv, then to Abe, then back to Betty, and grinned. *You can have him.*

"It wouldn't be right," Marv said. "I came here with Betty."

"Like Eleanor said, I live right there," Betty said.

The only light on in her house was the screen porch, no less obvious than the lighthouse beacon. It was half past ten, according to Betty's watch. Nannie and Zaide wouldn't be awake to ask her about her walk with Marv. And by breakfast time they would be too busy to ask.

"I'll see you tomorrow then, Betty?" Marv asked. Eleanor grabbed his hand and Marv didn't pull away.

"Of course you'll see her tomorrow, silly," Eleanor said as she skipped away dragging Marv behind her. "She owns the place."

"Eleanor's too much," Abe said.

"That's a nice way of putting it." Betty spun around and looked at the few couples necking on the beach. The fire had been doused with water. Stars were now hidden by a layer of clouds. She faced Abe. "I'd say that was my good deed for the day, wouldn't you?"

"You played right into Eleanor's hands."

"I may have."

"You didn't want Marv to walk you home."

"Well, let's just say Eleanor wanted it more than I didn't want it."

Abe laughed. "Would you let *me* walk you home, Betty Stern?"

Her heart thumped. Had she heard him correctly? "Didn't you come here with someone?"

"No."

"I thought you said most people don't come to bonfires alone."

"I *said* no one leaves alone."

Abe smiled a slow, wide smile, one that made his eyes crinkle at the sides. Sure, he was flirting. Thank God.

He cast down those eyes as he reached out a bent arm. And then, a moment later, he made eye contact with Betty. Even in the dark his eyes sparkled when she looked into them. Had she ever looked at anyone this way before, right into the center of their eyes as they looked back? If she had, surely their eyes hadn't glistened like sapphires. She'd have remembered that. She'd remember this.

As Betty looped her hand through Abe's arm, she rested her palm on the hill of muscle in his smooth forearm. Blood rushed around her body and she burned from head to toe. Abe's smile broadened without effort, and his gaze coated her skin like a drizzle of warm summer rain.

"I would very much like you to walk me home, Abe Barsky."

It was the loveliest name she'd ever said aloud.

As they started up the beach, Betty silently rehearsed the best way to say, "Thank you for walking me home."

She was content to hold his arm, to walk in wordless company. Then he laid his hand atop hers and patted it three times—three times! She was certain those were not platonic or brotherly pats—she'd have been able to sense that, wouldn't she? His hand lingered. Was that by accident or intention? Abe didn't strike her as someone who did anything by accident. He set his hand back to his side.

"I hear you're going to Barnard in September," Abe said. "You must be really smart."

"I guess."

"Don't be modest," Abe said. "You should be proud. It's hard to get into college. Especially for a girl. And Barnard is like an Ivy League, isn't it?"

"Ivy League colleges are for boys. The Seven Sisters are their counterparts, I guess."

"I'm sure it'll be great. Have you ever been to New York?"

Now Betty felt foolish. "No. I applied by mail and met an alumnus in Chicago. Have you been?"

"No," Abe said. "But it's a dream of mine. I'm going to design skyscrapers."

"I'm going to work in one!" Betty sensed it was safe to match his honesty.

Abe laughed but it wasn't dismissive; it was playful. "We're a good match then, I guess. Maybe I'll work on the skyscraper and you'll work in it. What do you want to do inside my skyscraper, Betty?"

Betty's heart pounded as they stood by her porch steps. "I want to write for a magazine." She outlined her plan for working her way to fashion editor.

Any other night, with any other boy, dreaming aloud would have been pointless. Boys weren't interested in her plans or her dreams. Most boys were like Marv—tolerant yet glib. But Abe listened. Abe nodded. Abe did not smirk.

"I have a feeling you'll be whatever you want to be. It's nice to meet a girl who isn't going to college to find a husband." Abe inhaled. "You're not, are you?"

Betty shook her head.

"I can tell. You have more in your head than room for recipes. Not that there's anything wrong with marriage and kids and all." Abe blushed. *Oh my God, he blushed.* "I should shut my trap now."

Betty laughed. "You're right. I have a lot of plans. But this summer I just want to have fun." There. She said it. "Can I ask how you ended up working here?"

"I need extra money to help with tuition next year. I asked around. I wrote to your grandfather and explained my situation. I sent references from three professors and my hockey coach. He was really kind to hire me at the last minute."

"That's Zaide."

"I'll always be grateful."

"I heard your family owns a store. What kind of store is it? My friend Georgia's family owns the department store in town. Lemon's."

"It's a five-and-dime, nothing fancy," Abe said.

"And you didn't want to work there?" Betty hadn't meant to sound like she wished Abe hadn't come to South Haven. "Obviously you didn't want to, or you'd be there. I'm glad you're here."

"Me too. Usually I work for my father, but business dropped off some and we had a falling out." Abe clammed up. "If I don't want to get canned my first week, I should let you go inside."

Betty didn't want to go inside. She wanted to know more about his skyscrapers, his family's business, his rift with his father.

"Maybe we can talk again soon?" Abe asked. "Real soon?"

She skipped up the steps but turned around and nodded. It was as if he'd read her mind.

Betty fell backward onto her bed and smiled at the ceiling. She couldn't help it. Had there ever been a more beautiful ceiling? White and smooth like her favorite frosting, by lamplight it glowed a muted amber, as if cast by a thousand familiar sunsets.

There were zero sunsets to count until she could see Abe Barsky again.

Betty rolled to her stomach and rested her chin on fisted palms, kicking her legs like she was swimming a mile. Her smile stretched until her cheeks ached with the tall handsome reality of Abe Barsky. She closed her eyes and imagined his blue ones staring at her, but not as if she were watching from above, as happened with some of her daydreams, but as if she were inside herself looking at him again, at the very moment their eyes met, before either of them had glanced away. She could still smell his aftershave.

He was *the one*.

Not just a summer beau or a passing fancy. He was her *bashert*, her intended, sent by God and a summer job.

It had happened this way for her grandparents. Their families owned neighboring farms in the Fruit Belt, so they'd met in grade school. Zaide said he never looked at another girl. That's when Nannie would always roll her eyes, but when she was sixteen—finished with school and taking in sewing to help her family—she married him.

Heck, it had happened this way for her parents too. Joe Stern met Tillie Feldman the one summer her parents came to South Haven from Chicago. They hadn't even stayed at Stern's, but the two met at the arcade, wrote letters for a year, and then eloped.

Maybe true love ran in her family.

Betty scrambled to her feet and grasped the bedpost with one hand, stretching out her arms. It was too late to call Georgia. She walked to her desk, opened the top middle drawer, and retrieved a piece of monogrammed stationery and her favorite pen so she could write to her Barnard roommate, an Italian girl from New Jersey named Patricia San Giacomo. Betty thought she must be worldly and exotic, and she couldn't wait to meet her.

Someone knocked on the door and opened it. Betty laid her hands by her sides and tapped her legs. What would she write to Patricia when her thoughts were overwhelmed by Abe?

Nannie poked in her head. "Did you have a nice time tonight?" There was no accusatory hint in her voice, but she hadn't said "with Marv," so Betty didn't have to lie.

"Yes, I did."

"Good. See you in the morning, honey." Nannie turned and pulled the door behind her.

"Wait," Betty said. Omitting was the same as lying. And someone might have seen them. "Marv walked Eleanor home, so Abe Barsky walked me home."

That was the truth, or it was enough of the truth.

Nannie stepped fully inside the bedroom. "It doesn't seem like Marv to leave you when he asked you to go for a walk with him."

"I said I didn't mind. Eleanor had much farther to walk than I did."

"I imagine you didn't mind. Marv is a nice boy but Abe's very handsome."

"Nannie!" Betty's cheeks grew even warmer. She contained a smile and hoped her grandmother couldn't hear her heart pounding or see it forcing its way out of her chest. She wished she could tell Nannie how her whole body had turned hot and cold when she'd looked into Abe's eyes—how she knew there were things they would say to each other that no one else would understand. That there was so much more to him than that handsome face, just like Nannie had always said there was so much more to her than a pretty one.

"Don't forget you leave in September," Nannie whispered.

"But would it be all right if . . . ?"

"If you went on a date? Yes. A date. As long as it doesn't interfere with work or preparing for the pageant, you have my permission. We want you to have a nice summer, but it's not the time for something serious, Betty. Don't go getting carried away."

"I promise." She skittered to the door and hugged Nannie hard and fast before she changed her mind. Betty closed the door, then placed the paper and pen back into the desk drawer. She'd keep her reveries to herself a little longer.

Chapter 6

BOOP

Boop focused on the present—Doris and Georgia staring toward the lighthouse, yelps from roughhousing teens on the beach, a rumble in her stomach, Hannah resting her chin in her hand and gazing at Boop as if she was waiting for more bits of the past.

Some bits were not for sharing. "You have a lot to think about," Boop said. "You should go home and talk to Clark."

"I will," Hannah said. "But not yet. I need to figure things out on my own. I'm so sorry I made you remember things you wanted left in the past."

"I'm a tough cookie. Don't you worry about me," Boop said.

Hannah kissed Boop and walked inside.

"Girls?" Boop said.

Georgia and Doris turned around.

"Enough about *yesterday*. Tomorrow afternoon is square dancing. Get ready to do-si-do."

"I'm not sure I have the right clothes," Georgia said.

"Oh, you don't need anything fancy," Doris said. "It'll be fun."

Georgia rolled her eyes. "Fine."

"You were brave to tell Hannah about the situation with Marvin," Doris said.

"It didn't feel brave," Boop said. "It felt right."

Much to her surprise, Boop loved remembering the girl she had been at eighteen. What *chutzpah* she'd had. What moxie. She'd known exactly what she'd wanted—and hadn't yet known she wouldn't get it, so she'd been light and free of constraints. It was a time when her feelings—love and lust and excitement and hope and anger—rushed through her like a snowball pushed down from the top of a hill, gaining speed and weight along the way.

Her footsteps to the bedroom were heavy but quiet, the same as her secrets.

She walked to the windows that had been manufactured to look like original double-hung paned glass to maintain the historic integrity of the house Zaide had built for his bride in 1919. The window trim had been repainted white, and after six years it still popped from the sand-colored walls, as her decorator had promised. When Boop had decided to move from Skokie and live in South Haven full-time, she'd sold her grandparents' walnut bedroom suite and donated the money to an organization that supported teenage mothers. She'd sprung for light oak beachy and contemporary furniture with clean lines.

She *potchkied* around her room, ruffling curtains, smoothing the bedspread, rearranging throw pillows, jotting down a grocery list even though the cupboards were jam-packed. Boop sighed. Contentment swirled and settled in with her deep breath.

This is why I'm here.

This was not an existential statement of being, but a practical declaration of resolve. She'd been asking herself, *What am I doing in South Haven, with its frigid winters and transient neighbors? Why am I living alone in an old house with a wooden staircase and enough bedrooms for a family?*

Hannah needed her to be there. Not forever, but for now. Hannah needed to know some of what happened that summer as much as Boop needed to acknowledge it, even relive it. After her granddaughter was settled and assured, and the girls had gone back to their own homes and lives, Boop would move to San Diego. Until then, she had memories to cherish, circumstances to unravel, and loved ones to nurture.

This time, when Boop left South Haven, she would be traveling light.

Boop pried off a blue lid from a plastic storage box and gently lifted out the itchy wool sweaters knitted by Nannie's mother, who'd died before Boop was born. Red beads the size of grains of rice were sewn across the front of the navy sweater, and iridescent sequins had been stitched across the beige one. Nannie wore the sweaters on High Holidays, and Boop had tucked them away when she died. She lifted the navy one to her face and inhaled. It smelled like an old sweater. There was a time she'd have detected a hint of talcum powder.

Under the next sweater—a white cardigan Nannie had knitted herself—Boop found just what she was looking for: her childhood tackle box. When she was eighteen it had been the perfect hiding place. As a child, Boop had loved fishing on the Black River with her grandfather. Then she grew more interested in looking for boys than for worms. But Zaide understood and didn't nag.

Boop walked to the taupe floral chaise—a reupholstered remainder of her grandparents' bedroom—tucked diagonally into the corner by the window, climbed onto it, and stretched her legs in front of her, not a varicose vein in sight, though her skin was more delicate and sheer than it had once been. She set the tackle box on her lap, the weight of the past pressing on her legs.

Rust embellished the box's edges—not because it'd been battered to look old, but because it was old. She'd seen things just like it at Eagle

Street Market, where someone could buy something like it to transform into a planter or a jewelry case or set it on a windowsill as an element in a vintage lake vignette. They'd make up a story to go along with the box, no doubt, though they wouldn't have needed to.

Thunder boomed in the distance, so Boop set aside the box, closed the windows, and watched a few cars drive down Lakeshore, away from the beach, when really it was the best time to stay. The lake became unpredictable, rampant with swells, its waves crashing onto the sand as it transformed into something different for the duration of the storm—perhaps living out its dream to be the ocean. Even in the dark, she saw rain roll in from the north. She knew the sheets of water cut through the surface of the lake like a straight-edge razor. The storm would darken the beach from beige to brown and in the morning the sand would be packed tight like brown sugar.

She cradled the tackle box in her arms like a baby, and a long-lost love danced across her heart. His name caught in her throat, as if she'd taken too big a bite of the past.

There would never be an accidental encounter, an explanation, or a second chance. He would never show up in South Haven. He would be eighty-seven or eighty-eight now. The memories were all she had, and this summer she would honor what she had ignored for so long.

The next morning, sunshine slipped through the opening in the bedroom curtains. Boop rose slowly, carefully. She shuffled to the window, pushed one panel left, the other right. She unlocked and pushed on the window sash. The breeze nudged her eyes closed again, and Boop held the sill so she wouldn't wobble. When she opened her eyes, she saw one boat gliding way out on the lake, set amid blue water with sky to match.

Two kites dotted the sky to the south, way beyond the lighthouse. Boop smiled, pleased she could still see so far down the beach, and as far as the horizon.

Hannah jogged up the street and disappeared from view when she ascended the porch. A few moments later the front door slammed. What she was thinking as she ran, jostling the baby, Boop didn't know.

Dressed in red twill capris and a light-blue embroidered blouse she'd have favored in the seventies, Boop went downstairs and stood at the threshold of her kitchen. "What's going on in here?"

Doris swiveled around, showing off her flour-dusted, once-peacock-blue shirt, which was speckled with lemon zest. "Is that a rhetorical question?"

"Come, sit with me, have coffee," Georgia said. "I'm checking the blueberries for stems."

Hannah flipped on the hand mixer. "We're making your Nannie's blueberry lemon cake," she yelled over the whir. "Did we wake you?"

Boop chose a mug and poured a cup of coffee. "No, I had to get up to eat cake."

Hannah tipped back her head and laughed.

Boop sat at the kitchen table with Georgia. "When did you plan this little baking party?"

"No plan," Doris said. "I woke up earlier and heard . . ." She glanced at Hannah.

"She heard me throwing up," Hannah said.

Oh.

"And then fifteen minutes later she was digging through the kitchen cabinets looking for something sweet," Doris said. "So here we are."

"By then, I was awake," Georgia said.

Georgia picked stems and tossed blueberries from one bowl to the next. "Why don't you look happier? Whatever else happens or doesn't, there's going to be a baby!"

Boop's own unplanned and outside-of-wedlock pregnancy was a *shanda*; her grandparents had been so ashamed. It was something to be hidden. *She* was to be hidden. For Hannah it was coffee klatch fodder.

"Hannah, come sit," Georgia said.

Hannah shut off the mixer, balanced the blades on the side of the bowl, and sat at the table.

"As far as I'm concerned, there's no right or wrong," Georgia said. "Get married now, later, or never. It has to be right for you."

"Wasn't it ever right for you?" Hannah asked.

If Georgia answered, this would officially be the summer that nothing was off-limits.

"All I wanted to be was a doctor. Not a wife, not a mother."

"I don't think you ever allowed yourself to want those things," Doris said.

"Perhaps. But I wanted to be a doctor because I had a sister who died when she was three days old. I never met her. She would have been the oldest, so twelve years older than me. My whole life I just wanted to keep babies healthy."

Boop held Georgia's hand. How Georgia had wished there had been a gravesite to visit nearby for Imogen, but her parents had moved to South Haven from Detroit. By the time they had moved away, Imogen might have been married with babies of her own.

One winter around Imogen's birthday, Boop and Georgia had collected frozen sprigs of fallen pine, tied them with a pink ribbon, and set the bundle on the river, where they saw it resting on the ice until the spring thaw.

"I didn't get married until I was twenty-two," Doris said. "My parents thought I was going to be an old maid. I do think good things come to those who wait."

"You're old but you're not an old maid," Georgia said to Doris. Hannah chuckled.

"It wasn't funny back then," Boop said.

"Do you have regrets?" Hannah asked. "Any of you?"

"No," Doris said. "I mean, I regret that my husbands died and that two of my marriages failed. So, I guess that's my answer. But I don't think of them being regrets as much as being sad reasons for brand-new opportunities."

"My regret might be not being closer to my nieces and nephews. I spent so many years taking care of children that when it came to my family I only got involved if someone was sick," Georgia said.

"You were always good to me and Emma," Hannah said.

"My sometimes granddaughters." Georgia leaned over and hugged Hannah.

"What about you, Boop?" Hannah asked.

Boop hesitated, but if she meant to finally be honest this summer—with Hannah and herself . . . "I'm sorry I didn't have a chance to go to college and push myself. To be someone in addition to a wife and mother." Or other than. "But I'm not sorry I married your grandfather if that's what you're asking. I wouldn't have your dad or you or Emma."

"What do you think you would have become?"

"Your grandmother wanted to be a fashion editor," Georgia said.

"At a big fancy magazine," Doris said. "In New York."

Hannah grinned. "Your grandparents didn't want you to take over the resort?"

"They never pressured me. Not when it came to my education. Zaide thought he'd run the resort forever. Never talked about retiring. They didn't count on the whole industry and all the resorts failing in the late sixties."

"What happened?"

"Highways, affordable airfares, summer camps, working mothers."

"So it would have worked out for you to stay in New York. Magazines didn't start to tank until the 2000s."

"Who knows what would've happened to me?" Would she have been encouraged or discouraged, redirected? Would she have been able to compete with the other girls? Boop still believed she would have liked New York, and that a future built on her abilities, intellect, and passion would have differed from the one she built on the top of a Magic Chef.

Hannah poured the blueberries into the batter, and the batter into a cake pan. She placed it in the oven and set the timer.

Georgia patted the chair next to her. "Marriage is a big decision, and if all this is a surprise . . ."

"It might be a surprise but maybe this baby is what you need," Doris said.

Georgia shushed Doris. "Hannah, would you want to marry Clark if you weren't having a baby?"

Boop should have been the one to ask, but she couldn't. Even hearing Georgia say it singed her heart.

Hannah slouched. "Probably not now. But maybe eventually. We weren't talking about kids yet. We both wanted them—but later."

"No time like the present," Doris said. "Take it as a sign."

"Please don't tell her to take one of the biggest decisions of her life as a sign," Boop said. "This should be a deliberate and joint decision. You know what? That's what's wrong here."

"What?" Hannah asked.

"This isn't about a fairy tale, or what happened to me. It's about you and Clark. No matter what you decide, the baby will be fine. But you have to be happy—really, really happy, Hannah. And frankly, so does Clark."

"What should I do if I'm really not sure?"

"You should go home and talk it out with Clark."

"But not until after we eat," Doris said as the oven timer dinged, and the four women pushed back their kitchen chairs and stood.

Hannah removed the cake from the oven and set it on a wire rack to cool. Boop didn't bake much—her harmless resistance to one vestige of housewifery—but thanks to Nannie she had all the correct equipment. Doris found the cake knife. Georgia gathered plates and forks and napkins. Boop whisked lemon juice into powdered sugar until it transformed into a shiny glaze.

Hannah drizzled the glaze over the cake and carried the pan to the table. Everyone sat, and Hannah served.

"So, did you end up 'going with' that guy Abe? Isn't that what you called it?"

"She did," Doris said. "He was a good-looking boy. Dimples, right?"

Boop huffed. "Must you, Doris?"

"He was, but it's irrelevant," Georgia said. "We were young. Everyone was beautiful or handsome."

Not true.

"Do you have any pictures?" Hannah asked.

Boop shook her head. "Not a one." At the time she didn't think it mattered.

"What happened between you?"

Boop revised her revisionist history. "It just ended."

"And you started going with Pop after that?"

"She did," Doris said. "Marvin was like her knight in shining loafers."

"Ixnay the opinions, Doris," Georgia said.

Hannah smiled at Boop. "I don't mind. Without Abe, you wouldn't have ended up with Pop. There would be no Dad, no me, no Emma, no twins. It had to happen for all of us to be here."

In almost seventy years Boop hadn't thought of it that way, that the events of that summer had served only as her circuitous pathway to Marvin. That *he* had been her destiny all along.

Even during good times—and there were many—Boop had always believed she and Marvin were each other's runner-up. What if she'd always been wrong?

"No matter how you ended up with Pop, I'm glad you did. Obviously." Hannah laughed.

"Me too."

"Do you know what happened to him?"

"What happened to whom?" Georgia's voice rose and she dragged out the *m* sound.

"Abe. Who do you think?"

Boop's heart pattered. Mentioning Abe in the past or thinking of him in private was one thing, but talking about him as if he were part of her present? She had stopped doing that a long time ago. She'd locked the vault and thrown away the key.

"How on earth would I know about him now?" Boop asked.

"People are always looking up their old boyfriends and girlfriends online. I can check for you, if you want."

"That seems a little meddlesome, Hannah." But it piqued Boop's interest anyway. Was it wrong? Who could it hurt? Silly question. It could hurt her. He might have forgotten her. He might have no memories. He might be dead. He was probably dead.

"That's what the internet is for, Boop! Aren't you curious?"

"No, she's not curious," Georgia blurted.

But questions fluttered inside Boop like a flung deck of cards. Could it really be that simple? Why hadn't she thought of it before? She knew how to use the internet. "Well, maybe a little curious now that you mention it. But don't do anything. Not unless I ask. The last thing I need is a surprise."

Chapter 7

BETTY

Betty loved summer Shabbos. The aroma of chicken noodle soup floated into the dining room on a magic carpet of sweet brisket, roasted hen, and just-baked challah. Her stomach gurgled as she walked to her grandparents' table in the center of the room, set with simple silver candles, a pewter *kiddush* cup, and a bottle of Manischewitz Concord grape wine. Georgia called it the Jewish holy trinity.

"Good Shabbos, *bubbeleh*," Zaide said.

"Good Shabbos, Zaide."

"You look very pretty tonight," Nannie said.

"Thank you." Betty wouldn't have considered her seafoam circle dress with the white wing collar worthy of notice, but along with her new white gloves, it was appropriate for Shabbos. And it was pretty enough for Abe.

"My girls sure are lookers." Zaide stood at attention, his natural stance, as the guests flowed into the room. On Shabbos Zaide didn't schmooze, or maybe he schmoozed less. Most of the meal he stayed by Nannie, his own Shabbos queen. Once, Betty had seen Zaide pat Nannie on the bottom.

"Ira!" Nannie had said.

"It's a mitzvah on Shabbos, Yetta."

She looked up at Zaide and waggled her finger. Betty could have sworn Nannie winked. It was years before Betty understood what Zaide had meant, and then she didn't really want to think of her grandparents being romantic, even if it was a mitzvah.

Tonight, Nannie, Zaide, and Betty were to dine with the Goldblatt family—Mr. and Mrs. Seymour Goldblatt from Indianapolis, along with their sixteen-year-old twins, Marsha and Marna, who wanted all the details of Betty's senior year.

Mrs. Alice Goldblatt, nicknamed Mrs. Gallbladder by the staff, crowed about extensive dietary restrictions, though no one at the resort had witnessed an attack during an entire decade of summers. Still, when the Goldblatts arrived for their three-week stay, Chef Gavin prepared ample portions of boiled chicken and steamed vegetables at every meal, as requested. But every day, after feasting on a platter of bland, medicinal food, Mrs. Goldblatt finished off her family's plates in full view of the other guests and staff, right down to wiping the fattiest bits of chicken skin in gravy. She tucked Danish into her handbag each morning and shnecken into her evening clutch. Rumor swelled one summer, something about a cheese blintze found between the sheets.

Maybe Mrs. Gallbladder had thought *that* was a mitzvah.

Betty loved this craziness as much as she loved the familiar view of her lake. These were her people, her family. She knew their quirks and foibles, and they'd watched her grow up—more so than her own parents, who feigned interest no more than one weekend a summer during a break in their performance schedule. That's when they showed up in South Haven, gussied up and gorgeous, both of them. They talked about cities and theaters and musicians and even soldiers, when they toured with the USO. They talked to Betty as if she were someone else's child, cooing over how tall she'd grown, or how she had all the brains in the family. Zaide never said much while they were there. Zaide was the best talker Betty knew, so this unsettled her. Nannie spoke higher than her usual voice and was on her best behavior, not uttering one "Nannie-ism" during the visit.

Betty bet Nannie would have done anything to get her parents to stay in South Haven.

Not Betty.

She learned one thing from her parents—the one thing she'd never do: abandon a child. She gulped a mouthful of air and scolded herself.

"Self-pity isn't pretty," Nannie would have said.

Nannie, inspecting the rosebud-embroidered challah cover, was right: Betty couldn't really pity herself when she had full-time doting grandparents and a revolving door of quasi aunts, uncles, and cousins three months a year.

Mrs. Goldblatt pulled off her right glove, finger by finger, revealing a double-strand iridescent pearl bracelet with a diamond clasp. Her wrist, as slim and fragile as a chicken wing, didn't seem strong enough to support it, belying Mrs. Gallbladder's reputation. Then she smoothed her napkin between her thumb and forefinger, no doubt planning for her evening snack. A few tables away, Betty noticed Marv in a fashionable black suit with narrow lapels, looking more dapper than she'd have expected. He stroked his chin. She looked at the Teitelbaum table to avoid his gaze, rather than be rude should he glance her way. She'd dodged crossing Marv's path since he'd trailed off after Eleanor on the beach two nights ago. How easily boys were distracted.

A reverent hum swirled around the room like a distant swarm of bees. Soon all the adults had settled in their seats and the children had been shushed. An anticipatory silence signaled the start of Shabbos as brashly as cymbals.

Nannie and Betty stood.

"Good Shabbos." Nannie turned to greet all her guests. Betty's grandmother was as at ease in the spotlight as a pinup on a poster.

"Good Shabbos" reverberated through the dining room as the women and girls at each table pushed back their chairs and stood to say the prayer over the candles set out for each family. This was one thing the men couldn't do. Oh, there were other things, of course, but women striking matchsticks on the surfaces of matchboxes distracted Betty. Flames glittered. Nannie struck a match and set the wicks aglow on their smooth white candles. She circled her hands over them three times, and then shielded her eyes.

In faux contemplation, Betty squinted at the basket chandelier hanging above the table. Her thoughts had already skedaddled to the kitchen, where Abe, in his waiter's white tails, would be gathering soup-filled bowls for his table and balancing a silver tray on his shoulder with his hand. The flickering candlelight rebounded off the crystals like a pinball, from praying to playing and back again. The female voices blended to bless the Sabbath. As Nannie recited the ancient prayer in Hebrew, Betty lifted her palms to her face and whispered along in disobedient unison.

> Dear God,
> If you could possibly have Abe waiting
> the way he did last night,
> I'll take it
> from there.
> And let us say amen.

As dinner dishes were cleared, Betty lifted the edge of her glove to uncover the coral-gold face of a wristwatch that had once belonged to her mother. The color reminded Betty of apricot and strawberry jams mixed together—more orange than pink or more pink than orange, depending on the light. She couldn't deny its beauty and hadn't the strength to decline the gift. She'd admired it each time she'd seen Tillie wear it over the past decade. Her mother must have noticed. The watch had arrived special delivery the day before Betty's graduation with a note that read, "Time flies. Happy graduation. Affectionately, Tillie and Joe."

Her parents weren't known for their sentimentality, yet Betty preferred to think of the Hamilton as an heirloom rather than a hand-me-down, something she could show off.

The minute hand suspended between the X and the XI. One, maybe two minutes had passed since the last time she'd looked, and it would be a lifetime until she was excused from the Shabbos table. As Betty bounced her knee like a jackhammer, the napkin on her lap slid toward the floor. Nannie whisked it away before it fell.

"Abe is working," Nannie whispered. "And shaking us all won't change that."

Heat rose all the way up Betty's cheeks. Abe set plates of apple cake and cookies onto his table on the other side of the room. It was the same table he would serve three meals a day, all summer.

For the first two weeks Abe had waited on the Mason family, and when they departed for St. Louis tomorrow morning they would be replaced by the Tisch family. The Tisches would stay through July Fourth.

"Maybe the girls want to play a game of hearts with you after dinner." Nannie nodded once toward the twins. There was no music, no skit, no scheduled entertainment on Friday nights, so the guests played cards and board games or headed back to their cabins earlier than usual. Zaide said Shabbos was reserved for family time. Unless you were a waiter.

"I have plans tonight, Nannie. You said it was okay."

"You have plans?" Zaide placed his hands on his hips, and even while seated it was an imposing stance. Or it would have been if Betty didn't know he was a big pussycat who cherished her. "Does that mean I get a rain check for our Friday night Scrabble game?" he asked.

"Oh, Zaide, I'm sorry."

Betty should have asked to be excused from the table while everyone devoured their apple cake. She remembered Marv had said it was his favorite. Betty whispered to their waiter to wrap a big slice in wax paper and hand it to him before he left the dining room. It was something Zaide would have done.

But sitting at the table through the requisite coffee and cigarettes would only lead to trouble getting away at all. She needed to change out of her Shabbos dress and into something more suitable for what she had planned.

Zaide tapped the table. "It's fine. Have a good time with your friends. Girls, you can snag Betty during your calisthenics one morning to tell you all about her senior-year academics. And her antics." Zaide winked at Betty, who hoped he was teasing her.

Betty rose and stepped to Zaide's chair, kissed him on the cheek, and leaned in for a little squeeze around her grandfather's shoulders. In the summers he rarely sat still long enough for this kind of affection.

Betty had asked Georgia to meet her in the lobby, so of course she was there, leaning against the wall, gazing into the air. She grabbed Georgia's hand and pulled her into Zaide's office, closed the door, and turned the lock. Changing here would save Betty time—at least five full minutes—instead of running home and back.

"Okay, now tell me what I'm doing here instead of the arcade," Georgia said.

"You're here helping me look blasé."

"This is about Abe."

"Of course this is about Abe. Unzip me, would you?"

Georgia unzipped Betty's dress and she stepped out of it. Georgia lifted it from the floor and slipped it onto a wooden hanger, as if she were a handmaiden. Then she harrumphed. She grabbed the dungarees and white cotton blouse from the back of Zaide's desk chair and flung them at Betty.

"Remind me why you didn't go home to change clothes?"

"I didn't want to waste a second." Betty stopped fussing and laid her hand on Georgia's shoulder. "Thank you for going late to the arcade on account of me," she said, not wanting to take Georgia for granted.

Lickety-split, Betty was out of her silk stockings and satin slip and on with the dungarees. She buttoned the blouse almost to her neck and flicked her hair out of the collar. She tucked in her shirttail and added a thin white patent-leather belt.

Georgia fixed Betty's collar. "You're keeping something from me."

"I just want you to wait with me, is all."

"Abe walked you home twice. I didn't even know about the second time until now. What happened?"

"He walked me home from the bonfire, and again last night after dinner."

"That's why you didn't go to the movies with us?"

"I suppose it is."

Betty perched on the step stool in the corner and pulled on white bobby socks, then slipped her feet into her new penny loafers and cuffed the pant legs. She set her elbows on her knees and her chin in her hands. "And we talked for two hours."

"Two hours? And all you did was talk?" Georgia smoothed her bold polka-dot skirt behind her bottom, sat on the floor in one fluid motion, and wrapped her arms around her knees. She stared at Betty like a child ready for story time.

Betty never hesitated to tell Georgia anything, but the conversation with Abe was tucked into her heart and not for sharing. "What do you want to know?"

"Did he kiss you?"

"I told you, we talked."

"I thought you were kidding."

Betty stomped as she stood. "I wasn't. It was wonderful. Maybe it was better than kissing." Betty didn't believe that, but she did believe the simple act of talking had jump-started their romance. Which was more than just romantic. "We talked about our families and what we want to do with our lives. He cared about everything I said. Every single word."

Georgia stood. "Be careful. All the girls have their eyes on him."

"You included?"

"Don't be crabby. I'm just telling you what I've heard. He's big man on campus up in Ann Arbor."

"This isn't Ann Arbor, and I don't need to be careful with Abe. He—" Betty stopped. She'd already said too much. Let them all think she was just having fun.

"He *what*?"

"He's different." Betty wasn't going to tell Georgia that after two days she felt like she'd known Abe all her life. She slid from the stool and hugged her best friend tight. "Don't worry about me." Then Betty opened the door of Zaide's office storage closet and tugged on the chain dangling from a naked bulb. She looked into Zaide's full-length mirror and traced her index finger around the perimeter of her lips, then retrieved her purse in search of Revlon's Stormy Pink and a Kleenex. She applied a fresh lipstick coat in front of the full-length mirror. "Abe really cares about me." Betty blotted her lips. "He's not going to hurt me." She blotted again. She looked into the mirror at her face, then up and down at her body. She turned to the side, then the back, to investigate her curves from all angles. "I thought you could get to know him a bit tonight before he walked me home, but maybe that's not a good idea."

"Oh no," Georgia said. "I think it's the perfect idea."

After saying good night to her grandparents, and circulating through dawdling guests in the lobby, Betty grabbed a peach from the fruit bowl on the lobby's side table. *God forbid anyone go hungry before the midnight buffet.* She held the ripe fruit out to Georgia as a peace offering.

"Is it poison?"

Betty cocked her head. "That's only apples, silly."

Georgia accepted the peach, but set it back into the bowl and slid her hand into Betty's. "Don't be angry with me for watching out for you."

"You don't have to protect me from Abe. But I adore you for wanting to, I really do. Now come with me and say hello."

"And then *leave?*"

"Yes, please. Anyway, isn't the gang waiting for you at the arcade?"

"They won't miss me if you want me to stick around."

Betty shook her head as she squeezed Georgia's hand, and then released it to push open the front door. The sun had set, and the bluish-purple sky was fading to ink.

Abe stood on the bottom step, just as Betty had hoped. Just as she'd prayed. A smile of relief and joy tugged at the insides of her cheeks. He leaned against the iron railing, hands in his trouser pockets, with one foot crossed over the other in a casual pose. He faced the beach, then leaned back and laughed, his voice bellowing like a love song. His demeanor was suave and serious, but fun—a combination usually reserved for men in cigarette advertisements.

Then Abe stepped aside.

There stood Eleanor. Again. Betty had heard the crowd call her "Easy Eleanor" behind her back. Insults like that one made her stomach churn, and she refused to take part or chime in—as long as Eleanor stayed a respectable distance from Abe.

"Well, there she is." Eleanor's voice reverberated like wind chimes and was equally as irritating. "*We've* been waiting for you."

Abe turned and smiled at Betty. She combed her fingers through the tendrils hanging near her face.

"You're a goner," Georgia whispered so softly that had she not been close enough for Betty to feel her breath, she wouldn't have heard her friend at all. "I'm not leaving until *she* does."

Betty turned around. "Thank you," she mouthed.

When Betty looked at Abe again, he stretched out his arm toward her and opened his hand as if revealing a tiny treasure. She could see the muscles in his forearms, and she shuddered, remembering the softness of his skin, the solidity of the muscles beneath.

"What are you waiting for?" Georgia whispered, and poked Betty's back. She turned and saw Georgia's apricot painted lips stretched into a wide grin, her eyes crinkled closed by the smile.

Betty skipped down the steps toward Abe, but truly she could have floated. When she arrived at his side she leaned in, knowing one day it would be natural to push onto her tiptoes and kiss the day's stubble or his dimple. No, she'd kiss both. She swallowed hard, imagining his rough jawline against her lips. He smelled earthy, like sandalwood mixed with crisp lake air. The aroma was delicate considering his size, but it was also warm and safe, which fit him. She wished Eleanor would disappear, and even Georgia—though that wish tinged her with guilt. When Georgia met someone, she'd get it. All Betty wanted was to inhale deeply, his scent as vital as oxygen. Once on their own, she and Abe could tumble back into the rhythm they'd found. Betty wanted to know every little thing about his day. Had anything funny happened in the kitchen tonight? Had he overheard any gossip while serving the guests? Had he taken a nap? Swapped a shift? Received a letter from his parents? She wanted to tell him about Mrs. Gallbladder, how Betty possessed a wristwatch in place of a mother, how his outstretched hand had already endeared him to Georgia. Instead of speaking, Betty linked her fingers with Abe's as Eleanor watched. *He's mine.*

Abe squeezed her hand. "Eleanor was just telling me about her date last night with your friend Marv."

"Is that so?"

"Yes. We went to Sherman's Dairy Bar for ice cream and then walked on the beach," Eleanor said.

"Well, good for you."

Eleanor swung her hands behind her back and shifted side to side, as if humble and shy. But Betty saw how Eleanor narrowed her eyes when she looked at Georgia, and then blinked three times when she looked at Abe.

"You do know Georgia Lemon, don't you, Abe? She hails from South Haven, and she's practically an honorary Stern, aren't you, Georgie?" Eleanor asked.

"Georgia, not Georgie," Betty and Georgia said in unison.

"Of course, we've met," Abe said. "Nice to see you again."

"Nice to see you too." Georgia stood on the ground next to Eleanor, who looked up at her. Georgia's ginger hair was curled and styled half-up, half-down—a little fussy for the arcade—unless she had her eye on someone. Did cautious, clever Georgia have a crush?

"I have the car tonight," Georgia said. "Let's leave these two. I'll give you a lift to the arcade, or wherever Marv is waiting."

Eleanor didn't budge.

"Eleanor?" Georgia asked. "Did you hear what I said?"

"Oh, you mean me?"

Georgia grabbed Eleanor's arm and led her away. "Yes, you."

Chapter 8

BETTY

For more than half an hour, Betty and Abe stood off to the side of the steps and talked. Guests nodded and smiled and stopped to chat. Betty was a Stern, never ignored.

"Have you ever had a normal summer?" Abe asked.

"This is a normal summer."

"I mean one where you're not on a three-month vacation?"

"Is that what you think this is for me?"

"Isn't it?"

"I know that's what everyone thinks. My grandfather says, 'Let them think it.'" But she didn't want any miscommunication with Abe. "Did you know we're getting ready for a month before the staff arrives? I have to not only iron all the sets of curtains for every cabin, but pin up the lace panels to dry after my grandmother has cleaned them. And when I say pin, I mean with hundreds of pins. We clean the cabins ourselves. And do most of the landscaping. And while you might think leading calisthenics is easy, all those women doing whatever I say like we're playing a game of Simon says, well, they also blame me when they can't fit into a dress for Saturday night, when all week they've been feeding like horses at a trough! Oh, and don't forget the five a.m. toilet plunging with my grandfather because he didn't want to pay a plumber or having to cancel plans if someone calls in sick or quits. Last year I was a chambermaid all of August."

"I didn't realize," Abe said.

"No one does."

"But that's what family is for, right? I'd do anything my mother asked." Abe traced his finger down her nose to just above her lip. The sensation ran over her scalp and down her neck, into her shoulders, arms, torso, all the way to her toes. "I'm sorry," he said. "I know you grew up without your parents."

"I had a wonderful childhood. Sometimes I think more than I had a right to."

"You have a right to be happy, a right to whatever you want."

Abe pulled her close and Betty wanted to stand that way forever. "Honestly, sometimes I forget my grandparents aren't my actual parents."

That was a wishful lie. For the past fourteen years Betty only pretended to forget that the two people who were meant to love her most had left her behind. One day she would tell Abe how, for years, she looked for her parents everywhere—in crowds on the beach, at High Holiday services, on walks, in her dreams that took her under the sea and up in the sky. She looked for Tillie and Joe in everyone, especially strangers she noticed from the back who were the right height and build, or almost.

This summer she was still without parents, but she was with Abe. Attentive, caring, smart, dreamy Abe. They'd started something. They were building something. No way was she letting her parents ruin tonight's mood. "Will you take a walk with me?" Betty held out her hand and Abe clasped it.

She steered him across the lawn and toward the beach. They sprinted onto the sand and it scattered at their feet as if clearing a path. Laughter drifted behind but didn't follow them. Moonlight and the glow of a nearby hotel lit the way as they ran far from lights and sounds and the well-meaning passersby of Betty's life. Privacy was elusive but not impossible.

"Where are we going?" Abe asked.

"To one of my favorite places on earth."

Betty and Abe climbed the dunes that rose to the east past the cabins, the tennis courts, and the staff parking lot. Most people didn't know this was part of her grandparents' property. A natural boundary between her family's resort and the Atlantic Hotel, the dune remained untended and overgrown. That's what made it a perfect childhood hideaway, where Betty played house among the brambles, where she had a mother home after school and a father who read her bedtime stories.

She pushed through the brush and the grasses, eager to show Abe her personal refuge. Stepping on fallen branches, she kicked them out of the way. At the top she turned back toward the lake and sat in the sand.

Abe chuckled and sat next to her. "You could've done that on the beach."

"But then I wouldn't see this."

The not-quite-full moon hung as if by a string and its light cast a glistening vertical stripe in the water. They were backlit by distant resorts, and Betty knew without that remnant glow the air around them would be as dark as Mabel's dark-chocolate molasses cookies. Betty leaned her head on Abe's shoulder without hesitation or permission and pointed while gazing straight ahead.

"I used to play back there." Betty tipped back her head and Abe turned a bit, not far enough to see but enough that she knew he was listening. "I played house and school, but my favorite was cops and robbers. I was both."

Abe placed his hand on hers. "Of course."

"Why do you say that?"

"Because it's unexpected, like everything about you."

Betty had never heard herself described that way. All her life she'd tried to do what had been expected of her—more than was expected. She couldn't risk her grandparents changing their minds. Then what would have become of her?

Oh, her grandparents adored her, she never *really* thought they'd send her away, but Betty had never been prone to taking chances. She achieved good grades, was accepted to a fine college, kept up her appearances, pitched in at the resort, made her bed, used polite manners.

"What's back there anyway?" Abe asked.

"Dense bushes, I guess. I haven't been here in years." Betty popped up her head. "There used to be a patch of beach grass. I had picnics there. Stole cookies out of the cookie jar, although I always confessed later. I wonder if it's all grown over. It's too dark back there to check."

"Next time we'll bring a flashlight," Abe said.

Next time.

Abe tugged on Betty so that she'd turn to him. "Did it bother you that Eleanor bragged about a date with Marv?"

"Bother me? God no. Why would it bother me?"

"I think he has a thing for you."

Whether he had or not was of no concern to Betty. "I've known Marv since we were children. We're just friends."

"So, you're not upset they're together?"

Betty hadn't thought about it before. "I'm happy that they each found someone."

"Are you happy for *us?*"

Betty sucked in a breath and looked at her shoes, the shiny pennies in her summer loafers staring at her like a wide-eyed hopeful friend. "There's an 'us'?"

"There is for me."

Bashfulness washed over Betty. She said nothing, as if she had nothing to say. Pressure spread inside her chest, resulting in a shortness of breath like the times she'd swallowed mouthfuls of lake water. The ache was proof. This was really happening.

Betty raised her head and stared into Abe's blue eyes again. Neither of them glanced away. She was safe there, gazing at him, safe this close to him. She was not at risk of losing any part of who she was, or what she wanted. Abe liked her spirit, her ambition, her unexpectedness.

His eyes were rimmed in specks of yellow. His nose a little crooked from a childhood tumble from his bicycle. His lips curved and slim, but not thin, and a pale shade of pink she might have chosen for a silk slip.

Abe placed his hands on her waist and caressed her with his thumbs, but he didn't move his hands. Betty's reticence dissolved. Her shyness whirled into desire. She rested her palms on Abe's chest. He smiled in the way that deepened his dimples, and her longing.

When would he stop being such a gentleman?

Abe leaned toward her. He kissed her full on the lips, deliberate and soft. The touch was tender and new, but somehow familiar. Then he pulled away.

Don't stop. Did he have regrets? Betty stared at his smile as it brightened his face. She knew he wasn't sorry he'd kissed her. She smiled into his eyes.

Then she slid her hands up his chest and around his neck. This time he touched open lips to hers. She crushed against him as the sweet kiss accelerated. Abe was skillful and passionate, not boyish or clumsy.

She drifted, oblivious to time, unaware of the surroundings. Then she recognized the taste. Mint.

Betty's insides fluttered. Abe had planned to kiss her all along.

She pulled away and kissed Abe's cheek, his chin, the tip of his nose. She rested her head on Abe's chest. He lay back on the sand and she remained there, listening to his heartbeat. Did all hearts pound so loudly?

Summer stretched in front of her, but at the same time the season wasn't very long at all—just three months. How could it be that just days after she met him, she'd found a piece to her puzzle? And not just any piece—a corner piece, one that secured her to everything else in her life.

And just like that, she knew.

I love him.

It felt the way she believed it should. Safe and strong. Urgent and patient. Overpowering and liberating.

He traced his hand down her back. She laid her arm over him, pulling Abe as close as she could. Her next breath emerged as a sigh. She could be closer.

It wouldn't happen tonight, but it would happen. Abe would be her first.

She wanted him to be her only.

Chapter 9

BETTY

On Saturday night, traces of perfume and hair spray sailed around the dining-room-turned-nightclub. Cigarette smoke draped the air like a morning mist. Diamonds sparkled on wrists and necks, satin shimmered on bodices and lapels. Live trumpets blared, saxophones swooned, drums thundered.

Betty swept her hands behind her waist that had been cinched inside her pale-blue taffeta dress. She locked her fingers and stepped backward to the wall. Just one dance with Zaide and then she could go. Nannie had promised Betty could leave before midnight.

Her grandparents whirled around the dance floor as if stand-ins for Fred Astaire and Ginger Rogers, though in the dimmed room the spotlight remained on the Rudy Mazer Orchestra. Nannie and Zaide wouldn't have had it any other way. They spent the off-season booking top-notch entertainment. Fellow resort owners cursed Nannie for her charm and Zaide for his shrewdness, but the guests boasted to their friends and family and strangers on the beach. "Boasting boosts business," Zaide often said.

In her mind, Betty swapped out her grandparents for her and Abe, decades from now, a lifetime behind them. She imagined his broad shoulders filling a tuxedo jacket destined for dancing, not waiting tables, and herself in the aubergine organza gown with a trumpet skirt and an illusion neckline that was both alluring and sophisticated—the one she'd seen in *Vogue*. No matter how flattering, there would be no more modest pastel dresses with layers of petticoats once she entered college. She tapped one foot and closed her eyes, pretending she'd been transfixed by the music.

She visualized Abe leaning down to kiss her, and the way his mouth stayed parted when she removed her lips from his neck. Her heart rate quickened, and blood rushed through her veins. She remembered the piercing gazes they'd shared on the lawn, in the main house, by the tennis court earlier that day.

"May I have this dance?"

The voice did not belong to Zaide.

Betty opened her eyes. "No, thank you, Marvin." He smiled anyway. Had she blushed? Could he know what she'd been thinking?

"My mother calls me Marvin."

"No, thank you, *Marv*. I'm actually waiting for someone."

Marv turned toward the dance floor, then back to Betty. Zaide was waltzing with Mrs. Levine.

"Since no off-duty staff is allowed in the nightclub and your grandfather looks busy . . ." Marv cocked his head. "I'm sure Abe wouldn't mind if two old *friends* shared a dance."

Betty *would* mind but she heard Zaide's voice in her head: *Give the guests what they want.* Did anyone care what she wanted?

"What about Eleanor?"

"What about her?"

"Won't she mind?"

Marv shook his head and smiled but didn't smirk. "No, she won't mind." His tone was mild, without insinuations or demands. Then he held out his hand. "Please."

Betty nodded. It was just one dance.

And it *was* one dance with Marv. They whirled around the dance floor to "Till the End of Time." It was one of Nannie's favorites, but a little old-fashioned for Betty's taste, which made it perfect. The band played some new music, but mostly catered to the guests her parents' and grandparents' ages.

As the song ended, Zaide walked toward them wearing his new midnight-blue semiformal dinner jacket, a fashionable match for Nannie's peacock-colored dress, even when she was on the far side of the room directing cocktail waiters.

He dominated the crowd, guests stepping aside as if nudged. There was never a sideways glance or distasteful sneer. Of course, her grandfather was handsome, but it was something else for Betty to see the reaction to his stature and good looks, to realize that even at sixty-two he garnered the attention of men and the admiration of women. A cluster of guests—female guests—pressed to the side to make way for Zaide, as if it was their pleasure to stop talking and smash their evening gowns together like cotton rags. Betty thought perhaps it was. "Come back and have a drink with us?" one woman said. And why shouldn't she? Zaide always had a jovial anecdote or kind word for every guest. For the women he sprinkled compliments the way Betty had sprinkled daily fish food for a carnival goldfish.

Zaide patted the sheen from his forehead and slid his handkerchief into his pocket as he struck the shoulder of Mr. Horowitz with his other hand like they were old college pals.

Abe would be just as smooth when he was older, Betty was sure of it.

"May I cut in?" Zaide asked.

Marv released his hand from Betty's waist but maintained a light hold on her right hand, which he placed into her grandfather's left. Even after an enjoyable Lindy Hop, repugnance settled into Betty's stomach like soured milk. Marv was not being possessive, but chivalrous. Wasn't he? He wanted to be friends.

"Thanks for the dance, Betty," Marv said.

She wondered if he was off to see Eleanor. "You're welcome."

Marv nodded once at Zaide. "Good night, sir." He walked toward the door as the music grew louder and Betty began to fox-trot with Zaide by rote.

How lucky Marv was to be on vacation for the whole summer, away from his work and responsibilities. Did that mean he wasn't essential to his father's business? This thought tumbled through Betty's thoughts as she and Zaide danced.

He leaned in to her ear. "You seem a little distracted, bubbeleh. What's wrong?"

"I was just thinking about the Miss South Haven contest." It was better to be distracted by a beauty pageant than by a boy. At least to Zaide. "Nancy Green is in Europe."

"I heard about that."

"Do you think I have a shot? I mean, I'm going to enter anyway, but, oh, Zaide! I really want to win. Wouldn't that be a swell thing to do before I go to Barnard?"

"That would make Nannie and me very proud."

"We'd get a lot of free publicity, wouldn't we?"

"That's what I've heard."

"I'll do my best, I promise."

"You're a beautiful girl, and the judges would be fools not to see it, whether there's a Nancy Green or not." Zaide smiled, twirled Betty, and spoke into her ear. "I think someone is waiting for you by the door."

Betty craned her neck, but with the dancing and the crowd and the low light it was hard to discern one black or blue jacket from another. Still, Betty's heart felt as if it nearly skipped a beat, as though her feet were atop Zaide's like when she was a little girl as they turned in time to the music. Zaide was smiling. He approved. She glanced around the smoke-shrouded glamour to the door, the corners, no Abe. "Don't tease me, Zaide."

"Look."

Zaide motioned with his chin, and as if he were the conductor, the music stopped. Zaide kissed Betty atop her head, held her shoulders, and turned her toward the door. "He's a nice boy. Go, have fun."

That's when she saw Marv walking through the doors into the lobby.

Did Zaide think she was dating Marv? Did anyone else think she was dating Marv?

Betty wished she could have told Zaide she didn't like Marv, not like *that*. Zaide had urged her off the dance floor, so Betty pushed through the dining room doors. Marv paced the lobby, tossing and catching a peach as if it were a baseball.

His actions were cavalier and casual, in contrast to his tightly slicked-back hair and tailored semiformal. But she had to admit he *was* neatly groomed. And a decent dancer.

Betty turned toward the window before Marv looked at her.

Outside the window, light spilled onto the steps and the lawn. Moonlight brightened the sky to a bluish gray, and the beacon from South Haven lighthouse shined like a flame, casting its spell over the water.

Betty cupped her hands by her temples to block the glare. She needn't squint and strain her eyes to know that Abe hadn't waited for her this long; she was more than an hour late. A current of sadness pulsed through her; then a sharp pain pinched her chest. She laid her hand on her heart and felt it thump. Tomorrow. She'd catch a glimpse of him tomorrow. Betty didn't want to be one of those girls who whined and whimpered when her boyfriend was out of sight. She'd go home, set her hair, and go to sleep while the band played swing and jazz and the guests drank Manhattans and whiskey sours.

She hoped Abe would explain why he'd left. She'd certainly apologize for being late, though he'd likely say she didn't need to apologize for anything. He understood she was devoted to her family, because he was devoted to his. She was just doing her job—her *this-is-not-a-vacation* job—as the Stern granddaughter.

Betty tugged at the fingers of her left glove, yanked it off, and did the same for the right. Darn, she'd left her clutch on the table inside. She tucked the gloves into one hand. She didn't need her lipstick because the night was over, or her key, because her front door was always unlocked.

"I told my mother I was walking you home."

Betty adjusted her gaze and saw Marv's reflection behind her own in the window. She wasn't in the mood for polite small talk. "Why did you do that?"

"She likes you."

Betty fiddled with her gloves. "That's nice to hear, but please don't make up stories about me."

"It won't be a story if you let me walk you home."

"I thought we could be friends. We danced—and it was nice. But if it's all the same to you, I'll walk home myself."

"It's only a block and a half, Betty, but if I was your guy, I wouldn't let you go on your own."

"Well, you're not 'my guy.'" She hadn't meant to snap, but he had nerve. He didn't know anything about Abe.

Marv held up his hands in surrender. "I'm just trying to be a gentleman, that's all."

Betty rolled her eyes. "I think the last thing you're trying to be is a gentleman."

"Betty Claire Stern!"

Betty swung around. "Nannie, I didn't know you were there."

"Apparently not!"

Marv raised and lowered one eyebrow. Nannie had been just out of Betty's view and he knew it.

Nannie pressed the white beaded clutch into Betty's hands. "I think you owe Marvin an apology."

"But—"

"No buts. And I think it would be nice for him to walk you home. There isn't anyone else waiting for you, is there?"

As if Betty needed the reminder. "No, Nannie."

"It's settled then. Thank you for being so thoughtful, Marvin." Nannie gave Betty "the look" and walked back into the dining room.

"Don't get all bent out of shape about me asking to walk you home. I'm a nice guy. Ask Eleanor."

"I think we have different definitions for 'nice guy.'"

"Ouch." Marv held open the door.

"Thank you." Betty walked through. "So, it's official now?"

"Is what official?"

Betty skipped down the steps. "You and Eleanor."

Marv shrugged. He removed his jacket, hung it over one shoulder with a crooked finger, then loosened his tie.

"Truce?" he asked.

"You didn't answer my question about Eleanor."

"Why do you care?"

"Hey, I'm just trying to be friendly. Answer or don't." Betty could wrangle any staff gossip out of Mabel or the girls, no matter what Marv did or didn't tell her.

There was no point in being his enemy—her grandparents wouldn't permit it because he was a guest. Betty nodded to Marv and walked next to him with an arm's length between them. It was only a block and a half until she was home.

They crossed the street and walked on the sidewalk instead of the beach. Betty's shoes and hose were made for glamour, not sand.

Marv stepped around Betty and walked by the curb. Gallant even by Betty's standards.

"I'm not half-bad when you get to know me," he said.

Betty smiled. It was a half smile, but at this moment he was trying to be nice. "I'll believe it when I see it."

"Oh, Princess Betty is giving me a chance to prove myself?"

Betty stopped and stomped her foot. "I am not a princess!" Then she laughed and lightened the mood.

"You kind of are," Marv said. "Barsky'd better treat you like one."

Betty wasn't sure if that was a compliment or an insult. They walked the last hundred yards in silence and stopped at the bottom of the porch steps.

"We could sit and talk," Marv said.

Betty wanted to talk to Abe. She shook her head, almost apologizing, but she wasn't sorry.

"Can't fault a guy for holding out hope."

She could not. Betty smiled. Marv didn't stir her or interest her the way other boys had, the way Abe did, but he seemed sincere. When he could have been cold or flippant or handsy, he wasn't. Maybe they *could* be friends. She could use another friend. The warm porch light soothed her soul and softened her outlook.

"So, where do you think they are?"

Marv furrowed his brow. "Who?"

"Abe and Eleanor." It just occurred to her. "Neither of them were where they said they'd be." She didn't mean to insinuate that they were together, just that they might be at the same place. Lots of kids hung out way past midnight. Betty gulped. She knew what happened when kids were "hanging out."

Marv pulled a leather key pouch from his pocket and swung it like a hypnotist's pocket watch. "I have a car. We could go find them."

"Isn't that like spying?" She was strangely intrigued.

Marv shrugged.

She did want to know where Abe had gone, and she could justify the outing by helping Marv find Eleanor. And no one had to know; it could be their secret. A secret between friends. Betty held out one side of her skirt in a faux curtsy.

"You mean right now?"

"Do you have a better offer for tonight?"

She did not.

Chapter 10

BETTY

Betty handed Marv a flashlight. He pointed it low and straight ahead. They crouched beneath the still-open windows of the main house, and duckwalked close to the building, as the band played the lively "Aba Daba Honeymoon." Betty loved that song, but not enough to be distracted. The music faded as she turned to the back of the house and passed the kitchen. She and Marv stayed small, quiet, and imperceptible longer than necessary. Betty felt like Nancy Drew. *The Mystery of the Missing Boyfriend.*

Good thing she'd changed her clothes. The Skylark dress would have dragged, and the pedal pushers allowed her to strike these unlady-like poses and maintain her dignity. The peep-toe pumps would have slowed her pace. She'd rolled her hair into a bun at the nape of her neck. A ponytail would have been too bouncy.

With every step, Betty repeated to herself that she trusted Abe. But did she? Not enough to repress her curiosity. Plus, she was bored. She'd waited all night for the exhilaration of seeing him only to be disappointed.

Last year, the Saturday nightclub would have been enough to keep Betty buzzing with delight and fantasies. But her enchantment with glitz and glamour had been lost to that of summer romance. How could it not be? The sparkle in Abe's eyes outshined the crystal chandeliers, and the melody of his words whispering in her ear was more hypnotic than music. His lips against her skin were smoother than the fabric of any cocktail dress. Betty swallowed, and her skin prickled as if it were dusted with sand, though she didn't want to brush it away. She'd happily linger in that sensation for the rest of her life.

It had only been two weeks. *Not even.* It had been ten days since she'd seen Abe for the first time on the lawn. Three days since she'd let him walk her home, and twenty-four hours since the dunes. Time seemed an irrelevant inconvenience. She could have sworn it had been years.

Another few feet of crawling and she and Marv would be in the clear, far enough from the windows of the main house and the cabins.

It wasn't easy for her to go unnoticed in South Haven, let alone on the property, but the guests and her grandparents were still drinking and dancing. More important, no one was looking for her.

Betty and Marv stood upright at last.

"You did good bopping along there." Marv chuckled. "Betty Bop. Almost Betty Boop."

"Very funny."

"I think it suits you." Marv pointed. "We'll see if his car is here in the lot. If it's not, we'll take my mother's car and hit some spots around town. I have ideas where they could be."

Betty took a giant step forward. "I changed my mind."

Marv stopped, and Betty stood next to him. "Why?"

"I just don't think we should spy. It's wrong." What if she found Abe with someone else? She would have to bear not only the heartache, but the humiliation of Marv knowing her business.

"We're not spying, we're looking. Just trying to find our . . ."

Betty didn't know the right words to use either. She and Abe had acknowledged their relationship and their immediate connection, but it wasn't like he'd pinned her or asked her to go steady.

"Don't you want to know if Abe has taken off with Eleanor for the night?"

"He's not 'off with Eleanor.'" And certainly not for the night.

"How do you know?"

"He just wouldn't."

Marv shrugged, and started walking again. "Then his car will be in the parking lot, and when we go over toward the Palace he'll be playing poker with the guys or sound asleep like an angel." Marv drew a halo in the air above his head.

Betty skittered and kept up this time, shuffling through the grass, glad she'd worn her old saddle shoes. "I didn't say he was an angel. I just mean, I trust him. I was much later than I said I'd be." Betty felt the same jolt of tension in her neck as when Nannie announced Tillie and Joe's annual visits.

Marv stopped and skimmed the group of cars with the flashlight.

The patchy, unkempt grass of the staff parking lot was in stark contrast to the resort's pristine front lawn. This area wasn't even raked gravel like she'd seen at other resorts, or the pale, cracked tar of the loading areas. This wasn't a parking lot. It was a forgotten lot.

"What kind of car does he have?" Marv asked.

"It doesn't matter."

"We're here, it's not a big deal to just look."

Betty turned left, west, toward the lake, even though she couldn't see it. They were a block or two away by now. She leaned back on a blue car and pushed herself up to sit on the hood. The cold steel shocked her hands and the backs of her shins, but it wasn't half as chilly as the rushing breeze that seemed to pass through her, though the air was motionless. This close to the lake, that usually meant a storm threatened to drop in unannounced, but copious twinkling stars filled the sky like spatter dots on draped black fabric, and the *South Haven Herald* had called for sunshine tomorrow. It was rarely wrong.

"It doesn't matter because his car isn't here," Betty said.

Marv leaned on the car and looked away from Betty toward the abyss of vehicles she didn't care about. "I'm sorry," he said.

"No, you're not."

Marv turned to Betty. "You think you know me. But you don't. I *am* sorry. For your sake, I wanted to be wrong."

"This proves nothing."

"Okay, you're right. Your boyfriend said he'd meet you, he ditched you, and now you can't find him or a girl we know would be happy to do what you won't do."

"You are quite presumptuous."

Marv turned away. Betty was glad not to see his face and imagined his smug grin. Her cheeks grew warm, but she shivered. "If that's what you think of Eleanor, why are you dating her?"

Marv said nothing and confirmed what she suspected. She wasn't naive . . . well, maybe a little. But she was a lot optimistic.

"I bet she'll fall in love with you by the end of the summer."

Marv guffawed. "I don't think Eleanor is the 'in-love' type."

"Every girl is the in-love type."

It sounded like something Doris would say as Betty scoffed, but the words had come out of Betty's mouth. And she believed them.

"Is that so? I'll keep that in mind."

"You should."

"Are you in love with Barsky?"

She hopped off the car and ground her toe into a lonely patch of grass. "I don't think that's any of your business."

Marv walked the length of the row of cars and back again. "It doesn't mean anything, you know, that his car isn't here," he said. "He could be out with some of the guys, even over in one of the meadows. Your grandparents would have a cow if they caught anyone drinking, and no one wants to lose their job."

"You should look for Eleanor. Girls like to be pursued."

Marv smirked.

"What's that look for?"

"You surprise me, Betty Boop—oh, I'm sorry—Betty. You have very conventional notions of what girls and boys should do, don't you? I thought of you as modern and sophisticated, maybe even a bit of a rebel, but I was wrong. You're a nice girl through and through. Barsky doesn't know what he's in for."

"What's that supposed to mean?"

"Just that nice girls break your heart, and because you don't see it coming, it hurts like hell. Excuse my language."

"Is that why you don't have a girlfriend? Besides Eleanor, I mean? Did a nice girl break your heart?"

Marv looked away and Betty regretted her accusation. She hadn't meant her words to be hurtful, even if she was hurting. "I shouldn't have said that. It's none of my business."

He stepped closer to Betty but didn't touch her or look at her. "If you must know, I don't have a girlfriend because until a month ago, I had a fiancée."

Betty gasped. She didn't know as much about Marv Peck as she'd thought.

They retraced their steps in a courteous silence without dipping or ducking from anyone.

At the corner of Lakeshore and Avery, they stopped. Betty turned to Marv. "Do you want to talk about it?"

Marv shrugged. "No reason not to. Her name was Debbie. We were together for a year and engaged for two months. Until last month."

"What happened? I mean, if you want to tell me."

"She said she didn't love me enough to marry me, gave me back the ring, and I never saw her again. I called her parents a week later to see if she'd changed her mind. I told them I'd wait for her to love me. That I was patient and we'd make it work."

"She didn't buy it."

Marv shook his head. "I don't know what I did wrong. My father gave me plenty of ideas, though."

Betty found she felt sorry for Marv, even disbelieving he'd done anything wrong at all.

"Don't listen to him. You didn't do anything wrong. You lucked out."

"What are you talking about? Debbie was the only girl I ever loved." Marv's voice dropped to an almost indiscernible whisper. Betty knew he hadn't meant to be so vulnerable. "Sorry. I do like you, you know that, Betty. I like you more than I should considering you're swooning over Barsky and I keep looking like a fool. Who would want a fool?"

"You're not a fool." Betty briefly touched Marv's hand. "She was the fool. If she couldn't commit to you as your fiancée, she wouldn't have made a very good wife. Most of the girls I know are dying for a ring and a husband. They would do anything to make it work with a boy like you."

"But not you."

"Not me." Betty whispered the words to round out any edges. She wanted to be honest, but not mean.

"When you do settle down, Betty, he'll be one lucky son of a gun, even if it is Barsky. I have a feeling Debbie was my last shot."

"Pity isn't pretty."

"What?"

"Pity isn't pretty. That's what Nannie would say. How do you expect to attract a wife if all you do is mope and put yourself down? It's time to leave Debbie in the dust."

"Is that your friendly advice?"

"It is."

Rampant truths spun through Betty's thoughts. She knew how Marv felt, what it was like to be left behind. The insecurity born out of her parents' dismissal stuck to her like it had been affixed with glue, even with Nannie and Zaide stepping in to do a bang-up job as parenting grandparents. Marv would always feel the wound of losing Debbie, no matter who else he loved. Even if he packed away the loss, it would exist under everything in his life as part of its foundation, and sometimes it would seep through.

"I'm glad we're friends," Betty said.

"Now that you know I was dumped?"

"No, because you're a decent guy. You'll find someone. Someone who makes a promise and keeps it."

Marv pressed his lips together, then exhaled. "From your lips to God's ears."

"You're spending too much time with your mother."

They laughed.

"You could be right. If you ever need anything, just ask me, Betty, okay? I'm more than just a pretty face. I can be a really good friend if you let me." He winked, and Betty laughed again.

"You can call me Betty Boop. Just not in public. Now, go find Eleanor. Make a nice girl out of her." Marv threw back his head and chuckled before releasing a deep and hearty sigh as Betty's house came into view.

"He's here." Her breathy words floated out in sighs of relief when she saw Abe's Sunliner parked across the street.

"I'll be damned," Marv said. Betty turned to him and scowled, partly in jest. "Go. But if he hurts you, he'll have me to answer to."

"You're a doll," Betty said. "But you don't have to worry."

Chapter 11

BETTY

Betty saw Abe sitting on the top porch step, long legs outstretched and crossed at the ankles. This was the porch where child-Betty had played hopscotch, where teenage-Betty had waited for dates, where every-Betty had watched her parents drive away year after year, and where she had stood to greet them, burdened by a swirl of manners, obligation, and reluctant longing. She'd watched the sunset so often from this porch. She had always thought it did so especially for her—a selfish belief, perhaps, but what else was she supposed to think? The horizon was just outside her home, separating her lake from the sky. She now knew it was all an illusion.

But Abe was real.

Betty stood with the toes of her saddle shoes scratching up against the riser of the bottom step. She was close enough to smell Abe's hair cream and to see his dimples dig into his cheeks as he smiled. He wore dark-blue work pants, faded and worn at the knees, like he'd had them for years. His belt was brown and worn, pulled so its tail circled halfway around his waist. His attire resembled that of delivery drivers or gas station attendants, not summer staff. It didn't fit Betty's image of a college boy.

His white shirt wasn't wrinkled but it draped softly down his torso, and the sleeves were short, unlike the traditional crisp white long-sleeved tailored shirts he wore waiting tables. How long would it take her to unbutton that?

Stop.

Betty swallowed away any hitch in her voice. She might be smitten but she wasn't going to be someone's patsy. Not even Abe's. If he didn't share her feelings, she'd adjust her daydreams and growing expectations. "Fancy meeting you here." The words sounded breezy, and not at all accusatory. Abe was clean shaven, and his skin smelled like talc and sandalwood. She bent to kiss his cheek, as if a man on her porch at midnight were commonplace, but Abe turned his face toward hers so the kiss landed on his lips instead.

Betty jerked back, or tried to, as Abe touched both sides of her face with his hands, grasping her cheeks with his fingers and drawing her into a hungry kiss. That was it—caramel! He tasted like her favorite candy—warm, sweet, and almost buttery. Betty steadied herself on the step, melting more and more into each sweep of Abe's tongue against her own.

"My grandparents. They'll be home soon." Betty whispered each word without separating from Abe. He nodded and released her with tenderness. He traced her lips with his finger. Betty sat next to him but wrapped her arms around herself. This erased nothing. It didn't matter how delicious he tasted. How much she wanted her world to be filled with kissing Abe. She wouldn't be one of those girls who was courted on one side of the street and mocked on the other.

Betty stared ahead. It was easier to ask a difficult question if she didn't look at him. It was also easier to hear an answer that way. She'd never taken any guff from anyone. And no matter how forcefully her heart hammered against her chest, she wasn't going to start now.

"Hey, look at me," Abe said.

Betty shook her head. "Where were you?"

"Is that what this is about? You walked home with Peck because I wasn't waiting?"

Betty stared into the night and her neighbor's wall. It was painted white—a blank canvas for her thoughts.

"I asked Eleanor to tell you I'd be late tonight," Abe said.

Betty guffawed.

"What's that supposed to mean?"

If he didn't realize Eleanor would drop Marv in a minute, Betty wasn't going to tell him. "Nothing." She crossed her arms.

"I'm sorry you're mad. Really, I am. I had somewhere I had to go." He wrapped his arm around Betty's shoulder and his hand dangled near her breast. Her heartbeat quickened even more. "I wouldn't just ditch you like that," he said. "I care too much about you."

Betty's throat tensed. She turned and looked into Abe's eyes, which was the opposite of looking at a white wall. "I know."

"No, you don't, or you wouldn't have been out with Peck."

"I wasn't *out* with him; he walked me home when you weren't there." She omitted the fact that Nannie had given her no choice. "Then I changed clothes and we took a walk, that's all. Since I didn't get any message from Eleanor, I didn't know where you were."

"Were you out looking for me?"

She couldn't lie. Well, she could have, but she didn't want to. "Yes. I was worried. And Marv didn't know where Eleanor was either. I think he really likes her." But who did Eleanor like?

"This isn't about them. It's about us. This isn't going to work if you don't trust me."

There was an *us* and a *this*. "I'm sorry I doubted you. You're not like other boys."

"You mean I'm not like Peck?"

"Marv's A-OK, believe it or not."

If Abe didn't want to be friends with Marv, that was fine, but two nice Jewish fellas should be able to find something in common. Something besides her. "So, can you tell me where you were tonight?"

"It's not important."

Betty reached for Abe's hand. In theory, honesty was easy. It was harder in practice. "Everything you do is important to me."

Abe smiled. "For me too."

Betty's heart swelled. How big could it get before it burst out of her skin? She laid her head on Abe's shoulder, gently at first, and she relaxed, allowing him to bear its pressure. He was sturdy and strong. He could support the weight.

"I want you to know I was telling you the truth, so I'll tell you where I was tonight. Where I'm going to be six nights a week," Abe said. He stroked her hair, still in the bun. "But you're not going to like it."

They settled onto the glider on the screen porch. Betty's shoulder fit under Abe's arm like a puzzle piece. "You can tell me anything."

Her head rested atop his chest. Her feet stretched to the end of the glider. Abe had his left arm around her, his hand gently on her hip. His heart thumped a rhythm that could have lulled Betty to sleep, had she not so badly wanted him to kiss her again.

She traced one of his shirt buttons with the pad of her index finger and wondered if hiding beneath she'd find a smooth chest or one covered in wisps of hair.

Abe turned his wrist without moving his arm from around Betty. "I'm not going to be able to walk you home at night anymore."

She began to perspire. Had her grandparents objected? Had someone seen them together and snitched? "Why not?"

"I got a second job. I'll be stocking shelves at night at the grocer's. Doing some odd jobs they don't want to take care of during business hours. This was the only time the owner could show me what to do. I start Monday after my dinner shift."

Betty averted her gaze as a lump formed in her throat. Their nights. There would be no more walks, no more dunes, no more cuddling on the porch. "Oh."

"Hey, it's not so bad. I'll be done before midnight. I need the extra money to send home. Well, I don't need to, but I want to."

Abe's voice tinged with equal parts sorrow and pride. Betty hugged him, not sure what to say.

"No deliveries on Sundays, so I'm off tomorrow night," Abe said.

Betty looked at him and lifted her eyebrows.

"I know you have to stay for the after-dinner show, but how about after that? We could go to the arcade or walk on the beach?"

"Sure," Betty said. But she didn't want to do either. She wanted to be alone with Abe, where they could talk just above a whisper without watching the clock. Where they could neck without fear of her grandparents waking up or walking in on them.

"We could double if you'd rather. Ask Marv and Eleanor?" Abe said.

"I was thinking maybe we could go back—" Betty's cheeks warmed. She pressed her lips together and smiled. She was sure Abe could see her redden under the porch light.

"To the dunes?" he asked.

Betty nodded. She knew just the blouse she'd wear. The one with round pearl buttons that slipped easily through the buttonholes.

She shifted to an upright position but still leaned against Abe. He pushed on the floor with his feet so that the glider rocked back and forth. They sat in silence for a few moments. Silence with Abe was as comfortable and complete as their conversations.

"What did your father say about your new job?" she asked.

"I don't really talk to him," Abe said. "But he wouldn't like it."

"I thought you were doing this to help your family."

"My mother. I'm doing it to help her. But I haven't told her either. She wants all my money to go toward senior-year expenses."

"I don't mean to pry," Betty said. "But are there any other family members that could help her?"

"You're not prying. My family owns a store but it's not like Georgia's family's store. It's a five-and-dime, and we get by. I'm on a scholarship. But that doesn't pay for all my fees and graduation activities. And unfortunately my mother's rich parents don't speak to her. I've actually never met them."

Betty knew she had met Tillie's family when she was a toddler, but only because there was photographic evidence of the gathering. Tillie was estranged from her entire family in Chicago, and they'd never reached out to Betty, something she'd pushed aside.

"Families are complicated. They shouldn't be, don't you think? But they are. My mother doesn't speak to her family either." Well, as far as Betty knew.

Abe bounced his knee like a jackhammer. "My grandparents disowned my mother. Literally wrote her out of the will and everything. My brother and I have never met them."

"Oh my gosh, that's horrible." No matter Betty's knowledge of strained families, disowning someone seemed worse than dumping them off with their well-to-do grandparents. "Why did they disown her? What did your mother do?" Surely parents had a reason for such a permanent decision and exclusion.

"She married my father," Abe said.

Holy moly. Nannie wasn't nuts about Tillie, but her grandmother would never disown Joe, her own son. All Betty's grandparents ever wanted was for Tillie and Joe to give up their life on the road and live in South Haven, participate in the family business while raising their daughter. "Why didn't they approve of your father?"

"Because he's Jewish."

The words rolled toward Betty with the rumble of a bowling ball. How could being Jewish be bad? Was he the wrong kind of Jew?

Conservative to their Orthodox? Perhaps nonpracticing? So were many of the guests at Stern's. But they were still Jews. "I don't understand."

"My mother grew up Catholic."

Images of Christmas with Georgia's family swirled in Betty's head. The tree, the treif, the midnight mass, the presents, the statues, the saints, the sign of the cross.

Woozy with understanding, Betty nodded. His mother had given it all up for love.

But Judaism was based on matriarchal lineage, and the matriarch of Betty's family wasn't going to like this one bit. If Abe's mother wasn't Jewish, *Abe* wasn't Jewish.

"You're not Jewish?" Betty wanted Abe to correct her, to recite some rule or law that made him so. "Did you lie to my grandfather? He only hires Jewish boys."

"I have a Jewish name, so people assume both my parents are Jewish. And if I hadn't fallen for you, it wouldn't have mattered. I'd leave at the end of summer. No harm done." Abe waved his hand as if swatting away Betty's concerns. "Does it matter to you?"

Betty wanted to blurt out "No!" but it caught somewhere between her heart and her lips. She'd never known anyone who'd married a gentile. She didn't know *how* someone Jewish even married a non-Jew. By a judge, perhaps. In secret, for sure. A few Jewish girls in her class had dated gentile boys, but even that had drawn looks and whispers, on both sides.

"No," Betty said. "It doesn't matter to me." She loved him, so she would make it be true.

"It will matter to your grandparents, though. Their entire livelihood is built on Jewish families. And coeds. I'm sorry I put you in this predicament. But if I'd told your grandfather, he wouldn't have hired me, and I wouldn't have met you—and I'm not sorry about that."

Betty's anger-tinged ache dissolved.

"I'll understand if you need to tell them. That I'm not really Jewish, I mean. I grew up going to shul and celebrating High Holidays if that helps. My mother did that for my father, not that he deserved it. It's too bad that half is not enough for anyone."

Betty knew there was no such thing as half-Jewish. You either were, or you weren't.

Looking at Abe, she realized their similarities and connections transcended their blood, their ancestry. They had similar values, a shared understanding of dreams. They were more alike than anyone she'd ever known.

It would have been okay with Betty if Abe said he'd grown up with Santa Claus and the Easter Bunny living in his backyard. Betty looked into Abe's eyes and didn't glance away.

She noticed Abe's eyes glistening as if he was about to cry. He'd been so brave to tell her the truth. He wanted her to know everything about him.

"We'll figure it out," she said. "Your father's Jewish, right? That has to count for something."

Abe stared at her. "My father isn't such a great guy."

"But he's Jewish." That's what would be important to her grandparents.

"I guess that's the bright side."

Abe was Betty's bright side.

They talked about Abe's family's five-and-dime, his sometimes-absent father, and his older brother, Aaron, who didn't attend college and who had been drafted into the army just six weeks after marrying his childhood sweetheart.

Betty didn't see any bright side there. She shared the story of Tillie and Joe "giving" her to Nannie, Zaide, and South Haven.

"Neither of us won the parent jackpot, I guess," she said.

Abe wrapped her hands in his. "No one has ever understood that like you do." It was a unique and reassuring bond. Abe gulped before kissing her. He quickly pulled back. "I love you, Betty."

She smiled—she couldn't help it, even though it might have been a silly smile that stretched her cheeks out to look like a squirrel's. A blanket of calm enveloped her. It warmed her more than need be on a summer night, but she wouldn't have changed a thing.

She kissed Abe softly on the lips. "I love you too."

Abe continued staring into her eyes. "When I graduate in May, I'll move to New York . . ."

Betty nodded. "You'll design skyscrapers."

"You'll continue at Barnard, and when you graduate we'll get married. You'll work at a fancy magazine in one of those skyscrapers."

Had Abe just proposed? Or had he promised to propose? This was everything she had wanted, everything her grandparents wanted for her. Half-Jewish would do.

"We'll be the toast of New York!"

"We'll vacation here in South Haven," Betty said. "I'm sure my grandparents would like that."

"Like an ordinary Jewish couple on summer holiday," he said.

They laughed, and Betty knew they would never be ordinary.

She pictured herself a guest at Stern's, a visitor like her parents. She had never thought she'd move back here after college or take over the business. It wasn't part of her plan, or her grandparents' plan for her.

Abe tapped Betty and she jolted from her thoughts.

"Don't you want us to raise our children here?"

Her stomach fluttered. "The career I want is in New York. There's no fashion industry or magazine industry in Michigan. As for my children—" It was then Betty realized what Abe had said—*our children*—and the substantial meaning behind the two words. He had placed them into a joint future. One where she was a wife with a career.

She playfully poked a finger at his chest. "I'll raise them wherever their father is."

Abe smiled a mischievous crooked smile. "I suppose you'll want to marry me."

She'd been content with the implication, never expecting him to say the words. Betty's temperature spiked; her face heated. Then she rolled her eyes. "Well, I guess so—for the sake of the children."

Abe kissed her. "Your grandparents aren't going to approve of these plans. I'm only half-Jewish and I'm getting in the way of your future."

"You *are* my future."

Nothing and no one would change that.

Chapter 12

BOOP

The next day, Hannah drove Boop and the girls to the nail salon before heading home to Kalamazoo. "If I want to work this out with Clark, I have to be honest with him, no matter what," Hannah said. "I'll let you know how it goes."

"I want whatever you want," Boop said.

Georgia patted Hannah's shoulder. "Same."

"Honesty is always the best policy," Doris said.

Boop sighed as she stepped out of the passenger's seat and as the girls emerged from the back of the car.

Doris was loving and lovely but sometimes stuck her in-need-of-a-pedicure foot into her mouth.

Boop set Hannah's quandary to the side of her thoughts, after repeating a short, silent prayer that everything would be easy for her granddaughter going forward—with Clark, the baby, and life.

"You have to stop looking so grouchy," Doris said. "Your face will freeze that way."

"I am not grouchy, I'm just concentrating." Boop forced a smile. She handed Doris a bottle of Ballet Shoes, grabbed Reddy or Not for herself, and chose Over the Taupe for Georgia, who already had her feet soaking.

The girls sat in a row of black faux-leather pedicure chairs at the front of the salon, and one by one, nail techs sat on swivel stools by the footbaths.

Natalie had been doing Boop's nails every summer since she'd opened the salon five years earlier, and every week since Boop moved to South Haven full-time.

Boop had admired her right from the day she'd wandered in without an appointment, drawn by the Grand Opening sign. Not only had Natalie opened a business on her own, she was a single mother with a nine-year-old daughter. Though Piper spent intermittent time with her father in East Lansing, Boop knew Natalie shouldered most of the parenting alone. She always tipped Natalie well, and these days befriended Piper as much as a now-fourteen-year-old girl would allow.

The salon buzzed with friendly banter and local gossip, just like her beauty parlor had back in Skokie. "It's busy season again," Boop said.

"Thank goodness." Natalie looked up and smiled.

"Remind me what Piper's doing this summer?" Boop asked. She often heard music floating—or pounding—out of the back room. Her weekly appointments created familiarity without baggage. She knew about Piper's hobbies and grades, and some of Natalie's dating escapades.

"She's spending most of it with her dad, but this week she's in Chicago with my parents. They love spoiling her, and I needed extra time to work on a new project."

"That sounds interesting," Boop said.

"I'll tell you all about it, but first, let's see your color." Natalie lifted the bottle from Boop's hand. "Red. Nice. I'll add it to my stash."

"Your stash?" Doris leaned toward them from her chair.

"Natalie goes to Maplewood Assisted Living every Monday morning and takes along colors I recommend. Isn't that right? Seems I have a knack."

"You certainly do." Natalie smiled broadly, the corners of her mouth puffing her cheeks. She was a pretty young woman—a little more worn and tired-looking than Boop's granddaughters, with an often-furrowed forehead. Business and motherhood had stolen some of her carefree youth, but Boop imagined they had given her more than they'd taken. She had a daughter.

Natalie's eyes were round, big, and brown, rimmed with dark liner and mascara on the top and bottom lashes, both artfully applied. Earrings dotted parts of her ears Boop never knew were meant for piercing. Natalie was thirty-five years old, as short as Boop but rounder and softer, yet still shapely, with a bouquet of flowers tattooed on her calf. Boop couldn't get close enough to see what variety, but they looked like poppies. Natalie and Piper lived in an apartment over the salon.

Boop adored Natalie for her fortitude as much as for the weekly pampering and conversation.

"So, what's this new project of yours?" Boop asked.

Natalie pulled off her gloves and stood. She reached for a stack of papers on a shelf below the reception desk to her right.

Natalie handed flyers to all the women in the salon. Boop would support Natalie however she could. Then she looked at the paper.

THE SEARCH IS ON FOR THE NEXT
MISS SOUTH HAVEN!
NOW ACCEPTING CONTESTANTS:
WOMEN AGES 18–22
MUST HAVE A CONNECTION TO SoHa
TALENT, DRESS, AND POISE CATEGORIES
REGISTER IN PERSON AT NATALIE'S NAIL SALON
SPONSORED BY THE SOUTH HAVEN CHAMBER OF COMMERCE

With her peripheral vision, Boop saw Georgia and Doris gazing at her. Boop stared at the page as it took on the weight of her past, a single pink sheet of paper, three words laden with memories: Miss South Haven. Boop's chest thumped hollow and cold, like a wind was blowing through her. She folded the paper and handed it to Natalie, who chattered on, unaware of Boop's discomfort.

"They've always done the Blueberry Princess and the Vacation Queen, but Miss South Haven?" Natalie leaned in as if that would give them privacy. "There hasn't been a Miss South Haven since 1951. Can you believe it? The records are vague but there was some kind of scandal."

"That's ridiculous," Doris said.

"Just an excuse because *someone* lost some town records, I'm sure," Georgia said.

Boop turned to her friends but averted her eyes when she smiled and nodded. Her tongue tasted like tin and felt dry, like she'd stuffed her mouth with cotton.

"I don't know," Natalie said, sounding self-assured, even argumentative. "At the chamber meeting they all seemed convinced that something had happened to the winner and the sponsor dropped out. But if there was some kind of town moratorium on the title, it's over."

"Says who?" Boop hadn't meant to challenge her, but she wanted to know.

"Says me." Natalie sat straight, stretching upright from her hunched pedi position. "I thought a pageant would be a way to boost business this summer, which I really need to do this year. I asked why there was no Miss South Haven and no one knew anything concrete. So, Miss South Haven it is. Seems like a no-brainer."

"The town has done fine without it," Boop said.

"Maybe, but it could be just the thing I need."

"How so?" Doris asked.

Natalie glanced around. "Business is great in the summer but really falls off during the rest of the year. I need it to pick up before Labor Day to make up for the slower months."

"And doing nails for a few girls will make a difference?" Georgia asked.

"Yes, but it's more than that," Natalie said. "My name will be on every flyer, every poster, every program, every ad. I couldn't pay for that kind of publicity."

Boop wished she could argue that Natalie was wrong.

"And now I'm curious too," Natalie said. "What could have been so horrible that they wiped a whole pageant out of South Haven's history?" Natalie led Boop from the pedicure chair to her manicure station. "You and your friends grew up here—do you know anything about what happened?"

Georgia had followed and sat at the station next to Boop. "That was a long time ago. But if anything comes to mind, we'll let you know."

"It doesn't really matter." Natalie examined Boop's fingernails as if there were an answer hidden beneath. "It's water under the bridge."

Her voice faded into distant, muffled hums.

Boop was drowning.

The cab ride home was quiet until Boop sniffled.

"Are you okay?" Georgia asked.

Boop shrugged. She felt jostled and bruised, as if her memories had roughed her up instead of having appeared in type on a piece of pink paper. "I'm sorry this is how your visit is turning out. We were supposed to have fun like we did when we were girls."

Doris chuckled. "That would kill us."

Boop smiled. "You know what I mean. We're caught up in Hannah's drama and in my past."

"When did we have the most fun back in the day?" Georgia asked. "When we holed up in your bedroom and talked. About school, about boys, about clothes, about our parents."

"We're together. That's the important thing," Doris said.

"I know," Boop said. "But you came back at the same time, after so long, and *that's* when all heck breaks loose in my life? It's like the universe conspired against me."

Doris leaned her head back and chuckled. "You don't think the timing is a coincidence, do you? The universe didn't conspire against you. No sirree. The universe *armed* you."

Back home, Boop excused herself to her bedroom. She flipped the brass hook into its eye on the doorjamb, though the hardware served more as a delay than a blockade. Anyone who was to turn the doorknob and push would encounter only slight resistance, which was fine with her. There was a precarious nature to living alone. Boop was independent, but not foolhardy. If there was an emergency, someone could get inside to save her.

Talking about Abe with Hannah and the girls was one thing. She could temper the story, omit details, paint it pretty. But who could protect her from her recollections of the long-ago Miss South Haven pageant that served as her life's turning point?

She'd never been glad Marvin was gone, but now, God help her, she was relieved he wasn't there to hear about the new pageant. During the first years of their marriage, any reference to a beauty pageant had set him to sulking, as if he had needed to remind Boop of the past without mentioning it. Later, the televised Miss America and Miss Universe contests were discouraged in their home, and Marvin had always harrumphed and snorted at the idea that a girl would want to do such a thing. He knew she had been such a girl, but Boop kept her promise and had never mentioned how she'd longed for the title of Miss South Haven throughout her girlhood. After all, Marvin had been a kind husband, and she found no reason to upset him, even when he involved himself in every part of her life—except for her outings to South Haven.

He'd chosen her clothes from Marshall Field's on State Street and preferred Boop cook meat loaf on Tuesdays, tuna casserole on Wednesdays, and roast chicken for Shabbos. Those were his favorite meals. But, in Marvin's defense, he had always complimented her cooking and her appearance, so Boop didn't see the harm in any of it. Marvin had encouraged Boop's leisure time activities like bridge and canasta with bellowing enthusiasm, neighborhood boasting, and gifts such as the best bridge table and chairs he could buy. He'd provided a hardy fund with which she could buy the latest cookbook or even cater a gathering of her friends, who were envious of her good fortune in landing a husband who was generous and stable.

She was a lucky girl.

Boop had never forgotten Nannie's words.

The trade-off for Boop was that Marvin had never balked at the summers she spent in South Haven with Stuart, or the weekends she escaped the suburban turmoil or trials of motherhood on her own, handing Stuart off to her mother-in-law on occasion.

She never said she wanted to go, but that she *needed* to go. This had always quieted what she sensed was a bubbling objection.

Marvin had never known that, on their wedding day, Boop had stood outside Zaide's office, dressed in her finery. She'd overheard Marvin and Zaide discussing something—or rather, someone. Her!

"She'll be a proper wife and mother, but she must be able to come here whenever she wants." Zaide's voice was deep but soft. Of her two grandparents, he wasn't the serious one, but her welfare was serious business, even when she'd disappointed him. Then she'd heard the slap she'd imagined was the handshake that had sealed her fate.

"Yes, sir," Marvin had said, sounding resolute and like a man. A husband.

"After the wedding I'll talk to your father about that promotion he promised you. Maybe I can help to speed things along. And Yetta and I will help out with the house. Make sure it's what Betty will like, where she can feel at home. All you have to do is keep your end of the bargain. All your ends."

In that moment, and in the wedding that followed, Boop had set aside the detail that her marriage was not just her agreement with Marvin but a transaction between him and her grandparents. She'd turned and headed toward the kitchen, pivoted, and then walked past the office again, feigning ignorance as Zaide opened the door, none the wiser that his granddaughter knew he had built her an escape hatch from her suburban bungalow.

Someone tapped on her bedroom door. Boop didn't want to talk about the memories that had stirred because of one measly flyer. It's not like she had anything to do with the pageant now. She could avoid the topic at home and at the nail salon. Heck, she'd been evading the topic for almost seventy years.

She opened the door.

"We should talk," Georgia said. She and Doris stepped inside.

They sat on Boop's bed. Their younger selves would have plopped and bounced and waited for tales of a date or a dance. Tonight, they sat gingerly. Doris wrung her hands.

"I didn't realize Marvin didn't let you talk about the pageant," she said.

Boop widened her eyes at Georgia.

"What?" Georgia asked. "Doris wanted to know why you were so flustered by the new pageant when Natalie mentioned it. I told her that Marvin forbade you to talk about it."

"He didn't forbid me. I agreed not to mention it because it bothered him. We focused on what happened after that day, not before," Boop said.

"But it was so important to you," Doris said. "Didn't that make it important to him?"

"He didn't want to be reminded of when we weren't together, that's all."

"I'm sorry I didn't realize. I thought you were so happy it just didn't matter anymore and that's why you didn't mention it. You'd won a better prize! You got married!"

Doris had a knack for forgetting unpleasant details.

"It was the right thing to do at the time," Georgia said. "But I guess times change."

"How about if I set out lunch on the porch?" Doris stood and walked toward the bedroom door. "And whatever you want to talk about is okay with us."

Georgia stayed seated on the bed.

"Thanks, that all sounds great," Boop said.

After Doris left the bedroom, Boop waited until the sound of footsteps on the stairs faded to a patter across the wood floor and then disappeared. She turned to Georgia.

"He didn't make me do anything," Boop said. "I agreed to be quiet. But Marvin's gone. Maybe it's time my family knew the whole story."

"After all this time, you're going to go against his wishes?"

"I'm tired of hiding a part of my life. That day of the pageant made me who I am—or at least who I was. It shaped my marriage. It's part of me, even now. God forbid I die tomorrow: Shouldn't my family know the whole truth, or at least as much as I know?"

"I always thought it was better for you to forget about it all, but that's the point, isn't it? You've never forgotten."

"No, I haven't." Boop wouldn't discount her life with Marvin, but it was time to acknowledge she had been someone before she'd become

Boop Peck. She had been Betty Stern—a smart and sassy girl. A bathing beauty.

"It's not just your family, you know. Your manicurist is mighty curious about the last Miss South Haven. I don't think she'll stop digging until she finds answers," Georgia said.

"She's going to be too busy organizing the pageant and wrangling all those contestants to worry about what happened in the past."

That night Boop found her tackle box right where she'd left it, sloppily stowed where anyone could have found it, had they been looking. She removed the box again, and like her heart, it felt too small to hold everything inside, so she set it on the bed in case it burst.

Her nightgown buttoned to her neck and fleece slippers on her feet even though it was June, Boop lost her resolve to open the box and backed away. Was it really time to unlatch the past? To touch it instead of just talk about it? She'd always considered herself brave, but when the act of bravery included baring her heart, she hesitated. Boop skittered around the bedroom, rearranging empty, decorative perfume bottles on her dresser top, grazing her hand along the top of the rocking chair that had belonged to a great-grandmother she'd never met. She fluffed the sheer curtains, and faint particles scattered into the air like fairy dust. The sky was blue and black and speckled with stars, reminding her of a navy Swiss dot pinafore she'd worn as a girl, back when her future was open, her possibilities endless.

Boop looked at the box and imagined the world it represented. Was she the only one who held these memories dear? Had Abe told anyone about their summer, about her?

Boop scoffed at her own vanity.

If Abe still had all of his faculties as he aged, he wouldn't be thinking about the girl from South Haven. She gasped and covered her mouth with one hand. She'd never thought of him aging. She'd always pictured him young and handsome, that dimple in his chin peeking out when he smiled. If he was alive, he'd be pushing ninety.

If.

"Dear God, I hope Abe was always surrounded by people who loved him. And that he didn't suffer in his life." Boop knew the odds. "Or in death. Amen."

Boop heard a tap on the door. She unlocked and opened the door. It was Georgia. "Doris is out for the count. Are you doing okay?"

"I'm not sure," Boop said. "I think it's time to face it all, or as much as I can." She motioned to the box. "I can't seem to open it."

"Is that what I think it is?"

Boop nodded.

"You've had it all this time."

"Yes."

"I'll open it for you, if that's what you want," Georgia said.

"I do."

With that, Georgia flicked the latch on the tackle box but left the lid closed. "Ready?"

Boop couldn't believe she was frightened, as if a physical reminder would have more heft than emotional ones. She was as jittery as she'd once been turning the crank of her jack-in-the-box. But in this box she'd tucked her happiest and her saddest memory—which happened to be the same thing. Love and loss, comedy and tragedy, past and future. It all had the same face, the same voice, the same touch—that's what would pop out this time.

She and Georgia had hidden the box so carefully that day so long ago. Boop had moved it years later, carrying the box as if it were as fragile and priceless as a Fabergé egg. Then, like the kids say, life happened. Most people might have been surprised at what she'd saved and have thought it an unlikely totem. Yet it had enraged Marvin.

Boop squeezed her eyes tight against the memory of flashbulbs and sunshine; she covered her ears against words of judgment and disappointment. Then she allowed herself to sneak into her past at the moment before her world shifted. Perfume. Pretty dresses. A purple swimsuit.

She opened her eyes. What was she waiting for?

Boop inhaled deeply. "I'll do it."

She lifted the lid, and the box unfolded like a child's pop-up book. Fewer lures in the top tray than she'd expected. A few pennies in the second tray. None of this seemed familiar, but then again, sometimes she forgot what she'd stored in her kitchen cupboards.

But she wouldn't have forgotten this. Boop's throat constricted. In the bottom section lay a box of twenty-four Crayola crayons and torn pieces of construction paper in a rainbow of colors, so faded and crackled it was as if they would disintegrate if she blew on them. She removed the crayons and scrambled the papers with a few frenetic slaps. She found a plastic protractor, a six-inch wooden ruler, random lengths of blue and yellow yarn, tongue depressors, and a jar of rubber cement.

This wasn't her box. She closed it and flipped it upside down. Scratched into the corner with a straight pin were her initials, BCS. It *was* her box.

"What is all this stuff? Did you know this was in here?" Georgia asked.

"No!" Boop dumped the contents of the tackle box onto her bed, fanned them out, flipped them over, turned the box upside down, and shook it, hoping her keepsake would materialize as if by magic. But it didn't. Her bed was littered with craft supplies a young Hannah or Emma might have collected then forgotten about by the following summer.

Boop spotted wisps of silky thread caught in a hinge. She yanked them loose and held them toward the glow of her night-light. She exhaled, and the translucent strands of pink fluttered from her breath.

The box was full but empty of meaning.

Boop closed her hands around the delicate fibers and, once again, prayed to find something she'd lost.

She rifled through her memories with the same fervor Marvin had flipped through his Rolodex when he'd wanted to negotiate a deal or beat out his competitor. The last time she'd seen the contents of the box was the weekend of their tenth wedding anniversary.

Ordinarily, Boop and Stuart would spend summers in South Haven while Marvin stayed in Skokie, buckled into his job running the five Peck's Popular Shoes locations on the North Shore. He was a workaholic before Boop had known what to call it, but she knew he also didn't share Boop's affection for her grandparents' resort and house. She had longed for the familiar food, scenery, and creaks on the stairs. She reveled in watching Stuart play with the children of the children she'd known growing up in town and at the resort. He followed Zaide around, and her grandparents set time aside from working to spoil him.

Boop hadn't minded time apart from Marvin. It seemed normal to her. The wives at Stern's spent summers mostly without their husbands, who would join them on weekends.

But the summer of 1961, Marvin was the exception to this rule, belying the norm, the routine, and the odd comfort of distance. He left the stores in the care of his father and stayed in South Haven for a full week, including the weekends on either end. Every time Boop had turned around, there he was behind her. On the beach, in the resort kitchen with Mabel, out in the garden, even while she was making the beds. At first, she'd found it charming, even romantic. Then she realized: Marvin was bored. In Skokie he would divide his time among the stores, golf, cards, and as Cubmaster for Stuart's Scout den. On Saturday nights they'd socialized as a couple with the neighbors or with people from the synagogue. But in South Haven the lack of an agenda made Marvin antsy.

"I'll take Stuart fishing. There must be fishing supplies here," Marvin had said, drumming his fingers on his pants. "Do you know where your grandfather keeps them?"

"Since when do you fish?"

"Since today."

Boop had been scraping Duncan Hines yellow cake batter into two round pans, greased with Crisco. She hadn't inherited Nannie's from-scratch gene but had wanted to create something for the occasion of Marvin's visit.

"You used to go fishing with your grandfather, and I know you wouldn't get rid of anything he gave you," Marvin had said.

She'd wiped her hands on her apron. "Please just give me a minute; I'll do it as soon as I get the cake in the oven." Boop didn't want Marvin going through her grandparents' things. Her things. She'd moved her tackle box into the shed when she'd filled her old bedroom closet with packed-away baby clothes she thought she'd need again one day. She had been only twenty-eight then, and still hopeful for another baby.

"Fine." Marvin had looked at her askance.

Betty had trembled inside but kept her gaze steady.

"I'll go fix the window in Stuart's room," he'd said.

Marvin had found Boop in the backyard shed, in front of an open metal storage closet. It had been just enough time for Boop to have finished with the cake, for Stuart and his summer friends to have licked the bowl and the wooden spoons, and for her to find what she needed. But not enough time to have hidden it again.

She'd felt like a child caught with her hand in a candy jar, when in fact she had been a twenty-eight-year-old married woman and the mother of a young boy. Still, Marvin had demanded she open the tackle box, as if he'd known what was inside. He had, hadn't he? He glanced at the box, then stared into Boop's eyes. He hadn't raised his voice; he never did.

"I'll take that." Marvin held out his hands.

"Everything in here is old," she'd said. "You should take Stuart to the tackle shop. They can give you some pointers."

"Give me the box. No need to keep it if it's old."

Boop had slammed the box and snapped it shut. Her throat had seared with pain from a muffled scream or a cry or a combination of both. She was angry with him for the first time in a long while, maybe years. She had done as she'd been asked and told for the past ten years. She'd fulfilled her duties as mother, homemaker, and wife. That day in the shed, tears had dripped onto her cotton plaid culottes. She'd kept her head down, maybe in an effort to be submissive, or respectful, or maybe because she hadn't known what would happen next.

"I'm sorry, Marvin. It's all I have." She hadn't let go of the box until he'd turned and left the shed.

They never mentioned that incident—or the tackle box—again.

And there she was, decades later, with the same box. The one that had been important enough to anger her husband, or maybe to break his heart, just as it was breaking hers at that moment.

Boop looked at Georgia. "It was all I had."

Chapter 13

Betty

The next Saturday night, Betty positioned herself sideways on the window seat in her bedroom. She wrapped her arms around her knees and wiggled her toes, to show off her toenails painted Petal Pink. She stared at the dark, clear night. The stars sparkled like rhinestones, glittering bold to the north, twinkling pale to the south over the lighthouse, as if a deliberate design. She supposed it was.

In two hours, she'd look at that sky with her head on Abe's shoulder, her heart pounding as it whispered a thousand wishes.

Betty glanced at her girlfriends, lying across her bed—as usual—still flipping through the issues of *Vogue*, *Seventeen*, and the latest Spiegel catalog she'd handed them thirty minutes earlier. Words like *hemline*, *neckline*, and *bustline* floated around the room with *rayon*, *silk*, and *tulle*. The girls didn't know much about fashion, but they knew it was important to Betty.

Doris dropped from her side to her stomach. "I can't believe you haven't decided on your dress *or* your swimsuit." She tapped a page in *Vogue* as if she were a teacher pointing to a lesson in a textbook. "This one's sophisticated." The photo showcased an elegant blond model wearing a black-and-white taffeta ball gown, nothing like what Betty needed for Miss South Haven.

Betty shrugged. "There's plenty of time."

"Plenty of time?" Doris asked. "I thought that's why we were here. The pageant is in August!"

Doris closed the magazine and rose from the bed. She lifted the dictionary from Betty's desk and held it out toward her. "For posture practice."

Georgia grabbed the book and placed it atop her own head. She held her arms out to her sides and looked as graceful as a ballerina, though Betty knew she'd never taken a dance lesson. Georgia's fingers were long and elegant, posed without effort, rehearsal, or knowledge. Those hands would save lives one day, Betty was sure of it. Georgia walked like a circus performer on a tightrope, and the book didn't fall until she tilted her head.

Betty accepted the book into her hands but laid it in her lap. Her posture was fine.

Doris closed *Seventeen* and stood. She smoothed out her shorts and sat next to Betty. "I can't believe you're head over heels for a boy who doesn't even take you out on a proper Saturday-night date. And then you gave up the nightclub for this?"

For years, Betty had waited for summer Saturday nights with the eager anticipation of a child walking into the lake, arms up, waiting for waves to crash. But she did not miss the nightclub. Not tonight. Not at all. "We all seem to be on our own tonight," Betty said.

"You asked us to come," Georgia said.

"You could've said no! I didn't want you to give up dates or plans for me."

"Don't worry, I didn't have a date," Doris said. "Maybe next week."

Doris had always been the most hopeful and romantic of their trio, although Betty seemed to be catching up fast.

"I'm just pulling your leg," Doris said. "Friends first, right?" She scooped Betty's hand into hers. They both reached out their hands to Georgia, and the girls linked together the way they had since they were children.

Gratitude stung Betty's throat. She squeezed their hands and they squeezed back.

"I have a secret to tell you," Betty said.

Doris dropped Betty's hand. "I knew it."

"Shush," Georgia said.

"You can't tell anyone," Betty said.

Without another word, the girls crossed their hearts.

Betty's conscience eased. Georgia and Doris would say it was okay. They would make it okay.

"Abe's not really Jewish," she said.

Doris smacked her hand over her mouth and opened her eyes as big as Ping-Pong balls.

"*Oy gevalt,*" Georgia said. "He lied to get the job?"

"No, his father is Jewish," Betty said. The statement sounded weak and apologetic.

"So he lied. You know his father doesn't count." Doris placed her hands on her hips, then crossed her arms in front of her, then folded them at her chest, all while tapping her foot. She was trying to be calm and nonchalant, but her jitters made that impossible.

"What do your grandparents say?" Georgia asked.

Betty glanced out the window as if they might be peeking into the second floor and eavesdropping. "They don't know. And they don't know we're . . . serious."

"What do you mean you're serious?" Georgia pursed her lips.

"We've talked about the future. Our future."

Georgia stomped around the room. "Your future is at Barnard."

"And Abe wouldn't have it any other way. He's going to move to New York when he graduates."

"A *gentile*," Doris whispered. "I guess that's why he's so handsome. He doesn't look like any Jewish boy I know."

"Don't be childish," Georgia said. "Jewish boys—Jewish men—are very handsome. Look at the husbands who show up every weekend."

"Eww, they're old." Doris giggled. "But you're right, some aren't half-bad in their swim trunks."

Betty rolled her eyes. "I don't care about the guests. What do I do about Abe?"

"I think you have to end it," Doris said.

Georgia shook her head. "If you want to be with him, even though you know it's wrong, there's only one thing I can tell you to do."

"Anything," Betty said.

"Pretend you don't know," Georgia said. "Sometimes it helps."

"You want me to lie?"

"She shouldn't lie," Doris said.

"It's not lying if you didn't know. You want to be with him the rest of the summer, right?"

"Right."

"And you don't want your grandparents to interfere."

"Right."

"Then forget he told you."

"But Abe wants to know I'm okay with it."

"You being okay with it and your grandparents approving are two different things. I wouldn't want to go up against your Nannie if she found out you're planning a future with a boy who isn't Jewish," Georgia said.

Doris nodded. "I wouldn't want to be there if she found out about the canoodling, let alone this!"

Guilt trickled into Betty's heart. She owed her grandparents every-thing. But that's what the pageant was for. If she won, they'd have brag-ging rights while she was off at Barnard. It was her way of contributing to the business when she wasn't leading jumping jacks or ironing curtains.

Canoodling with a gentile boy didn't change any of that.

As far as guilt for staying home that night, she'd only half fibbed to convince her grandparents. Betty *did* want to choose her dress and swimsuit outfits for the pageant, and this was the only time that she and her friends were off work at the same time. Nannie and Zaide had thought it a fine idea. They were all for having an advantage when it came to the pageant, and, like Zaide had said, "Three girls' heads are better than one."

Betty felt a twinge in her side, a reminder that she'd conveniently omitted another reason she'd wanted to stay home. Abe. The glamour of the nightclub, the rhythm and sway of the music, the elaborate displays of jewelry and fashion—yes, even fashion—didn't matter to her without Abe. If he couldn't be there, there was no way she'd spend an hour and a half primping, or dance with guests—even her new, old friend, Marv Peck.

Betty could see the lights in the main house from her window, but the music was muted by the distance. She flopped onto her bed next to Doris. Then Betty flipped open a magazine and turned pages one at a time and stared. She wasn't reading the words or noticing the advertisements. She was counting minutes till Abe arrived.

Betty's grandfather rarely summoned her, especially not in the middle of a summer Sunday. To Nannie and Zaide, summer meant tending to the guests, maintaining the property, and safeguarding their social status—each a full-time job on its own.

Betty inhaled and shook her hands by her sides so she wouldn't fidget once she stepped inside. She knocked.

"Come in." Zaide's voice rang clear, as if the six-panel solid-wood barrier between them didn't exist.

Betty turned the knob and opened the door just wide enough to poke her head in. "You wanted to see me? If you're busy—"

Zaide beckoned her with his crooked index finger, and Betty felt as if there was a string attached to her conscience and every motion weakened her resolve.

Betty gulped. Deny, deny, deny. Georgia wouldn't steer her wrong.

Betty stepped inside and shut the door. She was still wearing her shorts and staff-issue white blouse, her name embroidered in Stern Blue on the left breast pocket. "I can change out of these clothes first, if you want."

Zaide pointed to the walnut and leather captain's chair in front of his desk. "Sit, bubbeleh." Betty sighed. He wouldn't have called her that if he was angry. "You've been busy lately, haven't you?" Zaide said.

Betty wasn't sure if this was a trick question. "No busier than usual." Maybe she should have said yes, she *was* busy.

"Well, that's neither here nor there. I want to show you something." Zaide leaned to the right. The large bottom desk drawer clicked open and squeaked as it slid out on its tracks. Zaide reached down and seemed to jimmy something out of the drawer with one hand.

Betty tapped her toes in a rapid rhythm to match her heartbeat. She wasn't a liar. If Zaide asked her about Abe, she'd tell him. No, his mother wasn't Jewish. Yes, she was keeping her eye on the prize, as Zaide liked to say, though Betty wasn't always sure if that meant his prize or hers. No, she hadn't neglected any of her responsibilities at the resort. Had she? Yes, she still understood what it meant to be a South Haven Stern.

After a sturdy yank, Zaide placed a box with a crushed pink bow on his desk and slid it toward Betty. She breathed hard, like she sometimes did after calisthenics. This was a present, not a punishment.

"The pageant is coming, and well . . . what do you kids say? I want you to feel swell when you go up against those other girls."

Goose bumps danced down Betty's arms.

Zaide pushed the box again. "I know you're working more than other summers and you're getting ready for Barnard and you're seeing Abe Barsky. You're not a baby anymore." Zaide's voice caught.

Betty's throat burned as she swallowed her accusations, regret, and near-confessions. She fluffed the bow before untying it and set it on her lap. She glanced at Zaide, who was smiling at her. His eyes squinted small, his nose wrinkled.

"Go ahead now," he said.

She placed the lid to the side and turned two layers of white tissue paper like they were pages in a cherished book. Then she lifted fabric, which unfolded as she raised her arms.

"Zaide, you shouldn't have." Oh, but she was glad he had! Betty hugged to her chest the most glamorous structured swimsuit she had ever seen. She held it out again and it regained its hourglass shape. The suit was purple, but not Shabbos-grape-juice purple—a richly saturated lavender with sparkly silver straps and a matching embellishment at the bust. Betty had assumed she'd enter the Miss South Haven contest wearing her favorite yellow swimsuit with white pinstripes. She'd never been so tickled to be wrong.

She laid the swimsuit, silky but firm to the touch, across the box and pushed back her chair. As she stood, the pink ribbon cascaded to the floor. She bounded around the desk and climbed onto Zaide's lap the way she had when she was little and wanted him to read her a story. He'd always complied. Zaide had always made her feel special and safe and loved even though she wasn't an ordinary girl who wanted a house and husband right away. He loved her unconditionally. Then, now, always. She hugged him around his neck. At that moment she loved him more than anyone because he knew what was important to her, and he cared enough to show her. How would she ever leave and go to New York? How could she lie to him about Abe?

Betty banished the thoughts. "You're the best, Zaide. I never thought . . ."

Zaide pulled back and looked into her eyes. "If Nannie asks, you ordered this from Lemon's with my permission."

Betty nodded. "But where did it come from?"

Zaide whispered, "One of the girls knew just the store to call. Abraham and Straus."

"In New York!"

"Now how will the judges be able to resist my bathing beauty?"

Betty wrapped Zaide in another hug. She would do anything to make him proud.

Chapter 14

BOOP

Boop, Georgia, and Doris stopped into Natalie's salon the next day. Boop would prepare for this pageant the way she had prepared before— with an awareness of potential problems.

Natalie was standing behind the front desk.

"Smudges?" Natalie asked.

Boop glanced at her nails. "Oh no. I was thinking—" She shifted her weight from one foot to the other. "That you might like some help with the pageant. I could help with the registrations and even getting posters into local store windows."

"No one says no to an old lady," Georgia said. "And Doris and I will only be here a few more days."

Boop scowled but acquiesced. "I've been looking for something to keep me busy—and I think we'd have fun working together."

"I agree," Natalie said. "It would be fun. You're officially my cochairwoman!"

"Just like that?" Boop asked.

Natalie held out her hand and Boop shook it. "To be honest, I thought Piper might have fun helping me, but she'll be at her dad's most of the summer and she kind of rolled her eyes at me when I asked."

Natalie shrugged. "Oh! Since we're partners, I should show you this. Remember I asked you if you remembered anything about the last Miss South Haven pageant?"

"Right," Boop said.

"It was so long ago," Georgia said.

"Well, I found a photo online."

"You did?" Boop and Georgia said in unison.

Boop's pulse sped up and her hands went clammy.

"Yes, but just one. It's grainy and from the Benton Harbor newspaper. Nothing listed in the South Haven paper at all. Weird, right?" Natalie reached into her case and then handed Boop a piece of paper she'd never seen before. "The winner's not even looking at the camera," Natalie said. "There's a short article to go with it. But this is it. Nothing else about her. I couldn't find anything else online except her name."

"Holy Toledo," Georgia said.

"I know, it's amazing, right? All you have to know is where to look and you can find anything online." Natalie handed the paper to Boop.

Stern Granddaughter Wins Miss South Haven

SOUTH HAVEN, August 13—Mr. and Mrs. Ira Stern, owners of South Haven's premier property, Stern's Summer Resort, were as pleased as punch this year, as they had every right to be.

Their 18-year-old granddaughter, South Haven resident Betty Claire Stern, graduated with honors from South Haven High School in May and is planning to matriculate at Barnard College in New York, New York, in September.

Yesterday, brown-haired, blue-eyed Betty went on to win the crystal-encrusted crown and pink satin sash reserved for our Miss South Haven each year. Betty won the title over 19 other lovely girls representing local resorts.

The annual contest to pick South Haven's summer sweetheart was sponsored by B'nai B'rith and held at the North Shore Pavilion.

Much to the crowd's alarm, right after this photo was taken, our new beauty queen ran swiftly from the stage and fainted by the beach. At the time of this printing she is said to be resting comfortably at home, after suffering from exhaustion. Being a distinguished bathing beauty is hard work indeed.

We extend our best wishes to beautiful Betty for a speedy recovery.

Boop mouthed the words as she read. She felt Georgia's arm around her, holding on. She heard Doris's breathing. Boop stared at the photo of the girl they'd called beautiful, and felt no connection to her. That was a different person—which didn't seem right. She'd felt as if her life had been interrupted, so that there was before and after. The unidentifiable middle was in that photo.

Boop saw crisp lines, a purple swimsuit from a New York boutique, and a pink sash instead of grainy shades of black, gray, and white.

Of course it was the only photo or mention of her; Nannie and Zaide would have seen to that. They didn't even announce her engagement or marriage to Marvin in the newspapers. "Too many questions, and not enough answers," Nannie had said. Rumors had swirled. Lies were told.

Boop traced her finger along the sash, which looked dull and ordinary.

"Do you remember something?" Natalie asked.

"The suit was purple."

"That's a lovely detail. Does this mean you were there? Did you know this girl?"

Georgia held her tighter, and Boop didn't know if it was an attempt to encourage or discourage what came next.

Foggy moments drifted back to her consciousness. Her parents in the audience. Marvin too. The beach. All the images in her head looked faded by sunlight.

"I'm that girl, Natalie." She folded the paper and handed it back. "I'm the runaway bathing beauty. Or I was." Even for Boop it was hard to believe. The girl in that photo had been trim and toned and giddy. She was rich with dreams and expectations. Her disheveled appearance in the photograph made it almost look like she had known what would happen next.

Natalie gasped, then leaned over and hugged her. "This is more than I could have hoped for. I'm going to look so good at the next meeting, saying, 'My friend, Boop Peck, was the last Miss South Haven.' Can you tell me what happened that day? But if it's too much or you want me to keep it a secret, I will."

"No more secrets," Boop said.

"She was suffering from exhaustion," Georgia said.

"Oh, that's terrible," Natalie said.

"It was," Boop said.

Before she said anything else, the girls ushered her away.

Boop's next few hours passed in a blur of box kites, beach umbrellas, and oversize SUVs that blocked her view of the lake. Remembering the

Miss South Haven contest, where the threads holding her life together unraveled quicker than a ball of wool chased by a rambunctious kitten.

It was there, on that day, that her life lay in temporary ruin and permanent redirection. What did the kids say? *Own it.* Still, it was *her* redirection, *her* life that followed. Hannah's thoughts about how Abe had led her to Marvin applied to the pageant as well. Perhaps every event had been preordained. She'd never been meant for another life or another love. Maybe even without the pregnancy it all would have ended—Abe, Miss South Haven, Barnard. But if that were so, the longing inside her would not have resurfaced, the memories wouldn't pinch her heart. She wouldn't be in her eighties and wondering *what if.*

Doris stepped onto the porch and set a light shawl over Boop's shoulders. Georgia followed with a cup of tea. Boop didn't want any tea. They thought she was sick.

"I knew it was a mistake to go poking around in the past," Georgia whispered.

"Should we call Hannah? Or Stuart?" Doris asked.

"I'll call them later," Boop said. "I'm fine." She would be fine—wasn't she always?

Gathering the corners of the shawl with one hand, she felt the widening stitches and the wearing yarn. Nannie had crocheted this shawl for herself when Boop was seventeen. For years Boop had stored it in a tight-lidded plastic shirt box, folded in layers of white tissue paper and sprinkled with mothballs. Whenever she would open the box, the pungent and toxic smell would mean the shawl was safe, that she could wrap it around her as if it were Nannie herself. She was older than Nannie had ever been, but she was also that young girl sometimes—lately more so than usual, or maybe than was healthy.

The weight of the shawl transmitted only the wonder of Nannie to the forefront of Boop's thoughts. Her grandmother had knitted, sewed, cooked, baked, operated a resort, sustained a marriage, raised a son, watched him leave home to rarely return, and then raised her granddaughter. Yetta Stern had been the small, strong, grand dame of South Haven, who accomplished much and who had dared to dream on behalf of her granddaughter. That was, until her and Zaide's guidance had gone askew.

Boop had tried to right the wrongs of the past. To teach Hannah the lesson Boop wished she had learned.

Energy surged through her. A jolt of recognition of a forgotten tenacity—to help herself.

Hannah doesn't need to learn from the past; I do.

Boop should have been using those long-ago experiences as a way to understand what Hannah needed from her. Not what Hannah should do or think or feel. If they wanted to get married, Boop would support it. Clark was a good young man, just like Abe had been, maybe not someone she would have chosen for Hannah but that wasn't her job. Boop didn't need to see it, feel it, or know it; she needed to trust Hannah the way she wished she'd been trusted.

Boop left the shawl on the back of her chair and walked into the house. The girls followed.

She lifted her cell phone from the end table.

"Who are you calling?" Georgia asked.

Boop placed her index finger to her lips and turned to the window. Gulls dipped and soared and spun as if she had a front-row seat to a bird ballet. The phone clicked its connection.

"Hi, Boop," Hannah whispered. "I'm sorry I haven't called, but I was just about to."

"Am I on speakerphone?"

"No."

"Well, push the button. I think Clark should hear this."

"He's gone."

"When he comes back, tell him I get it."

"Get what?"

"My family got in the way of me and Abe. I won't get in your way. I pinned my past onto your future, and that was wrong. If this is where your life is leading you, Hannah, then I'll support you any way I can. And I bet your dad and Emma will agree."

Behind Boop, the girls clapped lightly but tittered loudly. On the phone, Hannah gasped then went silent. She was crying.

"Oh, Hannahleh, I'm sorry, I should have said that right away. You just caught me off guard and it brought back so many memories. But that was my past, Hannah. It has nothing to do with your future."

"We don't have a future," Hannah said. "Clark changed his mind."

"We'll see you soon, then," Boop said, then pressed the button to disconnect the call.

"What's going on?" Georgia asked.

"Clark broke it off with her," Boop said. "He *changed his mind.*"

"How dare he," Doris said. "There's a baby."

"There are two sides to every story," Georgia said.

Boop stepped back. "Whose side are you on?"

"I'm on Hannah's side. I'm just saying we don't know what happened."

"What happened was that she went home to tell him she loved him and wanted to marry him and he said 'no thank you.'"

Georgia shook her head. "I bet it was more complicated than that."

"Poor Hannah," Doris said. "What can we do?"

Boop scampered through the living room, collecting framed snapshots from the end table, the bookshelf, and the wall. "We can get rid of the evidence." She headed into Zaide's old office.

"What are you doing?" Georgia yelled.

Arms full, Boop emerged holding every picture of Hannah and Clark she could carry. If Hannah had given it to her, Boop had displayed it. Hannah and Clark in Mexico. Hannah and Clark in kayaks.

Hannah and Clark skiing, gardening, posing with silly faces. Now these would be reminders of her breakup—as if her belly wouldn't be enough.

"You're going to throw away all those photos?" Doris asked.

"Yes." Boop tipped her head toward the screen porch so the girls would follow her. "But not the parts with Hannah in them."

Settled on the screen porch, Boop, Georgia, and Doris hunched over their laps more from intention than age. They sliced through photographs, sometimes cutting around Hannah's image as if playing paper dolls, sometimes just cutting out Clark's head to preserve the scenery.

"What are you doing?"

Hannah? They looked up in succession. Boop, Georgia, then Doris.

Boop shuffled the scraps off her lap as if she were brushing away crumbs, then stood. She hugged Hannah and turned so that her granddaughter wasn't facing the girls. Boop waved her hand back and forth, hoping they'd know to hide the evidence. Georgia swept clippings into a wicker trash bin and Doris tucked a few under her bottom. Just in time too. Hannah pulled back and whirled around.

"I thought you were coming tonight," Boop said.

"I said *soon.* I didn't want to worry you, but I was already in the car when I called."

"You're with family now," Doris said. "We'll fix you up right as rain. I leave in the morning but that's plenty of time."

Hannah reached out her hand and Doris grasped it. "That's okay," Hannah said. "I'm glad I got a chance to see you." She glanced around. "What are you doing?"

"Nothing," Boop said. She'd never have started this if she'd known Hannah would arrive and catch them. It was meant to be a subtle change. There would be no visual reminders of Clark in South Haven. It would be a safe place for Hannah to heal.

Hannah plucked a discarded scrap from the trash can. "What are you *doing?*" she yelled.

Boop grabbed the photo. "I'm not going to have photos of Clark around. You don't need to see that."

"These are my memories!"

"I told you we shouldn't have done this," Georgia said.

Boop narrowed her eyes and scowled at her best friend.

Hannah plucked out six pictures of Clark and held them like playing cards. "You can't just throw him away. For God's sake, bubbes, turn the frames facedown, put them in a drawer. Don't decapitate him."

"It was her idea," Doris said.

Boop placed her hands on her hips. "Best one I had all day. How dare he abandon you and the baby like that."

"He didn't abandon the baby. He said he didn't want to get engaged now."

Boop slumped. She'd panicked. Overreacted. "You left that part out."

"I didn't think you were going to mastermind a photo slaughter in the time it took me to drive here."

After a few beats of silence, Hannah covered her mouth with her hand and the photos, and chuckled. Nervous that she was misreading the situation again, Boop kept silent. Then Doris hiccupped and laughed, and Georgia downright cackled. Only then did Boop join in as she collected Clark bits from the rubbish bin and set him on the arm of the glider. Later they'd find a way to put all the pieces back together.

That evening, they gathered at the kitchen table for Chinese food from Delightful Buddha.

"How about a little soup?" Doris asked, pouring wonton soup from its carton into a small bowl for Hannah.

Georgia dumped five fortune cookies out of their waxy bag onto the table. Doris reached for one; Georgia shook her head. "Pregnant ladies pick first."

Hannah chose a cookie and waited because she knew the rules; everyone has to have a cookie before anyone can crack hers open. Boop and Marvin had invented this rule with Stuart, and it stood now as part of Peck family lore.

"You pick, Boop," Hannah said.

Boop reached for the cellophane packet farthest from her. "Your turn, Doris."

Doris picked one, which left two for Georgia.

"When I say 'three' we open them," Boop said. "One, two, three."

Hannah laughed as they pulled open the packages. If a silly game of paper fate was what it took to make her smile, Boop was in.

"I'll read mine if I can see it." Georgia squinted. "Never forget that a half truth is a whole lie."

"Well, of course it is," Doris said. "Listen to mine. 'Big journeys begin with a single step.'" She looked up, eyes wide. "I think it has to do with marrying Saul."

Boop shook her head. "I'm opening the last one."

"Why? What does yours say?" Hannah plucked it from Boop's hands and read, "A truly rich life contains love and art in abundance." She tore the small paper into two pieces. "There won't be art in my life anymore. Not like it used to be. I don't know why they call them fortunes anyway. A fortune is a prediction of the future, not just a quote. Excuse me, I have to pee." Hannah pushed back from the table. The bathroom door closed a few moments later.

"We need to change the subject," Boop said. She gathered cookie crumbs and plastic into the empty Delightful Buddha bag.

"She'll talk when she wants to," Georgia said.

Doris set out the take-out containers and Georgia grabbed plates. She picked up a piece of white paper from the floor. Hannah's fortune.

"What does it say?" Georgia asked.

"Those who care will make the effort."

"Oh, that poor dear. I wish we knew what happened," Boop said.

"She has a good head on her shoulders," Doris said.

"That doesn't always help," Georgia said.

The bathroom door squeaked open. Boop and the girls opened the cartons, stuck an appropriate utensil into each, and started filling their plates.

"Sit with us, even if you're not hungry. Unless the smell bothers you," Georgia said.

Hannah covered her face with her hands. "I don't know how it happened."

"Do you want to tell us what *it* was?" Boop stretched her arm around Hannah.

"Do you think he'll forgive me?" Hannah asked.

The girls stayed quiet as Boop selected her words with great care. "For taking time to decide about marriage? I should hope so, Hannah. Not everyone says yes right away, especially if he caught you off guard with the proposal."

Hannah looked up at Boop. "You don't understand."

Boop saw Georgia's lips tighten and Doris gaze into the lo mein. This was a job for Boop. "Explain it to me then."

"Clark changed his mind because I told him I met someone else."

A gentle vertigo swayed the room from side to side. Boop held the edge of her chair. "Excuse me?"

"What do you mean, you met someone else?" Doris asked.

"I met a guy. Online. I really cared for him. Or I thought I did."

Georgia stood and lifted her plate. Doris did the same. "We'll be on the porch if you need us."

Now the girls gave them privacy? When Boop would have liked a little backup? Her thoughts jumbled together. There had been two men in Hannah's life.

The front door shut.

"I thought you said the baby was Clark's."

"The baby is Clark's," Hannah said. "It—I mean he or she—can't be anyone else's. I just thought I should be honest with Clark that I'd had a . . . I guess you could call it an emotional connection with someone else. He wanted more, but I realized I didn't. I just thought that I should be honest."

"This happened while you were living with Clark?"

Hannah nodded.

"So, it was like a crush."

"It was different than a crush."

"What does that mean?"

"We were really good friends, but I knew he wanted more." Hannah looked away from Boop. "I liked the attention. The thing is, I used to lie to Clark about who I was texting and who I was with when I went out sometimes."

"Oh, Hannah."

"I know, I know, it's awful. But I never even kissed him, and we always met in public, in this one coffee shop. Then all of a sudden it was like he had never been listening to me. He wanted me to break up with Clark to be with him, and I freaked out. I ended the friendship. I never should have said I miss him sometimes. I think that was the clincher. And I didn't want to lie to Clark anymore. Or to myself."

"You realize this made Clark insecure, right? He's worried you'll replace him."

"That's ridiculous. I reminded him that no one can ever compare to him. He's the one who encouraged me to get my master's. And how much I love going to craft shows with him and listening to him talk about his sculptures. He's so talented, and I'm proud as though I had something to do with it. He remembers everything I tell him about all my students. He's my best friend, Boop. What am I supposed to do without him?" Hannah coughed, and then sobbed her words. "I thought telling him the truth was the right thing to do."

"What did he say when you told him all this?"

Hannah spoke in gasps. "That he felt like he was the safe choice, not the passionate and exciting choice. But he's wrong. He's the only choice. But he may never fully trust me again."

Boop wouldn't tell Hannah that it would be okay, Clark or no Clark, that her life would fill with love and happiness, even if at first there was heartache.

It wasn't the right time for acceptance. It was time for action.

Chapter 15

BOOP

Hannah headed to bed early. Boop and the girls sat at the kitchen table amid the scraps of food and leftover conversation.

"I'll clean up," Boop said. "It helps me think."

"I thought ironing helped you think," Doris said.

"I haven't ironed since, I don't know, the eighties?" Boop said. "These days, I settle for drying dishes by hand."

Georgia set dishes by the sink. "We can help."

"I'd rather have some time to myself."

"I know you're thinking about Abe," Georgia said.

"How can I not? I would have forgiven him anything. And look at Marvin and his forgiveness, his acceptance. I know he wasn't perfect but love means giving someone a second chance. Maybe a third. If Clark doesn't see that—"

Georgia nodded. "Then maybe a baby isn't the right reason this time."

"Exactly."

With the dishes dried, Boop and the girls settled alone onto the porch to watch the sunset. But they weren't alone. A dozen people walked by and waved on their way to the pier—the best spot in town for skygazing, unless you had a porch.

A sloop cruised north toward the lighthouse. The boat traveled into the wind, sails angled forward, appearing as its predecessor may have hundreds of years earlier, when, as a merchant vessel, it transported furs, or while serving in the War of 1812, before it had been captured by the British and later burned.

Oh, the things Boop remembered from grade-school social studies.

That day *Friends Good Will* curved around the pier, to the cheers of the crowd that had gathered, the sky aflame.

Without forgetting its past, the ship had been bestowed new life, new purpose, as a tourist and educational attraction. No one had erased or disregarded the calamitous past, like Boop had. Those stories were part of its legacy; they made the ship's story whole.

The calamity of Boop's life was what made her whole as well.

The cantaloupe-and-honey-colored sky deepened to cider near the surface of the lake. Boop glanced away and toward her friends. Doris was leaving in the morning. It was time to hurry things along.

The next morning, Boop shook Hannah's foot through the lemonade-colored comforter. "Rise and shine, sleepyhead. It's almost nine. Doris's cab will be here soon to take her to the airport. Come say goodbye."

Hannah's eyes remained closed. "I'm awake. Just resting." She sat up straight. "Doris deserves a proper goodbye. And then you, me, and Georgia will go out for brunch."

Hannah's slim build and thin cotton nightshirt revealed a curve—the "baby bump," Boop had heard it called. Hannah had entered her second trimester, thank God. The changes would be rapid-fire from here on out. Boop wanted Hannah to revel in each experience, not have it serve as a reminder of anything other than the future.

Boop had once been forced to hide the shifts in her spirit and the burden of her symptoms, lest they confirm what everyone suspected: she was pregnant before she'd married Marvin. The fact that it was true was one thing. Admitting it would have been a shanda, a disgrace, and shame would have been unflattering to the South Haven Sterns' reputation.

There would be no shame for Hannah. Not because of the baby, not because of any mistakes or Clark's doubts. Boop would make sure of it.

She removed the only dress hanging in the closet and splayed it over the foot of the bed. The navy knit with bright-pink roses and green vines and leaves featured a familiar halter-style top. "Do you think this will fit?"

Hannah shrugged and glanced at her chest as she stood.

Boop tugged on the fabric. "It's got some give. Go in the bathroom, wash up, and try it on."

Soon Hannah would wear clothes designed to accentuate her figure and draw attention to her baby's upcoming arrival instead of wearing tent dresses like expectant mothers in Boop's day. Boop had set aside her love of color, prints, waistbands, and cleavage for the drab tent dresses, modesty, and big bows that maternity wear had demanded. Those dresses she'd worn when carrying Stuart had brought her both sadness in what she'd lost and joy in what was to come. She wanted only joy for Hannah.

Boop pushed her hair behind one ear, knowing the asymmetry flattered her face, which had droopier cheeks than she would have liked, and no amount of makeup could hide that fact.

Hannah plopped back onto the bed and scooted under the covers. "I don't have much of an appetite, so you go without me."

Boop usually avoided playing the old lady card but kept it in her back pocket for just such an occasion. "You know you might never see the bubbes again, right? You'll be sorry if the next time you see them is at a funeral."

"Don't say that."

"We know it's likely the last time the three of us will be together, especially here."

Hannah sat and swung her legs over the side of the bed. "I get it, but I don't . . ."

"Don't 'I don't' me, Hannah. The girls want to see you before they go, and not while you're in bed. Today this isn't really about you."

Hannah flipped back the covers. "You're right. I'll try the dress. What restaurant are we going to?"

"It's a surprise."

Hannah slipped the dress off the hanger and carried it to the bathroom. When the door closed and the sound of water gushing through the pipes resounded in the walls, Boop peeked out the window. She drew the curtains even though they were sheer linen, wanting to focus only on what was going on inside that room. Boop fluffed the pillows, tucked in the sheets, and smoothed the comforter atop all of it. She precisely arranged three throw pillows and set a stuffed bunny in front of them. No chance of Hannah wiggling back into bed, or out of what was next.

The dress fit beautifully.

Hannah twirled. She and Boop laughed as the skirt spun out around her. When Hannah and Emma were little girls, they'd played dress up in Boop's bedroom closets in Skokie and in South Haven, and twirl-tested all of the dresses. They'd emerged transformed, shuffling and stomping around in Boop's high heels. They'd adorned themselves with costume necklaces, clip-on earrings, shawls, and hats. Boop and Marvin would watch the fashion shows as if they'd been flown to Paris for Fashion Week. Marvin had whistled through his fingers to the girls' squeals of delight and their exaggerated and adorable curtsies.

Boop lifted a paddle brush from the dresser. "Can I brush your hair?"

"I'm not a little girl anymore. But yes."

Boop brushed the ends of Hannah's hair, then pressed the bristles at the top of Hannah's head and dragged them all the way down. "I know, but it's important to allow yourself to be pampered. And to pamper yourself. There are a few lipsticks on the tray over there."

"I don't really wear makeup, Boop."

"A little lipstick never hurt anyone." Today Boop's color not hurting anyone was Exotic Orchid.

Hannah sighed, stepped away, and gazed into the mirror over the dresser. She leaned close without pressing her stomach into the drawers, ran her fingers around her eyes and over her cheeks, then applied a layer, then two, of a sheer rosy pink to her lips.

It wasn't much, but Boop would take what she could get.

That was true for lipstick and life.

"How do you feel?" Boop asked.

"I feel okay. Thank you for this."

"You look better than okay. You look lovely."

"Thanks, Boop."

"Now, I want you to do something for me." Boop led Hannah to the bed and they sat. "I want you to keep feeling okay, drive back to Kalamazoo, and tell Clark all the things you told us last night. You owe it to yourself to remind him how good you think you are together. How what you have is stronger than anything else, that he isn't your safe choice or your second choice."

"Who are you and what have you done with cynical, Clark-doubting Boop?"

"You have to grab the opportunity I didn't have."

"What are you talking about?"

"I never had the opportunity to tell Abe everything." Boop gulped. "But everything you said last night about Clark is how I felt about Abe."

Hannah laid her hands atop Boop's. "You loved him, didn't you?"

Boop looked away. "I did."

"Marrying Pop was the safe thing to do."

Boop looked away and nodded. Then she met Hannah's gaze. "It was the only thing I could do. I did love him, though. You have to know that."

"I do. But Abe was the one who got away."

"In a way, yes. That's why if you love Clark the way I think you do, you owe it to yourself, to him, and to the baby, to tell him how you feel. If it doesn't work out, or if he doesn't feel the same way, you'll always know you fought for love."

"What if he won't forgive me?"

"If he loves you like you love him, this will just be a speed bump. One of many if you're lucky." Boop would have forgiven Abe for leaving, for staying away, for not coming back.

Hannah kissed Boop's cheek. "Can I ask you something?"

"Of course, but then we'd better get downstairs."

"Why did your grandparents disapprove of Abe?"

"It sounds silly now, but he wasn't Jewish. That was a huge deal back then."

"You had just graduated high school. It wasn't like you and Abe were going to run off and get married." Hannah gasped. "When did you start going with Pop?"

Boop shivered inside the way she had from a cold flash during her change of life. Her friends all had hot flashes. But no, Boop became her own personal subzero freezer. "I don't remember exactly."

"Yes, you do. It was a whirlwind romance and then you got married."

Boop looked at the yellow comforter, the color that had been appropriate, like mint green, for either a boy or a girl. "You know the story."

Boop felt Hannah staring, her granddaughter knowing something without being told.

The front door slammed with a thud. "Cab's here," Georgia bellowed up the stairs.

"We're not finished talking about this," Hannah said.

"We are for now."

On the upstairs landing outside the bedroom, Boop grabbed her cane and linked arms with Hannah. She held on to the railing as well as Hannah's arm. Boop might have been in okay shape for eighty-four, but the stairs could be a challenge.

Left foot onto the tread, then the right foot. Left foot, right foot. Left foot, right. Hannah walked in time—patient, understanding, and strong.

She'd make a wonderful mother.

On the back patio they each hugged Doris as the cabdriver stowed her suitcases in the trunk.

"Call us when you get home," Boop said.

Doris stuck her thumb up as an "okay" sign. Or so Boop thought.

"Go get him, Hannah," Doris said from the back seat.

Boop, Georgia, and Hannah waved until the cab turned the corner and was out of sight. She might never see Doris again. This had always been a possibility, but it seemed more palpable now as they hit the mid-eighty mark. Even if they all stayed alive, at some point one of them would lose touch with reality or lose control of their bladder. Or worse.

"Boop?" Hannah said.

"Go home, we'll have brunch another time."

"Well, I won't be here," Georgia said. "Take a short walk with me before you go?"

"Of course," Hannah said. "Are you sure you don't mind me skipping brunch? I just want to get home."

"Georgia and I will be fine, and she leaves tomorrow. That's when I'll call your dad and plan my move. But I'm not thinking about it until then."

Hannah and Georgia linked arms.

The women she loved most loved one another. No matter how much longer any of them were on this earth, no one could take that away. She walked inside and started a pot of coffee. She and Georgia would rehash everything that happened with Hannah, Doris's romantic life, and the weather forecast.

Anything to avoid talking about Georgia leaving.

A few minutes later, Boop had barely settled into the porch chair to read when Hannah ran through the kitchen door alone. "Come with me," she yelled. "We have to go to the hospital."

Boop shot to her feet. "Is it the baby?" It was too early. Boop had never even considered . . .

"The baby's fine," Hannah said, her eyes wide, her voice shaking. "It's Georgia."

Chapter 16

BETTY

A car turned the corner and drove down Lakeshore. Betty leaned against the house and slid her hands into the pockets of her pedal pushers. She looked down, the cordovan leather of her penny loafers buffed to a shine, her socks folded neatly. She crossed her left leg over the right and glanced south toward the lighthouse and the disbanding hordes of visitors who'd gathered to watch the sunset she and Abe had missed.

Somehow she knew it wouldn't be Abe, yet inside her pockets she crossed her fingers, inside her head she whispered "please." He was five minutes late.

The car, heading south, stopped and idled in front of her house. Betty turned and looked right at Marv, leaning his left arm and head outside the open car window.

"Hey, Betty Boop, I thought you might be here. We're going for ice cream and then to the arcade." He tapped his car door as if it were a bongo drum. "Hop in."

Betty stepped closer to the edge of the porch. "No, thanks, I'm waiting for Abe." She leaned at the waist and waved to Marv without looking at Eleanor. She'd never confronted her about the message from Abe or about flirting with him.

"He can meet us there," Marv said.

Eleanor turned her head toward the passenger window.

"You go." Betty would have said "have fun" but she had trouble being *too nice* around Eleanor.

"Everyone will be there."

"Then you don't need me." She hadn't meant to be snide; Marv was trying to include her. Isn't that what she'd always wanted? "Maybe next time."

Marv pulled his arm inside the car, gripped the wheel with his left hand, shifted, then rested his right arm atop the back of the seat.

Eleanor slid next to him and looked out the driver's side window. "Don't wait too long," she said. "It sends the wrong message." She tipped back her head onto Marv's shoulder and they drove away.

Eleanor knew what to say to rile up Betty's insides. What if Abe stood her up? Maybe he'd changed his mind and didn't love her after all. Boys were the fickle ones, not girls.

Betty exhaled a long breath. No. Love like theirs lasted forever. He'd have an explanation. It was only a few minutes, yet it weighed heavy on her, like the first days of a cold or flu.

Just then two headlights cut through the deepening darkness.

Betty turned to the street and folded her arms across her bosom. Then she dropped her hands to her sides, mitigating her cleavage. This was not the time.

She swore if it wasn't Abe, well, she'd march right into the house and write another letter to her roommate. They'd have grand adventures at Barnard. Who wanted a boyfriend anyway?

She did.

A horn beep-beeped and the car slowed to a stop. Betty's pulse thumped against her chest and her throat burned as she swallowed back fury. Underneath, her heart swirled with relief.

Betty slid into the passenger seat and clicked the door closed. She smoothed the sides of the navy-blue fabric along her thighs, as if primping, when really she was wiping off her clammy palms. She folded her dry hands atop her lap. She did not slide over next to Abe or lean in for a kiss. While the silent treatment wasn't really her style, she didn't know what to say. The only words ping-ponging around her brain were unkind and crass. Had she no patience or tolerance? He was only ten minutes late.

Nannie's voice echoed in her head. "Always be on time. Punctuality is a sign of respect."

But that was an old-fashioned sensibility, and this was a modern relationship. Surely he had a reason for being late, so she didn't know why it bothered her so.

Marv drumming the car door. Eleanor laughing. Why did anyone have to *know* Abe was late and see her standing on the porch checking her watch?

Anger wove through her thoughts, trickled along her veins. She wished it wasn't so, but appearances mattered. How was she to convince Nannie and Zaide Abe was the right guy for her if this behavior continued?

Betty's jaw hurt from clenched teeth. She shuddered with fear. Did this mean she and Abe were over? Was love compatible with anger and disappointment? She'd always been careful not to rile up her grandparents. They loved her, but she wouldn't take any chances.

"I'm sorry I'm late." Abe held the steering wheel at the twelve o'clock position. "Do you want to know why I was late?"

Betty's pulse quickened. She creased the fabric of her pant leg between her fingers. It was fidget or cry. She looked at Abe. "I was so embarrassed when Marv and Eleanor came by and invited me to go with them to the arcade. I was just standing here, waiting for you, not knowing if you were even going to show up. I had to cover for you. I'm not a very good liar, you know. I'm sure your friend Eleanor got a real charge out of that."

"I would never stand you up. I was on the telephone with my mother."

His mother. He had been on the telephone with his mother. That was something that never happened to Betty, not even on her birthday.

After an hour at the arcade and a double scoop of fudge ripple to share, Betty locked fingers with Abe as they stepped from the street to the sand. In his other hand, Abe swung a Big Beam lantern like a lunch pail, the same way Zaide had when he and Betty had walked to the Black River before dawn, fishing rods over their shoulders, tackle boxes stocked with supplies. She hadn't fished with Zaide in years, but that tackle box held some of her fondest memories. Abe pointed the Big Beam toward the lake, past the resort, and it shined a glowing path as if reaching toward the unknown, where it all went dark again. The farther they walked, the farther the light would reach.

"I know you didn't ask, but I told my mother about you," Abe said. "She asked me if you were pretty, but I told her no."

Betty stopped. "Pardon me?"

Abe threw back his head and laughed deep and loud. He looked at Betty and placed one hand on her cheek. He set the Big Beam on the sand and placed his other hand on her face as well. "I told her you were the most beautiful girl in the world. Inside and out." He kissed her forehead, grabbed her hand, scooped up the lantern as if his arm were a digger, and started walking again. They headed toward their dunes.

Betty welcomed walking in silence, piecing together parts of Abe's story. Long-distance telephone calls cost a lot of money. Abe's mother didn't just telephone to say hello when stamps cost a nickel. "You know, you can tell me anything," Betty said.

Abe didn't turn around. He walked faster, holding the beam out at shoulder height as if the answer was out there. "She wanted to tell me about my father."

"What's happening with your father?"

Abe dropped his arm to his side and the light brightened only a small circle ahead of their shoes. The muscles in his forearm tightened as he squeezed the lantern's handle. "He's gone again."

"What does that mean?"

"It means he took money from the store and he'll be back when it runs out."

"Where does he go? What does he do?"

"Who knows?"

Betty cringed. "It must be awful to worry about your mother like that. Is there anything else you want to tell me?"

"Just that I'm not my father."

The way Betty was not her mother. She wondered if Abe looked like his father, the way she favored Tillie. Was it as disconcerting for Abe as for her? Betty would have preferred not to look like the mother who gave her away even though she could not imagine doing anything similar.

"I know you're not like that," she said.

They continued down the beach, hand in hand.

As if reading her mind—which she was sure he could—Abe looked at Betty like he was reminding himself she was there. He stared into her eyes and didn't blink. Then he pulled her into a kiss. And time stopped.

When they arrived at the bottom of the dunes, Betty released her grip on Abe's hand and removed her shoes and socks. She folded one sock into the other as if Nannie were watching. Then Betty stashed them inside one of her loafers and set the pair in a patch of tall grass. Feet in the sand was better than sand in the shoes, Nannie would say.

Without talking, they followed the flashlight's beam up the hill, treading and sinking into sand, stepping over the thickets of grass and through bushes of thistle. If someone ever cleared this, the view from the top would be vast and spectacular, like the ones of exotic locations she'd seen in *Vogue* and *Seventeen*. Her heart pounded at the thought of privacy. If she didn't love Abe and trust him, she would have mistaken the thumping and shaking for fear.

175

When they'd almost reached the top, Betty saw a neatly folded cardigan atop a patch of beach grass. Abe shined the light on it. Aquamarine with pearl buttons. She'd seen it before, but it was a popular color this season according to *Seventeen*. It could be anyone's.

Then Betty heard an indecipherable sound. A deep voice. Guttural. An animal? It sounded more like a grunt or a pant than a feral cat's howl or a lost dog's whimper. With one more step, Abe fell to his belly as if hiding in a foxhole and shined the light up at the shed. Betty lowered herself next to him and saw two pairs of feet—human feet. Knees, pale skin, a bare behind? She closed her eyes and covered her ears with her hands.

"Oh my God!" Betty whispered. "They're . . ."

"Having sex." Abe kissed her cheek and pressed his lips to her hand.

Betty dropped that one hand away but kept her eyes closed. She was horrified. They were doing it outside? On the ground? "Are they gone?"

Abe chuckled. "They scooted as soon as they saw the light. I guess that's one way to forget about what's going on at home."

Betty opened one eye, then the other, and rolled onto her back. "How dare they!" They'd ruined her night and her favorite place.

"Who do you think that was?" Abe asked.

"Marv and Eleanor."

"What makes you think that?"

Who else could it be? Although an aquamarine cardigan seemed a little conservative for Eleanor. And hadn't she been wearing pink earlier?

She stared through the leaves and broken branches. The stars twinkled brightly and seemed just out of reach. Sometimes she felt that way about Abe. "It has to be them," Betty said. "Marv has grown up coming to Stern's. Not many people know about this place. Who else could it be?"

"It could be anyone," Abe said.

"Not here. It had to be Marv. Didn't you see who it was?"

Abe laughed, but it wasn't a mean laugh. "I tried not to!"

Betty burned with embarrassment, yet at the same time she knew Abe's humor wasn't at her expense. Her heart was safe. "They don't even love each other. Not really," Betty said.

Hand in hand, they skittered and slid back down the dune in the dark. "I'd like to go home now," she said. "I think that was enough excitement for one night." That really wasn't what she meant but Abe didn't argue. Nor did he let go of her hand.

If she slept with Abe, would everyone be whispering about her the way she had just whispered about Marv and Eleanor? If they'd been making out, would someone have seen them? Would she become just another girl who'd succumbed to summer romance, or was it different because she and Abe were in love, planning a future?

Abe squeezed her hand. "Let's pretend tonight never happened."

After Betty's earlier tryst with anger, they had talked, laughed, kissed, and shared ice cream. She'd learned about his father. They'd grown closer, linked by disappointment. She wasn't sure she could forget such a lovely evening, even if she tried.

The next day, instead of eating lunch with her grandparents, Betty stood in the foyer of their house, licked one of the three-cent stamps she'd found in Zaide's desk drawer, and affixed it to the corner of the envelope addressed to Patricia in New Jersey.

The correspondence filled both sides of Betty's engraved and monogrammed cream-colored, linen stationery. Beneath the black engraved, swirling "BCS," Betty's A+ penmanship filled the page. She exaggerated her preparations for Barnard—the book she was reading, the clothes she was packing, the anticipation she was feeling. Truth was, Betty hadn't been thinking at all about leaving South Haven—because that meant leaving Abe.

Betty looked out the window, then pushed open the door. "I thought you'd never get here."

"Not everyone can come and go like you can," Georgia said. "These are real jobs for us."

Betty huffed and flared her nostrils. Georgia could be such a spoilsport.

"Let her be; can't you see she's excited?" Doris turned to Betty. "We're here now. How can we help?"

Betty tossed the envelope onto the Parsons table and led her friends upstairs where three skirts and three blouses, in various shades, patterns, and combinations of red, white, and blue, lay on Betty's bed. Betty, Georgia, and Doris stood across from the patriotic fashion display.

"Are you okay?" Georgia asked.

"Why do you ask?" Betty said.

"You haven't mentioned your date so I thought maybe it didn't go well."

"It was peachy." Betty planned to keep the incident on the dunes to herself. She never wanted to think of it again.

"Peachy? That's all? That's not like you," Doris said.

"Well." Betty tapped her toes on the floor. "I'm just focusing on these outfits now, I guess." *That* her friends would believe.

"They're all pretty," Doris said. "I hate to say this, but does it matter? You'll look fabulous no matter what you wear."

"Independence Day is not a holiday about fashion, you know that, right?" Georgia said in a meek voice that sounded more like an apology than a fact. "It's about independence."

Exactly. "Everything is about fashion. Or have you forgotten?"

Georgia laughed and slouched into the pillows. "Pardon me." She pointed. "That one and that one."

Betty bounced and clapped, then grabbed the navy skirt with gold buttons and the white-and-navy-striped sailor blouse with gold buttons. She showed Georgia and Doris the small red anchor embroidered on the breast pocket.

"Well, then you're set. Red, white, and blue," Doris said.

Betty held the blouse under her neck and the skirt at her waist as she twirled. "What about my hair?"

"Since when do you care about your hair on the Fourth of July?" Georgia said. "We're going to serve a thousand hot dogs and hamburgers on the lawn, play games with the kids, and then watch the fireworks on the beach. Like every other year."

Doris pushed on Georgia's arm. "Don't be silly. This isn't like every other year."

"Oh, because of *him*." Georgia smiled and rolled her eyes.

Betty set about returning all the clothes to her closet. "It's not just about Abe," she said. "If I'm going to finally compete in Miss South Haven, I should take extra care of how I look no matter what day it is. Don't you think?"

Doris ruffled her hair. "You're dazzling. I'm doomed to be cute for the rest of my life. That's if I'm lucky."

"You're both perfect," Betty said. "Any fellow would be lucky to have you. I only asked because, well, don't tell anyone, but Abe and I are going to sneak off and watch the fireworks alone."

Georgia rolled her eyes.

"Don't be a wet rag," Doris said. "It's romantic. I hope I have at least one great romance in my life; otherwise, what's the point?"

"What's the point? The point is to do something whether or not you have a man in your life," Georgia said.

Doris turned to Betty and twirled her index finger by her temple.

"I like the idea of a love affair, don't get me wrong. I just think there's more to life," Georgia said.

"I said *romance*, not *affair*; there's a difference."

Georgia smirked, but in a playful way. "How would you know?" Doris huffed.

Betty laughed, stepped back to her closet, and rifled through the clothes. "Try this." She thrust a white cotton eyelet sundress toward Doris. "I think it will fit you. You can wear your blue Keds and red lipstick, maybe a flag pin on the lapel. I'm sure I have one, or Nannie does."

"You're a doll. I'll try it on."

"You don't have anything in that closet that will fit me," Georgia said.

"You don't need anything, and any boy who doesn't think you're a knockout with those legs needs new glasses."

A flush of pink rose on Georgia's cheeks.

"You're blushing. You *never* blush." Betty placed her hands on her hips. "Tell!"

Georgia raised her eyebrows, then she walked to the closet. She leafed through the clothes like they were pages of a book she didn't want to read. "There is nothing to tell."

"Oh my God! You like someone. Who is he?" Betty scoured her memory. "One of the fellas taking tennis lessons? Someone on staff? Jerry? Sol? Bob? Herman?"

Georgia turned around, her cheeks as purple as Nannie's beet borscht, her eyes wide and shiny. "It is not one of those *boys*."

Doris skipped into the room. "How do I look?"

"You look terrific," Georgia said.

Betty tugged on Doris's waistline. "I don't know why I didn't think of it before." She held Doris's shoulders and pivoted her toward the dresser and away from Georgia. "Borrow my red patent belt. It'll pull you in and add a little extra flair."

"You're the best," Doris said, then she glanced at her watch. "Can I pick this up later? I have to get back. I'm taking kids to the beach after lunch and I want to stop in the kitchen and grab a sandwich. You coming, Georgia?"

Just as Georgia said yes, the telephone rang. The girls ran downstairs.

"Georgia, this isn't over! You don't get to have a secret crush."

Georgia tipped her head back and laughed like Betty had told the funniest joke.

The telephone rang again and Betty answered. "Hello?"

"Come see me in the office, bubbeleh. I'll be here for another half hour."

"Zaide, what's wrong?"

"There's a little hitch in your plan."

Betty hung up the telephone, her mouth dry, and her head starting to ache. What plan? If only Betty knew to which plan Zaide was referring, she could prepare. Did she forget to do something she'd promised? Should she plan a defense for her relationship with Abe? Did someone else see Marv and Eleanor and notice Betty scampering away? Or maybe he needed help plunging toilets.

For once, that was what Betty hoped.

Minutes later, Betty leaned on the wall outside Zaide's office, her thoughts atwitter, her arms and fingers prickling with cold even though the ceiling fans whirled a warm and comfortable breeze around the lobby. She knocked on the door, opened it, and stepped inside.

The afternoon sun sneaked through the closed venetian blinds. Her grandparents didn't want anyone looking and seeing their powwow. Zaide shuffled a stack of pink invoices and set them off to the side. Nannie nodded and shut the file cabinet drawer. What was Nannie doing in the office? She should be supervising the kitchen or *shmying* around the cardroom, chatting up the ladies. Betty had walked into the middle of a conversation. This couldn't be good.

"I'm sure Nancy's family is happy to have her back. She was gone for what? Six months? For no reason? *Meshuga!*" Zaide said. "It was an opportunity, they said."

"What *farkakteh* opportunity?" Nannie said. "There is only one reason a girl goes away for six months."

"Who are you talking about?" Betty waved her hands in the air to attract her grandparents' attention. "Who's back? From where? And what does it have to do with me?"

"Nancy Green is back from Europe," Zaide said. "And she's entering Miss South Haven. Her uncle told me."

Betty plopped into the captain's chair across from her grandfather's desk. "I'm doomed!"

"Don't overreact," Nannie said. "We just wanted you to know, since we knew it would be a surprise. There's no reason you can't win."

"No reason? She's won two years in a row. Why should this year be any different?" Betty asked. She would never win now. Nancy Green was perfect.

"You haven't won because you were too young to enter," Zaide said.

"I should just drop out, because I can't compete with a girl who looks like Lana Turner."

"You're not dropping out," Nannie said. "With that fancy swimsuit Zaide bought you, those judges won't have a choice but to reconsider their favorite contestant."

Betty bit her bottom lip and Zaide chuckled. "Can't hide anything from this one."

"It's time for someone new to win that sash and crown," Nannie said. "Someone who didn't need to *go to Europe*."

No one *needed* an extravagant excursion, but how glamorous it must have been for Nancy. How grown-up she must seem now, full of continental flair and sophistication. Why would she even want to be Miss South Haven?

Betty swung around and faced the small hanging mirror Zaide used to check his tie. She was a pretty girl with classic features. "A knockout," some said. She stepped back enough to see part of her chest. It was ample compared to her friends', but smaller than Nancy's. A smile tugged at the sides of her mouth and she willed it away.

"I do have some advice," Nannie said.

Betty swirled around. "Anything."

"If this is as important to you as you say, be sure to get your beauty sleep. I'm sure Nancy Green has had plenty of problems, but I'm betting she doesn't have circles under her eyes from late nights on the porch."

Betty's cheeks burned. She swallowed hard but didn't glance away. She wasn't sorry she spent hours in the middle of the night sharing stories and dreams and kisses with Abe.

"What am I missing?" Zaide asked.

"Seems Betty has taken up with Abe Barsky."

"You said I could date him." Betty prayed her cheeks didn't look as red as they felt.

Nannie waggled her index finger. "I meant *a date*, not a steady—that's what you kids call it, right? I see how you look at him but he's not the one for you, Betty."

"It's summer, Yetta, let her be. You're embarrassing her. She'll go away to college and meet a nice Jewish doctor. If not, you can play yenta and find someone suitable."

"He's a nice boy, Nannie. You'd like him if you got to know him."

"I never said I didn't like him, just that he's not the boy for you."

Zaide walked around his desk and reached out his hand. Betty grasped it and he pulled her into an uncharacteristic hug. "Socializing is fine. We trust you. As for the pageant, if you don't win, there's always next year."

Betty's rush of relief was sidelined by worry. Nannie and Zaide knew she might not be back next summer. Or any summer. Didn't they? Were they in denial? They'd nourished her potential throughout her schooling and then they'd set her future into motion by encouraging her to attend and graduate college—and to graduate with more than an MRS degree.

They knew. If they wanted to pretend, who was she to stop them?

But Barnard College and New York City—these places would change practically everything for Betty. Her relationship with Abe would change whatever was left.

She was counting on it.

Chapter 17

BETTY

Betty had never disappointed her grandparents and she wasn't about to start then. For the next week she walked around the property with her shoulders pinched back and her head held straight. After calisthenics Betty would stride around the women with her pageant walk to applause and good wishes.

At home, Betty slipped on high heels and an old swimsuit and walked toward the cheval mirror in Nannie's bedroom. Then she repeated. And repeated. She inhaled to compress her stomach and project her chest.

Better.

She smiled at herself in the mirror, trying to see what the judges would see, and gauge how she might stack up against the other girls.

Her complexion was fair and blemish-free, her eyes symmetrical— bright blue rimmed with dark lashes and groomed brows. Her nose and mouth were small and feminine, and the Strawberry Kiss lipstick was the perfect shade that said "look at me" but didn't invite leering. Betty's hair tumbled in waves past her shoulders, like someone was pouring caramel. She was proportionate but her figure wasn't showy.

Maybe she could win after all.

For Betty, *celebrating* Independence Day was more figurative than literal. After a day of organizing children's games of checkers, ring-around-the-rosy, and badminton, judging the resort's blueberry-pie-eating contest, and timing the annual beach run, she grabbed a pail full of sparklers from the supply shed. Holding the bucket by its metal handle, she was careful not to swing it too high behind her as she scampered across the grass toward the kitchen. The last thing she needed was to gather up dozens of spilled sparklers and delay her getaway.

Betty strode through the dimmed kitchen, its cleared and cleaned surfaces streak-free and shining like mirrors. The dishwasher, mixers, and electric knives were silent. No pounding of dough against the stainless-steel worktable, no banging of pots and pans on the burners and into the oven, no splattering of soup. The only hint that this room served as a bustling kitchen producing thousands of meals per week were the hooks hung with lonely aprons and chef coats that jostled as Betty moved past them. They wouldn't be worn again until morning.

That night there would be no midnight buffet, despite Mrs. Gallbladder's annual petition. Mabel and Chef Gavin were off to enjoy the holiday. An empty kitchen meant there was no one to slow her down with comments or questions, although it also meant there were no warm cookies, sips of soup, or ends of brisket to snatch from the *fleishig*—meat only—cutting board.

Betty ran from the kitchen, around the naked tables in the dining room, then diagonally across the lobby. She sidestepped the center marble table and did not topple Nannie's grand display of white hydrangeas and American flags. At last, Betty leaned with her back and pushed open the elephant-size doors that led to the beach side of the main house. "The money side," Zaide called it in private.

Betty exhaled as she stepped onto the veranda. Nannie forbade them to call it a patio. A patio was plain—a veranda you could charge for! Whatever name they called it, this location on her family's property overlooked a giant slice of North Beach and the expanse of her lake.

Any spot on it offered unobstructed views of the South Pier and the lighthouse, and therefore of tonight's fireworks.

Betty tossed her hair back over her right shoulder, then her left. Someone tugged at the bucket. "Can I help you with those?"

Betty turned to Marv. "It's okay. I've got it." She twisted the bucket from his grip. He reached in and withdrew a handful of sparklers. She pushed images of Marv and Eleanor on the dunes, in the sand, with their clothes off, from her mind. It was their business, not hers, but she couldn't help but think he could do better.

Betty and Marv spread out the sparklers across one side of the table, next to a plate piled high with vanilla-frosted star-shaped sugar cookies and a bowl of red licorice whips. The other end of the table was set with pitchers of lemonade and iced tea, along with a full bar. It was the one night every summer Zaide acted as bartender. Betty grabbed a swizzle stick and twirled it in her fingers like a miniature baton.

Marv leaned on the balustrade and looked out toward the beach. "I haven't seen much of you lately."

She thought back to the night on the dunes. *I've seen plenty of you.* "I've been here. Just busy, I guess. Where's Eleanor?"

Marv jutted his chin toward the beach. "With your boyfriend."

Betty sneered. "She's not *with* him; they're playing volleyball."

"Things okay with you two?"

"Why wouldn't they be?"

"I don't know, the night he didn't show up, I just assumed . . ."

"He did show up, so don't assume." Betty tossed the swizzle stick back onto the table and walked away. Why was he needling her?

"I didn't mean anything by it." Marv was following her. "I care about you. That's all."

Betty looked at Marv. "Do me a favor and care about your girl-friend. Not me."

"She's not really my girlfriend."

"You should be ashamed of yourself." Betty marched forward, alarmed by Marv's arrogance. She might not be crazy about Eleanor, but if he was willing to have sex with her on the dunes, the least he could do was refer to her as his girlfriend. Betty pushed through the doors and stopped quickly, before colliding with Mr. and Mrs. Bloomfield.

"Oh my." Mrs. Bloomfield laughed. Even flustered, Tammy Bloomfield glowed with rosy cheeks and sparkling green eyes.

Mr. Bloomfield's glasses fell askew from the near collision.

"I'm so sorry," Betty said. "I wasn't watching where I was going." Marv stood next to her.

"Rushing away from the best seat in town for the fireworks?" Mr. Bloomfield asked.

"A bunch of us are going up to the dunes," Marv said. He looked at Betty and raised his eyebrows.

The dunes? Really?

"Getting away from the adults for a little privacy, I suppose." Mr. Bloomfield chuckled.

"Sam, don't tease them." Mrs. Bloomfield patted her protruding stomach. "You kids have fun while you can."

The three Bloomfield girls barreled past and out onto the veranda. That seemed to signal to the swarms of guests walking through the lobby. People migrated in their direction, eager for fireworks and Zaide's cocktails.

Mrs. Bloomfield pointed toward the doors. "I'd better go make sure they don't burn the place down. Sam, are you coming?"

"I'm right behind you." Mr. Bloomfield stayed in place as his wife walked outside.

Betty didn't know what to say or how to extricate herself from this awkward moment. Marv should have been looking for Eleanor, and Mr. Bloomfield should have been looking after his wife.

"I'm going to check on some things for my grandparents." Nannie and Zaide stood on the far side of the lobby, chatting with some of the guests. Betty needed to skedaddle before they saw her. "If you'll excuse me."

"She's meeting her boyfriend," Marv said.

"And I don't want to be late. This only happens once."

"Go," Mr. Bloomfield said. "Tammy was right. Enjoy it all while you can." He slapped Marv's upper arm. "Before you know it, you'll have a wife and kids, and fun won't be so easy to come by."

Mr. Bloomfield was a rat. Betty walked away and ducked out the front door. Twilight had set the sky alight. She wasn't sure fireworks could make any improvements.

Abe was right where he said he'd be—perched atop the hood of his car. Betty exhaled as if she were blowing out a hundred birthday candles.

Though Abe had dressed unpatriotically in his short-sleeved white shirt and tan trousers, his style made Betty's knees wobble. She'd always been mad for the best-dressed boys at South Haven High. Maybe because Zaide always wore tailor-made suits, or because the times she'd seen Joe he'd been decked out in the latest menswear she'd recognized from the Sears catalog. The rough-and-tumble appearance of a day's manual labor or the odorous remnants of fruit farming didn't turn her head, as it did for some of her friends. To each her own.

Abe's narrow collared shirt and cuffed-hem pants, along with his combed-back hair, resembled the men in Betty's favorite magazine's advertisements for cigarettes and luncheon meats. Her heart pattered.

When Betty stepped closer, she'd smell the sandalwood notes in his aftershave. Abe smiled at her, unleashing his dimples and those crinkles around his eyes she loved to smooth beneath her fingers. Betty clapped her hands to her sides. She would not make a fool of herself by running or waving.

Instead, she raised her hand waist-high and wiggled her fingers with surreptitious zeal.

Betty hoisted herself next to Abe and slipped her arm around his waist. She pressed against him, and as she moved in to kiss his cheek, he turned his head and kissed her on the lips. She giggled that she'd fallen for that one. Still, Betty pushed him away but left her hand on his chest. "Not here."

Abe looked around. There were couples necking and groping in plain sight. "It's up to you, you know that."

Abe had better not think she was a prude. They'd gone to third base, almost. Betty leaned so that the weight of her breast pushed against his arm. He wouldn't mistake that for an accident. She was new to most of this, but she wasn't stupid. She stretched to kiss him intentionally, but with closed lips, and then pulled back slowly. "I'm just private."

"Too bad we rarely have any privacy."

He was right. The one place they could rely on for privacy had been tainted by Marv and Eleanor, at least for Betty.

Her thoughts tumbled. Her house was empty. Her grandparents wouldn't leave that veranda for another hour, at least. If they noticed she was missing, who would they ask? What would they do?

Who was she kidding? That night they wouldn't notice.

Betty slid off the car and stretched out her hand. Abe clasped her fingers. "Come with me," she said. "I know *the best* spot to see the fireworks."

Abe landed on the ground next to her. "And where might that be?"

"Do you trust me?"

He nodded. Betty tugged and Abe followed.

Anyone who noticed them would think Betty and Abe were headed toward South Pier or to a viewing spot on the beach. If anyone saw them go inside the house, they'd reason that Betty was grabbing a sweater or a headscarf or fetching something for Nannie. Betty quickened her step, then slowed. The more nonchalant she and Abe seemed, the better.

At the last moment she led him to the back door instead of the front. A little caution couldn't hurt.

"Are you nuts?" he asked.

Betty turned and looked up into Abe's eyes. She swore she saw glitter sparkling around the damp edges. The words *I love you* echoed in Betty's ears as if someone had bellowed into a cavern. If other sounds punctured the night air in those moments—the boom of the first fireworks, laughing children, meowing cats, slamming doors—Betty didn't hear them.

"Yes. I'm nuts about you. We'll be alone for at least an hour, maybe more." She raised one eyebrow, so Abe would understand what she'd intended the moment she'd slid off the hood of his car.

She'd also been sure of her intentions when she'd hurriedly gathered the sparklers, when she'd dressed that morning in new undergarments, when she'd fallen asleep last night, and when she'd fallen asleep every night for the past two weeks.

Betty opened the door and scurried inside, and Abe followed her into the kitchen. Without another spoken word, but with clear intention, she guided Abe through the living room and they climbed the stairs without pause.

When Betty tapped her bedroom door ajar, the sky visible through the open window sparkled with the first pops and sizzles of fireworks. *Oohs* and *aahs* drifted inside.

Abe embraced Betty and whispered into her ear, "I will always love you."

Shivers traveled down her neck and landed in her middle. Betty was grateful, giddy, terrified, and relieved. Abe scooped up her hand as if it were a delicate baby chick and kissed it. This was the right decision. He was the right boy.

"Are you sure?" he whispered.

Betty swallowed hard but nodded.

"And you're sure we're alone?"

"Yes, I'm sure."

"Then I'll be right back."

Abe ran out of the room and down the steps so quickly Betty didn't have a chance to stop him. Her heart twanged like she'd been pelted with ice. What had she done wrong? Was she too forward? Not forward enough? Did the idea of being in her childhood bedroom bother him? Then she heard the back door shut. No!

Betty slipped on her shoes, not sure if she should follow him and if she did, what she would find. Then the door shut again, followed by heavy, pounding footsteps on the stairs—he was running up two or three steps at a time. Abe was coming back. Back to her room and back to her. And there he was, standing in her open doorway. He was breathing fast but wasn't panting or out of breath. He held a white piece of cloth—his handkerchief—wrapped around the stem of one of Nannie's biggest in-bloom fuchsia-and-coral-colored climbing roses. He set it on Betty's nightstand with the blossom facing the bed.

"You deserve a whole dozen," Abe said. "But this was the best I could do on short notice."

"How?" Those vines were strewn with thorns.

Abe patted his pocket. "Pocketknife."

Betty stood on her tiptoes and kissed him. They walked farther into her room and headed away from the window but toward the foot of her bed. It was needless to waste time with more banter or flirting; they were in love and making fireworks of their own.

Twenty minutes later the fireworks had ended and Betty lay naked under her pink coverlet with her head on Abe's bare chest. They still had time, the party on the veranda would go on for at least another half hour, her grandparents hosting and hostessing their hearts out. Stern's Fourth of July bash was renowned. It would never end early.

She lifted her head. "What did you say?"

"I didn't say anything." Abe ran his fingers along her spine and Betty giggled.

The back door slammed.

She pushed Abe so hard he rolled off the bed. "Hide in the closet."

Without clothes or a moment to gather them, he opened the closet door, backed in, and pulled the door closed. Betty kicked his clothes under her bed as footsteps on the stairs pounded nearer. There was no way out of this now. She would be humiliated, and she would shame her grandparents. Abe would be fired. Oh God. He was naked!

"Betty!" The whisper-yell floated into her room. It was not Zaide or Nannie.

It was Georgia.

She stood in the doorway and glanced around the room, not once looking directly at Betty's face, but definitely looking at the messy bed and the dress she had fashioned out of the floral sheet.

"Your grandparents are asking for you. I told them I'd find you, that you were probably on the beach stargazing. But I saw you run off from the parking lot earlier, so I'm probably not the only one. You'd better hurry."

Betty's throat felt like she'd swallowed sand. "Thank you," she mouthed.

"Are you okay?" Georgia whispered.

Betty's cheeks warmed. She nodded and smoothed out her hair. She felt its unkemptness beneath her hand, and that was as embarrassing as her makeshift caftan.

"I'm going back to tell them you'll be along in a few minutes," Georgia said. "I'll tell them not to worry, that I saw you walking back from South Beach. Please make sure you're wearing everything you were wearing earlier. You know your grandmother will know."

"I will."

"And if you hurt my girl Betty, you'll have to answer to me, do you hear?" she added in her full voice, louder than was needed.

"I hear you." Abe's muffled voice seeped out of the closet.

"I'm leaving." Georgia stepped toward the closet. "I know one good turn deserves another but please stay in there until I'm gone. Then, hurry." She looked at Betty. "I hope he's worth it."

Betty smiled. "He is."

Georgia left the room and the house, and Betty pulled open the closet door and shoved Abe's clothes at him. "Get dressed."

Those were not the words she'd imagined whispering at the end of their night, but nothing mattered now as much as covering their tracks. Even with the next year spent apart, they had a lifetime of making love and lazing in bed ahead of them. A lifetime where no one would be hiding.

Abe left first, out the back door. She didn't ask where he was going.

Betty washed, dressed, freshened her face, and made up her bed—all in less than ten minutes. Her body ached in ways she didn't know it could, but she didn't mind; it was as if Abe was still with her.

Betty knew what she would say. She and Abe had stolen away to South Beach to watch the fireworks and lost track of time. She'd apologize for being careless and selfish. The beaches were filled with locals and summer people, so Nannie would trust there had been no shenanigans—that the evening was just as she described.

Betty inhaled a deep breath of night air and counted to ten, reverting back to the girl her grandparents knew. At least on the outside. She bounced down the steps, then with a twinge slowed to a stroll. In minutes she'd be holding a sizzling sparkler and reassuring her grandparents that everything in the world was about as right as a summer rain.

Chapter 18

BOOP

The doctor said Georgia had a brain bleed, a broken right cheekbone, and two pelvic fractures. Her face was bruised, her demeanor a little loopy. All anyone knew was that she'd tripped while stepping up onto a curb, and had gone down so fast there was nothing Hannah could have done. The doctor also said she was fortunate. Boop didn't want to imagine what unfortunate might look like, or what her life would look like without Georgia in it.

What if Georgia had died—and why was the hospital so darned cold? The hair on Boop's arms stood on end. Hannah walked into the room with a blue blanket and draped it over Boop's shoulders as if she'd eavesdropped on her thoughts.

Guarded from the chill, Boop stared at Georgia as her cheek, already purple, hinted at the array of colors to come. Boop always assumed she'd have time to say goodbye to her dearest friends, the way she'd had two years to say goodbye to Marvin. She was presumptuous, naive, or maybe just infinitely hopeful. One minute Georgia was off for a walk and chat with Hannah, shifting her turquoise flamingo-print fanny pack over her hip, the next minute she was in an ambulance. What if Boop weren't standing by her bedside in the ER but by a gurney in the morgue? This was possible, but it wasn't her time. Not yet.

Georgia was there in the bed. Georgia was breathing. The doctor said these were not life-threatening injuries.

But that wasn't always the way, was it? Sometimes people went away, you thought they were coming back, and then they didn't.

Boop whisked away her morbid thoughts. "You really don't remember falling?"

"No," Georgia said.

"I should have caught her, I should have known," Hannah said. "But we were talking and I guess I was looking away and then I heard her hit the ground."

"It's not your fault," Boop said. "If someone is going down, there's not much you can do to stop it. Thank God you were there to call the ambulance."

"I'm just glad I fell away from you and not on you," Georgia said. "A fall wouldn't be good for the baby."

Boop sighed. Georgia remembered Hannah was pregnant; that had to be a good sign, even if it was a bad sign that she'd fallen and didn't remember.

"At least I didn't miss my flight," Georgia said.

"You're not going anywhere. At least for a few days," Boop said. Georgia was on pain meds and hadn't looked in the mirror.

"The doctor said three or four days in the hospital to monitor you, then rehab," Hannah said.

Boop slipped her hand into Georgia's. Any other plans could wait.

"I'm just a little banged up." Georgia moved her arm and winced, belying her positivity.

"A little is too much," Hannah said.

"I'll take care of you," Boop said.

Georgia turned to Boop. "You're too old to take care of me."

There was the Georgia she knew. "Aren't you full of compliments today?"

"I talked to the social worker," Hannah said. "You'll have home health aides."

Boop squeezed Georgia's hand. "Your job is to get better. Leave the rest to me."

Georgia's voice was low and a bit husky. "Hannah, dear, do you mind if I talk to your grandmother alone?"

"Of course." Hannah walked out of the room. Boop knew when she finished talking to Georgia her granddaughter would be waiting on those uncomfortable molded plastic chairs in the waiting room.

Georgia folded her hands atop her chest. "This isn't how you planned to spend the next month or two. You have to get ready for California."

"I plan, God laughs," Boop said.

Georgia grabbed Boop's hand in both of hers. "I thought I was going to die," she said.

Me too. Everything seemed to be moving in slow motion, and Boop's words—the ones she thought and the ones she spoke, sounded cartoonish and elongated. "You were wrong."

"When I was in that ambulance, I could only think of two things. I was going to get to see my sisters again—"

"Georgia, stop! You're a little battered but a lot alive."

"My only other thought was about you."

Boop swallowed hard. "Don't." *I'm not ready for Georgia's deathbed sentiments.*

"I made a promise to God."

"Everyone does that. Do you know all the promises I made when I found out I was pregnant that summer? When Marvin was sick? I think God expects those promises to be broken."

"Catholic guilt." Georgia covered her mouth with her hand, and for the first time Boop noticed the unnatural angle of some of her joints, the collection of wrinkles on her fingers, all acutely visible when Georgia was still in the bed, not in perpetual motion. She spoke through her fingers like someone trying to hide rotten teeth. "I need to tell you something."

"Right now? Can't it wait until you're feeling better? We'll have lots of time to talk when you move in. I think God will understand a little reprieve."

"You might not. I think you should sit."

Boop pulled over a chair that slid easily on the linoleum floor. She sat as close to the bed as she could. Georgia inhaled and folded her hands at her chest, a little too corpse-like.

"Okay, what's so important?" Boop knew that Georgia's uncertainty, bordering on delusion, could creep in at any moment. She prepared herself for anything.

"You're the best friend I've ever had," Georgia said.

"I feel the same, Georgia. We don't have to do this now."

"Shush. Let me talk."

Boop turned an imaginary key at her lips.

Georgia cleared her throat. "When I was in the ambulance, I was remembering how glad I was to have you and Marvin living in Skokie while I was at Northwestern, and then in med school. I was never alone on holidays—even when I didn't go home for Christmas. Remember you sneaked a little tree into your house on Euclid Avenue? You and Marvin really treated me like family."

"You weren't *like* family; you *were* family. You *are* family."

"Things worked out for you. You were happy."

"Of course they did. Of course I was." Even though recollections had bombarded Boop this summer, reminding her of when she'd dreamed of a different life and another love, this wasn't the time to disagree with Georgia, or discuss it. At some point Hannah would find some information about Abe, and Boop would lock up the memories again.

"I would have done anything to protect you." Georgia's voice was strong, her words almost defensive.

"Protect me from what?"

"From being hurt again."

Boop patted Georgia's arm. "I know."

"But you deserve to know the truth before I die. Before you die."

Boop had no intention of dying anytime soon; she had the pageant to attend, a new great-grandchild to meet, and a move across the country.

"You're not dying, Georgia. The doctor says you'll be good as new. Or good as old, as the case may be."

"Well, you need to know."

"Okay, okay. What is it that I need to know?"

"Remember you asked me if I thought Abe ever came looking for you."

"Yes, I know, it was a foolish thought, but all of us together, all the memories . . ."

"Betty!"

Boop quieted and snapped to attention. No one called her Betty anymore.

"He did," Georgia said.

"Who did?"

"Abe."

Georgia's voice sounded far away but clear. She spoke slowly and loudly, as if she sensed Boop's confusion. Or maybe so she wouldn't have to repeat herself. "Abe did what?"

"Abe came back."

If Georgia said words after that, Boop didn't hear them. She was nauseated. Sweaty. Cold. Hot. Cold again. Shivering cold.

Abe had come back. To tell his side of the story? To apologize? To start over?

"Are you sure?" Georgia *had* been knocked on the head after all.

198

"Yes, I'm sure."

"When did this happen?"

"On your wedding day."

Boop drew in a breath and gasped unintelligible sounds. Georgia blurred, as if she'd appeared at the end of a dream tunnel.

"My wedding day?"

Had Boop whispered, spoken, or yelled? She didn't know. Maybe she'd said nothing. Georgia's voice echoed in Boop's brain.

Surely she'd misheard, or at the very least misunderstood. There was no chance Abe had come back and no one had told her. No way Boop's lifelong friend and confidante would have withheld this information for almost seventy years. The notion was ridiculous. Georgia was forthright, fun, and no-nonsense. She was not a liar or a secret keeper.

Boop jolted into acute consciousness as if waking up from a deep sleep, aware of the hum of the machines, the beeping of Georgia's life, the hospital-scented air sneaking beneath her blanket shawl. "I thought you said Abe came to see me on my wedding day." She slapped her hand through the air. "But obviously that can't be true."

In cinematic slow motion, or maybe it was all the motion she could muster, Georgia traced an invisible X on her chest with a shaky index finger.

The childlike display burrowed deep into Boop's memory, a catalog of girlhood promises tumbling forward. Crossing one's heart wasn't done in jest.

"You can't mean that."

Georgia remained silent and looked away, her hand covering her mouth again. Her lack of response was enough.

Abe had come back.

A small, dry lump lodged in Boop's throat. If she spoke, she'd scream or cry. She wasn't going to make a scene. Not in a hospital. She kept her admonitions and questions inside. She didn't want to look at Georgia, let alone talk to her. Not then. Not when minutes earlier Boop had been crushed at the thought that her best friend was going to die, once again someone leaving her behind. She wanted to leave Georgia behind, as quickly as possible. This news, these feelings, shattered everything Boop thought she knew about herself and about Georgia. And it was all wrong.

"How dare you!" Boop whispered, but her tone was icy and accusatory. "I *just* asked you about him and still, nothing."

Georgia still did not make eye contact. "I'm sorry but I'm also not sorry. You had a wonderful life."

Georgia had said these exact words throughout the years. Boop had believed it was her friend's loving observation, but, if the pronouncement about Abe was true, that statement had been only a salve for her guilt.

Boop trembled. "When could this possibly have happened? You were with me until minutes before the ceremony."

"The doorbell rang . . ."

Bile edged the back of Boop's throat. "And you went downstairs to answer the door."

Georgia nodded. "But your grandfather got there first and sent him away, told him you were getting married and not to bother you again. Your grandfather saw me and told me not to tell you. That Marvin would give you and the baby the life you deserved." Georgia gasped and words interspersed with breaths. Boop didn't care that Georgia was sad or struggling. In that moment, her well-being ceased to matter. "I believed him."

Boop couldn't move, though she wished she could run. Her eyes stung as they filled with tears and she tried to keep them from spilling down her cheeks, to no avail. "Did he see you? Did he say anything?"

"It doesn't matter," Georgia said.

"You don't get to decide what matters anymore. Did he say anything?"

Georgia nodded. "He said, 'Tell Betty I love her.'"

Boop doubled over, heartache spreading through her, hot and rampant like a wildfire.

"Why didn't you go after him?" she yelled.

"You were getting married."

Boop covered her face with her hands. "I was getting married because I thought he didn't love me."

When Boop lowered her hands and looked at Georgia, she saw that tears had soaked her face.

"I'm sorry," Georgia said.

"No, you're not. This is all part of my wonderful life, right?" Boop stood and backed away. "Hannah!" she shouted.

Hannah ran into Georgia's room. "What's the matter? Do you need me to get the nurse?"

"No. I want you to get a psychiatrist. Georgia has lost her mind."

Chapter 19

BOOP

Back at home, Boop pulled her suitcase out of the closet, lifted out shirts, dresses, and pants, and threw them in without any pairing ritual, forethought, or coordinating lipsticks. She retrieved the empty tackle box and zipped it into the compartment meant for shoes, or a blow-dryer, or another bulky necessity. She could have removed photos from the walls or tucked in an old photo album or cookbook of Nannie's, but Boop wanted the box.

Now it really was all she had left.

She didn't want to stay in the place Georgia had betrayed her in the past and then again in the present. Why tell Boop now? To assuage her own guilt, she supposed. To get her into heaven. Harboring the secret was cowardice at first. Telling it decades later was selfish.

"What are you doing?" Hannah stepped into the room and removed items from the suitcase one by one. Boop replaced them one by one.

"I'm leaving," Boop said.

"And going where?"

Boop stopped moving, hands full of pants. Linen, cotton, gauze. The fabrics reminded her that she had always been quick to embrace appropriate fashion—for the times, the situation, the weather.

But where was she going and what would she need there? They'd all told her what to pack when she left South Haven the last time. She had her trousseau and a steamer trunk with dresses and twinsets, shoes, and accessories chosen by Nannie. Boop had insisted on taking her dancing-ballerina jewelry box, and a binder with her recipe heritage, one she'd rarely used.

"How can I stay?" She looked to Hannah for an actual answer. Not only had Georgia broken Boop's heart, but she'd broken their friendship. Boop was disillusioned and angry—so much more hurt than she would have been if Georgia had died from that fall. At least that wouldn't have willingly removed herself from Boop's life. And to top it off, Boop would miss Georgia. Damn her.

Hannah lifted the collection of pants from Boop's hands.

"Oh my goodness," Boop said. "You were supposed to go home and talk to Clark."

"I'm not going anywhere."

"You have to go. You owe it to yourself. I missed my chance but you don't have to."

"I texted Clark and told him what happened and told him I'd like to talk when I come back. That's good enough."

"Good enough is not enough for you. I want you to go."

She would be alone again, naturally. Boop grunted only because of the song of the same title, and how she'd always switched the radio station in the Caddy because the lyrics and melody were gloomy. Now that would be her life again.

She was no longer accustomed to being alone.

How quickly she'd acclimated to talking to the girls instead of herself, to making reservations for three or four or five instead of calling for Delightful Buddha takeout, to walking around with a posse and a pocketful of memories and private jokes. Her cheeks still ached from all the smiling. Those weeks had filled up parts of her she didn't know were empty—parts that were draining fast. She'd have her activities and her appointments, but that wasn't the same as having someone close enough to hear their breathing, anticipate their habits, appreciate their imperfections. The same someone who might tell her to put her hands in the air if she started coughing, even if that remedy (which worked) had no medical soundness.

Hannah unzipped a section of the suitcase and pulled out the tackle box. Boop gasped as if she hadn't placed it there herself.

"I remember this thing." Hannah unlatched and opened the box.

"You do?" Boop lurched back, thinking memories would pour out, but when she leaned over and looked inside, it was empty.

She removed it from Hannah's hands and the words spilled out as easily as the crayons had. "I used it as a hiding place, but I must have emptied it because when I checked it was empty. Well, not empty, but empty of my most special keepsake. It was the only reminder I had of the summer before I married your grandfather."

Hannah stayed silent, her eyes intent. Boop knew she wasn't being judged.

"I won the Miss South Haven pageant when I was eighteen," Boop said.

"I wondered when you were going to tell me."

"You knew?" Was everyone keeping secrets from her, the hypocrites?

"Natalie was worried that she'd upset you with the article. She found me online and sent a message. Why didn't you ever tell us?"

"I promised your grandfather I'd erase everything from that summer that didn't have to do with him."

"Oh, Boop, I'm so sorry."

"What's done is done. I'd have liked to see that sash again though, especially with the new pageant this summer. So many memories." Boop laughed. "Like walking around with a book on my head."

"Could you do it?"

"Of course I could, but Georgia was better at it." Boop allowed her words to drop off. "The summer of 1951 was really something. In so many ways."

"And they gave you a pink sash embroidered with 'Miss South Haven 1951' in black?"

"How do you know?"

"Pop gave it to me and Emma one summer. He said to add it to our trunk of dress-up clothes."

Boop's limbs ran cold. Another betrayal. When would it end? Her throat thickened with sorrow and rage. "Pop gave you my sash?"

"We were little girls. We just didn't know. I'm so sorry."

"No one asked about it?"

"We went home to our mom's that summer. I guess she didn't think it was anything more than an old souvenir."

The sash had been the only tangible reminder she'd had of the happy times that summer, before her life split into before and after. And Marvin had given it away.

He'd thought it would remain a secret, just like Georgia had.

"It wasn't his to give away. It represented childhood dreams. College plans. Career goals. Summer love. I wasn't hurting anyone by keeping it."

Hannah cocked her head. Boop was wrong. Cherishing those memories hurt Marvin. She supposed giving away the sash had been his quiet revenge. She realized neither action had defined their life together.

"You need to talk to Clark," Boop said. "To find out if the good in your relationship outweighs the hurt."

"He's in Traverse City this week at a craft show."

"That's not too far."

"No, it's not, but I'm not leaving you alone, and since he's busy, it's good timing."

Few things were, so Boop would take it.

Later Boop walked downstairs and through the living room, where Hannah had sprawled onto the couch for a nap.

Boop smoothed the fabric of her periwinkle blue shorts that didn't need smoothing. Anti-wrinkle fabrics would have been a godsend at Stern's. She looked at her familiar surroundings, the ones she looked at every day but didn't always see. She'd chosen a clichéd (and somewhat inaccurate) nautical decor with navy and white furniture and accents. Antique wooden tables that had adorned her childhood—and had the dings and scratches to prove it—held books and candles, figurines and art projects. Area rugs camouflaged the most worn paths on the solid oak floors that had never been replaced, though they pitched and buckled in spots everyone had learned to avoid. She walked to the sideboard and tapped the pictures of her grandparents next to ones of her great-grandsons. So many tchotchkes, some cheap yet treasured, others pricey but meaningless. What of it mattered?

Boop sat at the kitchen table, the weight of still-unspoken questions sat on her shoulders.

Hannah stepped into the kitchen and set store-bought chocolate-chip cookies onto the table and pulled out a plastic-wrapped sleeve. Nannie would have cringed. Boop helped herself to two.

Hannah sat across from Boop. "I have to ask. Do you think you would have run off with Abe? If you had known?"

Boop had dreamed of that scenario many times. The answer always unclear. "The truth?"

"Please."

Boop had been so young, and scared, and her heart had been broken several times over. "I don't know if I would have. But I'd have wanted to."

Hannah furrowed her brow and shook her head. "Even though you were pregnant?"

The answer to this question would further undo Boop's lifetime of secrets. "I would have wanted to *because* I was pregnant. Hannah . . ."

Hannah's gaze flitted back and forth between the cookies and Boop. She furrowed her brow, then opened her eyes wide. Boop knew what came next.

"The baby was Abe's, wasn't it?" Hannah asked, but Boop knew it was rhetorical.

Boop was at once relieved and ashamed. She nodded, and a knot tightened in her belly that tugged and tugged, phantom kicks from that long-ago baby, simultaneously creating a bruise on her heart. Long beats of silence filled the space between them. Hannah didn't yell or scowl. Her expression was kind and understanding. Boop was grateful for the compassion in her granddaughter's face, and then in her soft voice.

"Abe didn't know, did he?"

"They didn't let me tell him. God, I tried."

"Did Pop know?"

"Of course." *Of course* Hannah assumed Boop was capable of honesty. And in some ways she wasn't.

"This means Pop wasn't my—"

"Stop it, Hannah. Pop was your grandfather, don't you say he wasn't!"

"Does Dad know about this?"

Boop shook her head. "No, but—"

"No buts, Boop. He deserves to know Pop wasn't his biological father."

Boop sniffled and her eyes filled and overflowed. It wasn't that simple, but Boop couldn't talk about it. Not yet. Maybe not ever.

"I will talk to your dad, Hannah. But not today."

Over the next two days, Boop didn't call Stuart or Georgia, and Hannah kindly gave her a wide berth. Boop eavesdropped when Hannah called the hospital, and knew Georgia was alive and improving.

When Hannah drove Boop to Natalie's for her weekly manicure, they idled as the Dyckman Avenue drawbridge opened. Two sailboats progressed slowly, on their way to the lake. Boop stared ahead at the raised road.

"I have to tell you something," Hannah said.

"I know I promised I will talk to your dad, and I will." Boop was procrastinating, and she knew it. Letting out secrets might have been cathartic, but it was also exhausting.

"That's good, but that's not what I wanted to talk to you about. Not this time."

"Oh."

"Georgia called this morning," Hannah said. "She's being trans-ferred to rehab."

"It's only been a few days."

"They say she's ready to go. And since you refuse to visit her, you can't really have an opinion."

"I can always have an opinion. Where are they sending her?"

"Lighthouse. Have you heard of it?"

Lighthouse Rehab was a geriatric facility, the last stop before a nurs-ing home, meant for old people who might not recover, or recover fully. "I am glad she'll be out of the hospital," Boop said.

"Really?"

"What do you mean, 'really'? I'm not a monster."

"Do you want to go see her?"

"No."

"I don't understand. She seems to, but I don't."

"She kept a very important secret."

"Pot, meet kettle."

"Very funny, Hannah."

The drawbridge lowered, the light turned green, and Hannah eased the car across. She flipped on the signal and turned right onto Broadway

Street, and turned right again onto Phoenix Street, with all the tourists. None of whom had ever heard of Betty or Stern's Summer Resort.

Boop reveled in the distraction of the summer bustle; she always had. Even though there would be no familiar faces before she saw Natalie's, when she set her mind to it, each visitor to South Haven reminded her of the welcoming arms of Nannie and the jovial camaraderie of Zaide. They had treated every guest as family, and anyone they'd met as a potential friend. Maybe that accounted for the warmth Boop still felt toward the tourists, even though she had nothing to gain from their presence or their pocketbooks.

Hannah double-parked in front of the salon. "You should forgive Georgia. I think the good outweighs the hurt."

"Don't use my own words against me." Boop unlocked the door. "I have to go in, I don't want to be late." She opened the door and balanced with her cane as she stepped away. Then she turned back. "I'm not mad at Georgia because I married Pop. I'm mad because she didn't trust me to make my own choice."

Hannah waved on the cars behind her. "No matter what she did or didn't do, I think you two deserve closure, Boop."

"How is that even possible when Georgia just opened everything up?"

"Anything is possible."

Chapter 20

BETTY

Betty scurried into her bedroom along with her friends. Nannie sat on a sewing stool, tapping her foot on the floor as if counting the seconds.

"You're lucky your grandmother can do this," Doris said. "Mine couldn't sew a button."

"I am lucky," Betty said. She knew it was brownnosing, but an extra-secure spot in Nannie's favor didn't hurt. Especially when Betty was going to ask for a tighter waist and a bit of a lower neckline. If Betty was feeling bold in addition to lucky, she planned to mention Abe—that they were getting serious—even though they'd already gotten serious.

They stole kisses by the tennis court with Georgia as a lookout. They skimmed fingers whenever they passed during the day. Each night after his shift at the grocer's, Abe and Betty sat on the porch, watching the sky, listening to the lake, and kissing while her grandparents slept upstairs. A few times they'd sneaked off to his car to have sex in the back seat—which wasn't as uncomfortable as Betty had thought it would be, with the blanket and pillow she'd pilfered from the supply closet. That's also where they mapped out their visits as they wiggled back into their clothes, giggling and whispering like they'd gotten away with something—which they had. They figured they'd see each other on

Thanksgiving break when Abe would come to South Haven for a day. By then Nannie and Zaide would have come around and accepted Betty and Abe were an item. Then, during Christmas break, Betty would head to Detroit for a week. They also schemed when they might each take a train and meet halfway—in Cleveland—and stay in a hotel under fake names!

Winter was hockey season, so that would be more difficult, but after graduation in June—less than one year from that moment—Abe would be in New York full-time. Maybe they'd marry while Betty was still in school. Why not? It's not like he'd insist she stay home to bake cookies and have babies. Not right away. Not for a long time.

Nannie looked up from her sewing and whirled her forefinger in the air like a lasso. "Stop daydreaming. Let's get started. No one has all day."

Georgia looked at her watch.

Nannie slipped Betty's dress from its wooden hanger and held it by the shoulder straps. Each strap was topped with a blue satin ribbon tied in a bow that matched the skirt's powder-blue overlay.

Betty stepped out of her blue gym uniform she sometimes wore for calisthenics. It fell around her feet. Nannie handed the dress to Doris, who held it open wide on the floor, so Betty could step in. She held out her arms, and the girls lifted the dress up over her torso and onto her arms, quite like the blue birds in *Cinderella*, although that would make Nannie one of the mice. Doris zipped up the back and fastened the matching belt in front.

"It fits like a glove," Georgia said.

Nannie removed a pin from her pincushion and pulled at the fabric at Betty's waist. "Almost."

"Gloves!" Betty tugged away from Nannie and skittered to her dresser. She opened the top drawer and lifted out a slim gold cardboard box, unwrapped a pair of white gloves from protective paper, and pulled one onto each hand. "They're practically new." Betty stopped moving, as if in a game of freeze tag. She looked at Nannie, who nodded.

"You can never go wrong wearing white gloves," she said. "Now come here and let me finish so we can all get back to work. No time for dawdling."

Following her grandmother's instructions, Betty stood at attention as Nannie kneeled, then pulled and folded and pinned the hem.

"I think it's a little loose at the chest," Betty said.

"You can win without showing too much."

Doris nodded, but Georgia covered her mouth, knowing Betty's plan had been foiled.

Then Georgia glanced at her watch again. "I have to go."

"Where?" Betty asked.

"Timbuktu," Georgia said. "Where do you think? I have a tennis lesson. Every guest deserves special attention."

"Who's this star student?" Doris asked.

"Not a star, Sam—Mr.—Bloomfield. He wants to be able to hit tennis balls with his daughters, so he's doubling up on lessons on weekends."

Nannie removed a straight pin from between her lips. "Good for him, Georgia. And that's because of you. The Bloomfields are lucky to have you."

Georgia blushed. "Thank you. See you later, girls?"

"Of course!" Betty and Doris said in unison.

"Doris, would you help Betty take off the dress without sticking herself? And then just leave it on the bed." Betty held Nannie's arm and helped her grandmother stand. "Georgia, dear, I'll walk back with you. Ira's got to be wondering where I am, and it's almost time to check in on the kitchen." She brushed off her dark-blue shirtwaist.

Georgia stepped aside and allowed Nannie to walk out the door and down the stairs first.

As they disappeared from view, Betty clutched Doris's arms. "Can I ask you something?"

"Of course. But take off the dress first."

She stepped gingerly from her pinned frock. In her slip and brassiere, Betty sat at the edge of her bed near but not on top of the dress. She wrung her hands in her lap.

"What's got you all wound up?"

"My grandparents aren't going to be happy about this."

"You're killing me, Betty. Spit it out."

"I've been thinking about my parents. I may invite them to the pageant."

"What would your grandparents say?"

"They're always happy to see Joe, but I thought I wouldn't mention it. In case they say no, which they probably will. I could just write them. Then no one would have to know. What do you think I should do?"

"Does that really matter?"

It didn't, but Betty appreciated that Doris allowed her to babble. If her parents agreed to come, Tillie and Joe could see her as the woman she'd become. They might even like Abe, and to get on Betty's good side they might help convince Nannie and Zaide that half-Jewish was enough—even if they believed it was the wrong half. Even if she didn't get their help with Abe, they'd still see her triumphing onstage before she headed off to New York to pursue her own dream, the way they had pursued theirs. The difference being, she wasn't abandoning a child to do it.

Over the next weeks, Betty's days became predictable yet dazzling. Abe could be around any corner—and he often was. Yet her work in the laundry room provided a short reprieve, and while she missed the rush of anticipation, the rhythm of the machines soothed Betty, reminding her of her origin. The machines thudded, whirled, and buzzed, and none of the laundry girls paid mind to Betty. She liked her hours here. This was where Betty knew what was expected of her and she didn't have to be poised or coiffed or even polite. One day she'd heard the girls swearing aloud, not caring one iota that she was nearby. It was as if Betty weren't their bosses' granddaughter. Since Betty's summer life existed in the spotlight and was governed by propriety, she loved standing a little bit slouched, leaning while she worked, wiping sweat with the back of her hand in lieu of a handkerchief. She had wanted to tell her grandparents how much she cared for Abe, but it never seemed to be the right time for that conversation—that argument. She'd promised she wouldn't "go overboard" but overboard she had gone. Headfirst, as if she'd ducked beneath a wind-forced wave.

Betty poured bleach and Cheer into the washing machine before adding the morning's white cotton napkins and tablecloths.

Francine fed a folded flat sheet through the decade-old rotary ironing machine, then she looked up. "How's your fella? That handsome waiter. Abe, isn't it?"

Betty wanted to say Abe was wonderful, caring, gentle, and loving, but didn't want to be a braggart. Or come off as smitten and silly. "He's swell, thanks for asking."

"Some girls have all the luck," Francine muttered.

Was it luck she was feeling? The upwelling that compelled Betty to skip instead of walk, hum lively tunes, daydream through hours? No, that wasn't luck; that was love.

Mabel barreled into the laundry room, apron covered in the morning's flour and butter stains. "Your grandmother wants to see you in the office, Betty."

"What's wrong?"

"I'm just delivering the message and hoping the shnecken don't burn or I'll need to bake another type of cookie for tonight's dessert plate."

Betty wouldn't shirk her duties. Not while Francine and the other laundry girls watched for her reply. "I'll head over as soon as I'm finished." What could they want now? Betty's heart thudded as she rifled through her ruminations about Abe. What she could say. How she could say it.

Mabel turned to walk away. "Make it snappy."

There was nothing snappy about hanging the laundry to dry, but her grandparents condoned the use of the electric clothes dryer only if it was too cold or too wet outside, and today it was neither. Betty knew they bragged about owning one of the first commercial dryers, but that didn't mean they used it. She loaded the sheets into a basket, and lifted the basket into her arms.

"Go," Francine said. "You can owe me one."

"You're a doll," Betty said. She set down the basket and resisted the urge to hug Francine, who seemed more like a handshaker than a hugger.

The kindness was undeniable, but Betty wasn't sure she wanted to hurry. Nannie couldn't be summoning her for a good reason, could she? Had she and Abe been too public? Too brazen? Too reckless? Or did this have something to do with Barnard? Miss South Haven was two weeks away—was there news about Nancy Green? The legacy of Miss South Haven thrilled Betty. If she won, she'd be part of South Haven history apart from her family's famous name and resort. Wherever Betty studied, traveled, and lived in her lifetime, she'd be Miss South Haven 1951. The free publicity? The *nachas*? That would belong to her grandparents.

When Betty looked up from her daydream, all the laundry girls were staring at the door.

There stood Nannie in a clover-green shirtwaist, her hair up in a tight bun with brown-gray tendrils loose at the sides, by an accident of wind or walking quickly, not due to style. Not on a weekday. She crooked a forefinger at Betty. Her expression was staid—not a smile nor a frown—but that meant nothing. Nannie didn't bubble with emotions.

Betty's heart felt heavy and she swayed with a bit of wooziness, in a premonitory kind of way. Something was wrong.

Nannie might have been less than five feet tall, but she strode across the lawn with giant steps.

Betty scurried to keep up, but her legs wobbled from fear. What was the hurry when Nannie could yell at her right then? Unless she wanted privacy. "Nannie, please. Are you going to tell me what's wrong?"

"Just hurry along."

Nannie said nothing as she pushed open Zaide's office door. He sat behind his desk, and Abe stood in front of it, dressed in the shirt and tie he'd worn the first time Betty had seen him. A worn suitcase sat on the floor next to Abe.

Betty fell to her knees, her legs unable to hold her upright.

Where is he going?

What's going on?

This was a mistake, a mix-up, an egregious error in judgment. Betty would take the blame for anything her grandparents were pinning on Abe to make him go. She'd stay away from him so he could keep his job. He needed his job.

"Don't be dramatic, Betty," Nannie said.

Betty stood.

"We're going to leave you two alone," Zaide said as he walked around his desk and shook Abe's hand and patted him on the back. That was odd.

"We'll be right outside," Nannie said.

After the door closed, Abe reached out his hand and Betty flung herself against him. They'd fired him, she was sure of it. But they hadn't been accusatory or angry.

"Tell me what's going on. Do they know?" Betty pushed herself away from Abe. "I'll tell them it was my idea—or better yet tell them you love me; tell them we're getting married."

"This has nothing to do with us, Betty. Or your grandparents." Abe held both Betty's hands and looked into her eyes. He'd been crying. He was crying again. Betty reached and touched his face and the boy she loved sobbed into her hands.

"I have to leave. It's my brother," he said. "He was killed."

Abe climbed into the driver's seat. Betty closed the door, and he rolled down the window.

"I'm so sorry about Aaron," she said. "Please drive safely." She leaned into the window opening and kissed Abe's cheek. "I love you," she whispered, and didn't care if anyone saw or heard.

"Me too," Abe said. He looked toward Betty but not right at her, his voice heavy, his words slow and laden with worry.

She omitted "come back soon" and "I'll miss you"; it wasn't the time. It was time for Abe to tend to his mother, to make arrangements, to be the man of the family. She swelled with pride at his sense of responsibility, though it was likely the wrong reaction for such a solemn day.

As Abe drove away, Betty inhaled the same deep breath as when she surfaced from under the lake, air in her lungs a new, lifesaving sensation—a welcome burn. Amid that familiar feeling, displaced facts tumbled together.

Boys on staff at Stern's hadn't been drafted because they attended college. Most of the housekeeping staff were women. The visiting husbands were either too old or they'd served in the war, which meant they weren't required to register for the draft. That much she knew, because the kids her age talked about it sometimes.

Betty didn't know why President Truman had sent troops to Korea or how long this conflict, as she'd heard it called, would last. Did Zaide know? Did the husbands talk politics between games of pinochle, or were they all too distracted by their weekends of glamour and gluttony? What about when they went back to their jobs and homes?

And why didn't the wives Betty saw at every meal, at calisthenics, on the beach, at every Stern's event, discuss politics in addition to bragging about their children, their figures, and their homemaking prowess?

Because they lived in a bubble of educated ignorance. As did Betty. She shuddered at her narrow range of concerns. She could care about fashion and family *and* current events. Couldn't she? Good fortune should heighten her interest in the world, not limit it. She had time. In New York, Betty would detach her halo of privilege and stay fixed outside her insularity—with Abe by her side.

Four days later, Abe telephoned the resort. Betty pressed her ear to the receiver, as if his words could otherwise slip away.

She learned that Aaron Barsky had been in the 24th Infantry Division, but she didn't understand other details, another example of being unaware. It wasn't the time to ask Abe to explain. It wasn't time to ask him anything. But that didn't stop Betty from hoping he would return soon.

"I have to take care of some things. More than I realized," Abe said. "I don't know when I'll be back."

What did that mean? Another week? Two? The words stayed inside but selfishness tore a little hole in Betty's thoughts, just big enough for worry to seep through.

"I've got to hang up now," Abe said. "I love you."

Betty gulped and released her bottled-up fear. Blood rushed around inside her chest. Had she really thought he'd stopped loving her in a few days? She wanted him to say it again and again. She missed their carefree "I love yous" that had been filled with hope and promise and kissing. She missed the three weeks of fervent, clandestine lovemaking. She gulped away an inappropriate twinge of desire.

Betty opened her mouth to reply with affection, to ask if he'd received the letters she'd written, to offer regards to his mother—but before she spoke, the line went dead.

"I love you too." Betty finished the conversation even though only the operator was listening.

Chapter 21

BETTY

Betty pushed cooked carrot medallions around her plate with her fork. It was the tactic she now employed to make it look as if she had eaten.

At any moment Nannie would tell her to stop playing with her dinner, but that was all Betty could do. It had been days since Abe's only telephone call, and while she'd written to him every night, Betty had received only one postcard with eight words on it.

Eight words she'd read a thousand times.

Rec'd your letters.

Will telephone soon.

Love,
Abe

Betty continued playing with the carrots until they lined up like little soldiers. Oh God. Anything but soldiers.

Nannie placed her hand on Betty's forearm. *Here it comes. Nannie is going to tell me to forget him.*

"You're not doing Abe any good starving yourself. Or hiding away from your friends."

"I want to be alone," Betty said. "And I'm not hungry." She hadn't been hungry in days. Rye toast went down okay when Mabel stopped balking that Betty wanted it dry, without butter or jam, and obliged her.

Nannie rubbed Betty's arm. "He's with his family, Betty. Where he should be."

Betty wanted to say *she* was Abe's family, but she swallowed the words. Nannie's kindness was proof she didn't hate Abe. That would be enough for now.

"That swimsuit won't fill out itself, you know," Nannie said.

Betty needn't be told again that the Catalina suit had cost four dollars. She lifted her fork and scooped a clump of mashed potatoes. She opened her mouth and pushed the fork inside and clamped her lips around it. Betty pulled out the fork and stared at the clean tines as she swallowed. Her stomach churned, threatening to retch.

"I know the swimsuit and dress cost a lot of money," Betty said. "I'll find a way to pay you back. But I don't think I can do it—I can't be in a beauty contest. It seems silly now."

"Don't be ridiculous. There is nothing silly about a time-honored tradition," Nannie said.

"Oh, we're so looking forward to the whole event," Mrs. Levin said from the far side of the table. "We've never been. And your being in it makes it extra special."

Betty resented how her life had become dining-room fodder. Where was Zaide when she needed him to distract a busybody with one of his stories? Betty looked at Mrs. Levin, who'd already gone back to picking the meat off a chicken thigh bone, as she ignored her two boys who were picking at each other.

Betty leaned toward Nannie but spoke toward her plate. "I can't."

Nannie whispered in Betty's ear even though Zaide was across the room shmying around with the guests. "I wasn't born yesterday. I know you're smitten with each other. And with summer half over, I know you wish he were here."

Betty's cheeks heated as if she were feverish. They must have been beet red. What else did Nannie know?

"By carrying on with your life, it shows him that you can take care of yourself. Don't make that poor boy worry about *you* when his brother has just died."

Nannie was smart. That was good advice. She hadn't asked Betty to break it off or forget him, but to change her behavior on Abe's behalf.

"I'll get back to acting more like myself," she said. "You're right."

Nannie tilted her head. "And this surprises you?"

"No." She didn't dare say yes. Nannie was being receptive to the idea of them together. For the first time that week, Betty was able to smile.

Days came and went with the usual bustle of resort activity, and a return to normal behavior for Betty. Every swipe of lipstick, curl of her hair, and jumping jacks count-off meant she'd again look like the girl Abe loved. She knew more important things were happening in the world—in Abe's world too—but this was something she could control. She'd have pink cheeks even without rouge, a smile that reflected the mood she wanted, and a skip in her step that meant she had faith in the future. She would not be that Betty's dowdy twin. Staring into her bedroom vanity mirror, Betty brushed her hair again and again along the same silky path. She wondered if shiny hair and a smart appearance truly disguised how she felt. Zaide said doubt and fear seeped out of one's pores like garlic. Betty sprayed English Lavender into the air and scampered through the perfume cloud as it floated to the floor.

"I wonder why he hasn't written to you," Doris said, leaning to gather crumpled paper from Betty's bedroom floor.

Betty dropped her hairbrush onto the vanity table as she leaped from her chair. "What makes you think he hasn't?" She snatched the wads of ink-flecked paper from Doris's hands.

"I wouldn't read them." Doris clasped her hands in front and pivoted away, as if offended. She sat sideways on the window seat. The light outside was fading from crisp to muted. "It was just a question."

"His brother died, you know. I don't want him worrying about me."

"We don't want you to get hurt," Georgia said as she stepped into view in the doorway. Too late. "Betty, it's been two weeks."

Georgia's unspoken meaning settled onto Betty. She didn't want Betty's heart strewn aside the way her and Abe's clothes had been on the Fourth of July.

Betty remained on the vanity stool, turned toward the mirror, and resumed brushing her hair. *One. Two. Three. Four.* The bristles massaged her scalp and then scratched her shoulder. *Five. Six. Seven. Eight.* "I don't want to hear anything negative. It upsets my stomach." *Nine. Ten. Eleven. Twelve.* "His brother died serving our country. Abe had a memorial service to plan, and then they sat shiva, and now he's the man of the house . . ." Betty clamped her lips. *Thirteen. Fourteen. Fifteen. Sixteen.* She'd said too much. Abe's home and family were private. *Seventeen. Eighteen. Nineteen. Twenty.*

Doris gasped. "He doesn't have a father?"

"His father is a louse. Abe is a mensch."

Betty opened the middle drawer and placed her silver-plated brush inside. She pushed the drawer shut with a thud. "I'll thank you not to go spreading rumors. And he has sent two postcards, I'll have you know."

Georgia and Doris looked at one another and shrugged.

"If I can't have the support of my two best friends, then what's this world coming to?" Betty's throat burned. Tears threatened to belie her confidence. "He loves me." A solid statement, but her voice was on the verge of cracking.

"I should hope so," Georgia said.

222

"I *thought* you might be in love," Doris said, tapping her temple with her forefinger. "I have a sixth sense about these things."

Betty wished Doris would go so she could talk about everything to Georgia. Sure, Georgia knew what happened on the Fourth of July—she'd practically walked in on them—but Betty hadn't told anyone their plans for New York and marriage and children, and right then she thought she might burst if she didn't.

"As a matter of fact," Betty said, "I wouldn't be surprised if he's here in time for Miss South Haven." The contest was next Sunday.

Doris placed her arm around Betty's shoulders. "If you love him, then we love him." Doris tittered. "You know what I mean."

Georgia peeked out the bedroom window. "Everyone's starting to gather by the pier. Let's go watch the sunset like the summer people. C'mon, it'll be a blast. Get your mind off things."

Georgia was right—focusing on her friends would get Betty's mind off herself for now. In just a few days she'd be preparing for Miss South Haven in earnest, and she'd make her grandparents proud.

The girls bopped down the stairs, Doris yammering about her perfect boy. Everything from temperament and favorite food to eye color. Too many musts for Betty to keep track. On her way out the door to the porch, Georgia said, "I want someone intellectual and sophisticated."

"Is that so?" Betty elbowed Georgia in the ribs.

"Knock it off," she said.

"Well, I think that happens *after* you marry them." Doris laughed; her romanticism, it seemed, was mixed with traces of realism.

The girls skittered down Lakeshore Drive, skirts swaying, hair bouncing. For a few hundred yards they chattered over and around one another; then they intentionally linked arms and fell in step. Comfort and safety enveloped Betty. It was a feeling warmer than the midsummer breeze, and more reliable than the beacon on the lighthouse. She'd felt it so many times before. This, too, was a type of love. Love from two people who didn't have to love her. They'd chosen her—with her penchant for theatrics, her attention on Abe for the past month, her impatience the past two weeks. And she'd chosen them right back.

Though they'd said it many times, it was that night's sky casting her friends in a majestic purple glow, when Betty knew for sure—in well beyond a pinkie-swear or cross-your-heart kind of way—they'd be friends forever.

"We won't make it to the pier," Betty said. "Let's just sit on the beach right here so we don't miss it. We can look for boys later." She leaned to Georgia. "Though I don't really think you want to."

Georgia looked as if she were about to speak, but she didn't. Betty watched the movement in her throat as she swallowed hard.

Then Georgia reached for Betty's hand and squeezed it. "I'm sorry about before," she whispered. "If Abe loves you, he'll be back."

The only word Betty heard was *if.*

Betty convinced herself that even though Abe's next postcard didn't mention Miss South Haven, he would be back for it. She didn't want him to shirk his duties at home, and she didn't want to be bossy or needy—but oh! How she wanted him to be there.

She flipped a curl behind her shoulder and sucked in her breath one more time. She held it and inhaled again, but no matter how hard Nannie tugged at Betty's waist, that zipper was not sliding up the back. Across the room, Betty's friends' lips sealed in tight lines, their cheeks puffed like chipmunks.

Betty set her hands together as if in prayer. "Please breathe. If you die, I'll have lost part of my cheering section."

The girls exhaled, their concern settling around Betty. She shrugged it off.

"Maybe I shouldn't have encouraged you to eat so much," Nannie said. "Or I measured wrong." She shook her head. "That can't be it. I had the girls in the laundry room do the sewing. That must be it."

"Try again," Betty said.

"It's no use. You'll have to pick another dress."

"But I don't want another dress. You said this one matched my eyes. And it cost eleven dollars."

"I'm not a magician, Betty. I can't fix things that are unfixable."

Two weeks earlier the dress, with its long, narrow torso and dropped waist, had fit Betty as if it had been custom-made for her hourglass figure. The boatneck had showed off her clavicles and accented her bosom enough to interest the judges but not enough to mortify her grandparents. Two weeks ago was also the last time she'd seen Abe.

Betty looked down. "I'll try a different brassiere."

It didn't help.

The next day, eight hours before the start of the contest, Betty readied herself in body and spirit. She stood in the middle of her bedroom with the dress pulled up and zipped to her waist with the bodice seams opened and splayed like drooping flower petals around her stomach, hips, and buttocks.

When Georgia and Doris walked in, Betty pointed to her dresser. Atop it sat a spool of blue cotton thread with three needles poking out. Draped across the back of her vanity stool were thin scraps of fabric in shades of blue. An avid and thrifty seamstress, Nannie always kept leftovers.

"What are you waiting for?" Betty asked. "Sew me into it."

An hour later, the blue dress of Nannie's and Betty's dreams lay in segments on the bedroom floor.

"We tried," Georgia said.

"I want to know what you've been eating," Doris said.

"Why?"

"Because the only thing that's bigger about you is your chest."

Betty glanced down, uncertain Doris was right, but uncertain she was wrong. Then she spun around and looked at her alarm clock. "Do you know what time it is?" she asked.

Georgia laughed. "I sure do. It's time to choose a different dress."

225

Chapter 22

BETTY

Betty smoothed the "Miss Stern's Summer Resort" sash along her torso. She pulled it taut—wrinkles were unacceptable—even though that meant the word *Resort* was hidden at her hip, under her left forearm.

She held up her head, her shoulders straight. No slouching. Arms at her sides, wrists slightly crooked outward to give her hands the subtle angles of a ballerina's. Betty inhaled to fill her lungs and calm herself. As she exhaled, the line she stood in started moving forward. Fourth in a procession of twenty swimsuit-attired girls, Betty followed instructions and entered North Shore Pavilion two paces behind Miss Glassman's Resort and two paces in front of Miss Mendelson's Atlantic Hotel, whose sash lettering was stitched indecipherably close together.

When Betty reached her designated spot on the stage, she smiled and turned forward to face the audience. She'd watched this contest every summer before this one. Had the pavilion always been this crowded?

Women fanned themselves with leaflets. Children fidgeted. Men watched and waited, also glancing at wrist and pocket watches. Mrs. Martha Bookbinder, the mistress of ceremonies, tapped the microphone. It was time.

Mrs. Bookbinder introduced the five judges from B'nai B'rith, which made sense to Betty, since the Jewish service organization was the contest's sponsor and the most active community group in South Haven. Betty didn't know how these men snagged the coveted assignment. Her destiny was in their hands. Literally. The judges held pencils and clipboards where they'd record impressions of the girls, along with their scores for the swimsuit and afternoon dress categories.

It would be better not to be caught staring, so Betty looked straight ahead toward the back of the pavilion, where people stood behind the last row of seats. She kept her gaze fixed above the heads of the crowd. She knew Abe wasn't there. If he had come, she wouldn't have to look for him, she'd know. But the hollowness inside her was certain. It wasn't laced with anticipation; she wasn't buzzing with glee. He wasn't coming.

The microphone screeched. "Welcome to the annual Miss South Haven pageant," Mrs. Bookbinder said. The crowd clapped, some boys whistled. "Now, now. Hold your applause. Today we'll be naming our Miss South Haven 1951." Mrs. Bookbinder continued with cursory announcements for all the B'nai B'rith committees and events, times for Shabbos services at First Hebrew Congregation, and a reminder about the meeting on the new Israel Bonds. Then Mrs. Bookbinder leaned into the microphone. "You can clap now."

It was as if permission had turned a switch. The mostly genteel crowd erupted in a standing ovation. Some boys and men whooped and hollered. The contestants hadn't done *anything*. It was as if the room full of spectators had been cooped up all summer, when in fact, summertime in South Haven was synonymous with activities, opportunities, and beaches full of bathing beauties.

Pretty girls made fools of grown men.

It was something Nannie would say, but Betty thought of it herself.

Still, beads of sweat trickled down Betty's back. As long as no one could see, she didn't care how she felt. It only mattered how she looked.

Alma Goldberg, Miss Fidelman's, was called first. She walked to the middle of the stage, stopped, and then proceeded to walk down the runway, which extended about ten rows into and above the crowd. She stopped, turned, and walked back to her place in line, all while her name, measurements, school, and ambition to be a homemaker and mother were announced, though Betty doubted any of it was heard over the ruckus in the room.

The judges glanced and scribbled whatever judges scribbled. Then they glanced and scribbled again. Betty's heart pounded. She hadn't expected to be nervous, but her eagerness drowned out most of the introductions for Miss Kellman's Cabins and Miss Levin's Resort. Each girl walked in peep-toe pumps, their swimsuits accentuating their bustlines and curves. They wore ordinary suits—one yellow gingham, one with nautical stripes. Betty's lustrous purple suit might have been too fancy for this off-the-rack runway.

Miss Stern's Summer Resort was called. She heard the words. Then her awareness faded into a faraway echo. Nausea hit her stomach like a punch from out of nowhere. Deep breath. Deep breath.

Miss Levin's Resort whispered as she reclaimed her place in line. "That's you," she said. "Go."

Betty stepped forward.

In a bingo-hall-turned-dressing-room on the west side of the North Shore Pavilion, the girls were allowed ten minutes to change from swimsuits into their afternoon dresses and freshen their makeup. Betty pulled on her gloves and slipped on the junior prom pink satin pumps she'd dug out of the back of her closet. The shoes coordinated with Betty's dress as if they'd been dyed to match.

"Do you want me to tie your bow?"

Betty turned around to see Nancy Green, Miss Grossinger's Resort—also the reigning Miss South Haven—in a pale-green taffeta dress with a dropped and curved waistline. The hem touched just below her knees. The scoop neck was trimmed in gold, highlighting the copper flecks in Nancy's brown eyes. Her complexion was creamy and clear, her eyeliner precise, her coral lipstick flattering. Nancy's not-so-subtle cleavage would sway the judges.

Nancy was not only sexy, but also glamorous and sophisticated. And she was nice. Betty groaned but disguised it with a cough.

Betty lifted both strands of ribbon at her waist. "Thank you." There was no way she could tie a proper bow behind her own back. "I didn't think it through."

Nancy stepped behind Betty and tugged and pulled at the wide ribbons. "There. You look lovely in pink."

"It wasn't my first choice, but thank you," Betty said. "Had a little mishap with a blue one."

Nancy leaned in. "I'll tell you a secret. This dress wasn't my first choice either. I had a lovely little peach number I picked up at a boutique in Paris."

Betty leaned in, ravenous for a story about Paris fashion. "Why aren't you wearing it?"

"*Little* is the issue. Even months later, it still doesn't fit. I got full up top too," Nancy whispered and glanced down at her bosom.

Betty hadn't known Nancy was so good-natured, or why she would be so personal.

"Time to line up again," she said.

The girls stood in the same order as before, except for Nancy, who scooted next to Betty. They all readjusted their sashes. "I'd wish you good luck, but I want to win," Nancy whispered. "It's my last chance."

"Mine too."

"Right. I heard you're going away to college."

"I am. In New York City."

"I know other girls who've said they're going to college."

"I *am* going to college," Betty said.

"Well, good for you," Nancy said. "I hope it works out for you."

For some reason, Betty believed her.

Nancy sighed. "You know if I win tonight I'll be the only girl to take the title three times. It would be the best day of my life." Her voice was wispy and longing.

Betty wanted to win, but even with the sash and crown, her best days were yet to come.

Nancy looked at the floor, then wiggled her shoulders and leaned closer to Betty. As close as she could get. "The nausea goes away," she whispered. "Try soda crackers."

"Okay," Betty said, but she didn't have the time or interest to decipher Nancy's meaning.

When her turn came to walk the runway again, Betty looked side to side and chose audience members and then smiled right at them, the concentration keeping her tears at bay. With each step, her legs weakened. He wasn't there. It had been silly to hope. But what if he never came back? With each step she thought, *He loves me.*

Marv sat between his mother and Eleanor. He was a decent guy, a good friend even. He deserved a nicer girl than Eleanor, one without a sharp edge. A girl who didn't want someone else. She smiled at him and before she pivoted at the end of the runway, he smiled back.

As Betty glanced at each of the judges, she smiled and nodded just a bit. Then she copycatted Nancy, and winked.

Back in line, and to the sound of applause, she noticed her grandparents at the end of the second row on the right, clapping and smiling wide. Next to them sat Betty's parents, also smiling. They came! Everyone was proud of her, just as she'd imagined. And just as she'd hoped, the day was almost perfect.

Mrs. Bookbinder shuffled papers, glanced at the judges, and grinned. She stood to the right of all the contestants, and four bouquets of red roses, one bigger than the next, lay on the stage, tied with pink ribbons. She lifted the first bouquet.

"Our third runner-up is . . . Miss Glassman's Resort."

The crowd applauded. All the girls clapped as they'd been instructed, and the third runner-up collected her roses and stood next to Mrs. Bookbinder. Betty thought she might throw up. She'd wanted this for so long, the possibility of it becoming a reality was making her dizzy.

"Our second runner-up is . . . Miss Fidelman's." Betty clapped and smiled but the sound faded away, as if she'd stepped inside her bedroom and closed the door and all the windows.

Her arms full of at least a dozen roses, Mrs. Bookbinder said, "Miss Grossinger's Resort is our first runner-up."

Nancy didn't win!

The crowd cheered. Betty squeezed Nancy's hand. Was it a congratulatory squeeze or one of sympathy? Betty didn't know, but she leaned over and kissed Nancy's cheek. Nancy smiled and waved to the audience. Betty knew it was a fake smile and the wave a rote gesture.

But this meant nothing. There were seventeen pretty girls on the stage, all of whom had practiced and primped. All of whom wanted the title for any of a hundred valid reasons. Should Betty have stepped away? She had so much—devoted grandparents, a boy who loved her, friends who cherished her, and her education and future ripe for the taking. She inhaled a deep breath and swelled with gratitude for her good fortune. No matter what happened next, she would remember this sense of peace and gratitude for the rest of her life.

Then, without fanfare—or a pause—Mrs. Bookbinder tapped the microphone. She loved tapping the microphone. Then she clapped like a teacher demanding attention from an unruly brood. The hurly-burly of it all settled Betty into a moment of unencumbered hope—yes, she wanted this as much as, if not more than, the other girls. She had the right to be here. Betty swept her hands around to the back of her dress and crossed her fingers.

Mrs. Bookbinder cleared her throat. "I'm so pleased to announce that our Miss South Haven 1951 is—" She turned and smiled at Betty then returned her attention to the audience. "Miss Stern's Summer Resort—Miss Betty Stern!"

Cameras flashed. Betty saw only bright lights. She was shocked—but was she really? She was rendered speechless as someone removed her Stern's sash—wait! Maybe she'd wanted to keep it—and laid another sash over her head, onto her shoulder, and across her body, and smoothed it over her chest and hips. She had no idea who was touching her, but she supposed it didn't matter. She'd won.

Betty was Miss South Haven.

Someone placed a bouquet of at least two dozen red roses into her arms, and someone else set something on her head. Oh! A tiara! She lifted her chin just a smidgen, so it would stay on for all the photographs. The photographs that would be published in all the newspapers. All the newspapers that would mention her grandparents' resort. She wished she could see their reactions.

Betty walked to the middle of the runway. Was this what it was like to be a movie star, or Princess Elizabeth? Her thoughts zoomed to Nancy Green in Europe, or the Europe Betty imagined from films and books. Ice water surged throughout Betty's body, leaving her cold, and woozy, and wondering. Another flashbulb popped just as she turned to look at Nancy.

A swirl overtook Betty's stomach and moved into her throat. *The nausea goes away.* How did Nancy know Betty was nauseated?

She'd also been light-headed, and her new dress hadn't fit. Come to think of it, most of her blouses had become tight across the bust.

No, please no!

"Excuse me, I have to go," Betty said. She whirled around. The microphone stand wobbled as she pressed her bouquet onto Nancy's chest, not knowing or caring if it had fallen to the ground.

When were her last monthlies?

Betty jerked herself away from random hands trying to hold her back. "I have to go." She was going to vomit. Betty pushed aside a burgeoning crowd of well-wishing girls. She dashed down the stage steps. Her tiara slipped off, but she didn't stop to retrieve it. Yes, she was going to throw up.

"Betty!" yelled either Zaide or Joe. She couldn't tell. Their voices were the only way they were alike.

Betty kicked off her pumps and ran down the aisle toward the front of the pavilion. As she reached the door and strode outside, she heard the fuzzy thuds of someone tapping the microphone.

Betty ran to the edge of the beach, stopping short. She vomited onto the ground. Empty, she moved with ease and without a churning stomach or spinning head and stepped onto the sand. It wasn't pale and warm and soft, no longer able to cradle her if she lay upon it. It stretched out in front of her, cold and wet like she imagined quicksand to be, ready to drink her in and swallow her up. The lake ahead was calm, but ominous, not wondrous. Betty stared toward the lighthouse, a beacon not only for ships. If she stared at its immense sturdiness, perhaps the ground would stop shifting beneath her feet. She swayed, legs like spaghetti, so she lowered herself to the ground, sand sticking to the vomit on her hem. Nannie would be mad. Betty heard the echo of Abe's voice faraway behind her while the lighthouse faded into pieces as if she were looking at it through the broken colors of a kaleidoscope. The bright blue day dulled to ominous gray.

Then everything went dark.

Chapter 23

BOOP

Boop wore white linen pants and a deliberately wrinkled lavender tunic. The crinkly cotton prompted her ironing instinct, but pressed, smooth, stiff fabric wasn't the style. She had swiped a pale-pink color across her lips, just enough to be summery but not so pale as to match her lips to the skin on her face. She'd seen that look in a magazine and thought the models looked washed out.

"You look so pretty," Hannah said as she walked into the living room. Her hair had been trimmed into a long blunt cut, and she'd let it dry with its natural wave, but it didn't look messy. Her loose knit navy T-shirt dress had no holes. Boop wouldn't say it aloud, but Hannah already looked like someone's mommy.

"You're all dressed up," Hannah said.

"This isn't dressed up. Not really." Boop thought back to the days of hose and heels, satin and silk. "I was thinking you could drop me off to see Georgia and then hightail it out of here and go home to Clark. He's back in Kalamazoo, I take it."

Hannah smiled. "Yes, he is."

"Well, you were right. The good outweighs the hurt with Georgia. And I have lost enough people I loved." Nannie, Zaide, Marvin, and too many friends. When she was a little girl, she'd lost Tillie and Joe. Boop wasn't going to lose Georgia. Not while she had a choice.

"That's one bit of good news this morning. Here's another." Hannah placed a small pink tissue-wrapped bundle onto Boop's lap.

"What's this?" Boop's heart rate quickened. She knew.

"Open it," Hannah said.

Boop needed only to unfold one flap and see a pink edge with a fragment of embroidery to know for sure. It was her Miss South Haven 1951 sash. Despite all of the yearning, she hesitated to look at it, let alone touch it. She laid her hand on her chest as if pledging allegiance to the flag, and her heart pounded, maybe as rapid and strong as it had the day her name had been called, her dream realized. Maybe this was a mistake after all. Had Georgia, though imprudent, been right all along?

"Where on earth did you find this?"

"You know our Emma. She doesn't throw *anything* away. I had her overnight it."

Boop smoothed away the remaining tissue paper but didn't lift the fabric.

"Pop shouldn't have given it to us."

"Emma had it cleaned. It looks like new, but it's the real thing. Do you want me to unfold it for you?"

Boop laid her hands atop the cool satin, the hills and valleys of the embroidery caressing her palms. She shook her head. "Not yet."

"You should own all pieces of your life, good or bad," Hannah said. "They make up who you are."

With her uncertain relationship and delicate condition, Hannah was brave, not afraid of the truth.

Boop could learn a lot from her granddaughter.

Betty closed her hands into fists, not as a show of anger, but as a way to garner strength. "Do you mean that?"

"Of course I do."

"Then I want you to find out about Abe. Even if it's an obituary, I want to know."

"Are you sure?"

Boop needed certainty, even if that didn't come with answers. "I'm sure. And there's one more thing that's nonnegotiable."

"What?"

"After you drop me off to see Georgia, don't stop driving till you're home. It's time for answers for both of us."

It was no accident that Boop's purple cane coordinated with her lavender tunic—not that she had ever needed an excuse to accessorize. Not only did Boop need the cane to help her navigate the grid of hallways that comprised Lighthouse Rehab, but she also needed the fashion to avoid being mistaken for a patient. Boop walked slowly and deliberately, using the cane to keep her steady and also to alleviate some pressure. She headed up one corridor and down the next, past rows of wheelchairs and a small collection of walkers with tennis balls stuck onto their feet.

Boop didn't yet need either of those contraptions. She was grateful to be getting old. To be old. She had outlived Marvin and most of her friends. The fact that Georgia and Doris were still alive was an anomaly, she knew that, and didn't want to take it for granted, waste it, or have regrets. If Boop had been a Catholic, she would have crossed herself, but instead she just stared ahead and continued with the confidence and purpose of a visitor on a mission.

Georgia needed her.

And she needed Georgia. No matter what she did or didn't do, Georgia was family. Boop didn't turn her back on family.

Boop stopped and checked her reflection in the glass of a framed generic floral print. She'd had a similar ritual every day before stopping to see Marvin in the nursing home. Even when he didn't recognize her, Boop had always insisted on recognizing herself.

A few moments later, with anger set aside—perhaps shoved aside—and her tote bag behind her back, Boop stood against the open door. Georgia lay back in bed against a stack of pillows. She was dressed in a zipped peach terry-cloth housecoat, though it wasn't even six o'clock. Her hair was combed but not styled. She looked paler than usual, smaller too. How could that be? It'd just been a few days. Weren't they feeding her?

Georgia looked at Boop and smiled. "I wasn't sure I'd see you again."

"Me either." Boop smiled. "You look awful."

Georgia ran her hand over her hair and laughed. "I do, don't I?"

Boop stepped inside. The space was less crowded than a hospital room. Though the bed still had sidebars, there were no monitors, machines, or IV poles. A TV protruded from the wall on a metal arm. There were three institutional-yet-padded chairs, a small dresser, a nightstand, and two wide windows with vertical blinds that let in the remaining summer daylight. Without a word, Boop set a paperback on the bedside table next to a stack of sealed Jell-O cups, and then sat in the chair by the foot of Georgia's bed.

"You should tell them you don't like green Jell-O," Boop said.

"Does anyone like green Jell-O?"

Years ago, Boop would have slurped it down without a spoon, simply because it was forbidden. As soon as she and Marvin had agreed they wouldn't keep a kosher home, Boop learned the fine art of making fruit-and-marshmallow Jell-O salads and colorful, layered Jell-O molds.

"What does the doctor say?" she asked Georgia.

"That I'll be here two to four weeks, depending."

Georgia would recover. Maybe she'd get out early for good behavior, as if it were a prison. Boop wiggled herself up straight and tall in the chair. "And then what?"

"I don't know."

"What do you mean, you don't know? They're just going to push you to the lobby and tell you not to let the door hit you on the way out? There has to be a plan."

There were two things Georgia always had: a plan—and a backup plan.

"My only plan is to apologize again. And to make it up to you, if I can. Can you forgive me?"

"I wouldn't be here if I couldn't."

Georgia sniffled and inhaled so deeply her whole body expanded. Then she cried.

Though the betrayal would stick to Boop like a burr, relentless and prickly, she'd continue to pluck it off each time she noticed it.

"None of that," Boop said, handing Georgia a tissue.

"I'm just so grateful to get a second chance."

"You need more than that—you need a place to heal and rest when they're finished with you."

"I'll go home. I'm sure I can get some of my friends to help. I can hire someone."

"You'll do no such thing. You're coming home with me."

Georgia couldn't go back to Boca, where she had no family. Boop was her family. Her plans to move would have to wait until Georgia was literally back on her feet. "We'll set up the TV room as your bedroom and you'll stay as long as you need."

Georgia placed her hand over her heart. "Are you sure?"

Boop nodded, her throat thick, her heart bursting with the memory of herself and Georgia as little girls who thought they'd grow up and be next-door neighbors. Now they would be housemates.

With that, Georgia closed her eyes, and her chest began to rise and fall with slow, deep breaths. Boop watched her friend the way she had watched a sleeping newborn Stuart in 1952 and their fifteen-year-old dog, Lizzie, in the seventies.

Once Boop was satisfied the breathing would continue, she lifted her tote onto her lap and peered into the abyss. Wallet, a comb, a deck of cards, tissues, Tic Tacs, Life Savers, a compact, a comb. She set the tote onto the nightstand, then dug her hand in and around to the bottom and pulled out two abandoned lipsticks. She fiddled with them, waiting for Georgia to wake up.

Minutes later, Georgia opened her eyes. "You're still here."

"You bet I am." Boop held out the lipsticks to Georgia. "Pick one."

She placed the closed cases on the bed and Georgia opened each and examined the colors. One, a neutral mauve. The other, a glittery peach. Boop didn't care which one Georgia chose. That wasn't the point. "If you look good, you'll feel good—or at least you'll feel better." Boop believed that. "By the way, when was the last time you had a manicure?"

At first, Boop's daily visits to Lighthouse Rehab were all about Georgia. Boop sat in on consultations with the therapists and doctors. They walked the hallway, and Boop brought in blueberry muffins to share with the staff. Another day she ordered in Delightful Buddha to give Georgia a break from rehab food.

"You've already done so much for me. But could you do me a favor?" Georgia asked after winning yet another hand of gin rummy.

Boop was prone to sarcasm at serious moments, and *I just did* rushed through her thoughts. She resisted in deference to the circumstances. "Of course."

"I'm pretty sure that Charlotte in 209 could use a little Mauve Luster. And maybe a friend."

Georgia had always been good with people and names, but now she was citing lipstick colors too. Just the way to Boop's heart.

"That's the favor?"

"Yes. She was here before me and she doesn't get many visitors. I met her in the PT room. A nice lady. A little pale, perhaps. You know just what to do to lift her spirits, I'm sure of it."

"Knock, knock," Boop said through the open door of 209. She peeked in.

A woman sat in bed with a beige waffle-knit blanket draped over her legs. Hannah had brought a lightweight floral comforter with matching pillowcases for Georgia's bed to spruce her room up a bit. No beige waffle-knit for Georgia.

"Come in, come in," the woman said. "I'm Charlotte Levy, meniscus tear."

"I'm Boop Peck—"

"The one with the lipstick, yes, I know. Any chance I could have a look?" Charlotte motioned to her face like she was Carol Merrill from *Let's Make a Deal*.

"I just brought my own lipsticks to make Georgia feel better," Boop said.

"I should have my niece bring me something nicer to wear."

"It'll make you feel better."

Boop realized this was what Charlotte was asking for, a way to feel better as she healed. No one here considered the woman herself in 209, just the patient. Boop pulled a zippered case out of her tote bag.

"I cleaned them with alcohol before I came. Try what you like." Boop set a small magnifying mirror on the bed tray.

"Really?" Charlotte pulled the cover off each lipstick bullet and examined it. Then she went in for round two before applying, as Georgia had predicted, Mauve Luster.

"That color on your lips makes your cheeks look rosy," Boop said.

"Which is so important here."

240

"If how you feel is important, and you feel good wearing this, then you're right. Keep it. It's not my color." It definitely was Boop's color. "So, how has your day been? Had any visitors?"

Charlotte smiled. "Yes. You."

The day after she met Charlotte, and then every day for the next two weeks, Boop showed up at Lighthouse Rehab with as magical a bag as Mary Poppins. She went on her own rendition of rounds, ducking out of the way of nurses, therapists, doctors, nutritionists, visitors, and uninterested patients.

One day, as soon as Georgia headed to physical therapy, Boop loaned a hand-painted silk scarf to Poppy Miller in 226 and showed her how to tie it into a perfect droopy bow around her neck and as a bohemian head covering, and to drape it like a shawl, but one that wouldn't fall off.

For Charlotte, Boop unfolded a cotton throw and draped it over the footboard. It was blue with sunflowers. Definitely better than beige waffle.

In room 202, Maureen Turner's catawampus wisps of gray at her hairline behaved like Stuart's cowlick had when he was a boy. *Catawampus* was not a word Boop fancied associating with seventy-nine-year-old Maureen and her hip fracture. Luckily, Boop discovered a set of delicate floral barrettes that served as the solution.

That particular day, Boop learned she and Maureen had more in common than a fondness for L'Oréal Peach Fuzz. (The color suited Georgia best, but Boop knew she wouldn't mind sharing "the look.") Maureen had been an army nurse and a war widow; she'd grown up in Detroit and then moved to the suburbs when she married—and, like Boop, had moved to Skokie.

Growing up in Detroit in the thirties and forties wasn't an unusual origin story for a Michigander. It was the biggest city, with the most jobs. Or that's how it once had been.

If things had been different, Boop might have ended up in Detroit with Abe. Though New York had been their plan, Boop possessed the wisdom of hindsight. She understood that had they been together, their lives might have been different than expected. *What if* was the only question for which there was never a sufficient answer, because no one knew. No one could know. But maybe she could get closer to knowing.

"Did you ever hear of a store owned by a family named Barsky?" she asked.

"Barksy? No, can't say that I did. Why?" Maureen asked.

"No, it was Barsky. B-A-R-S—never mind. Just a memory. It's not important."

"All our memories are important. You should hang on to them as long as you can, don't you think?"

Boop knew Maureen was right. But that wasn't why she was there.

"Why don't you ask your daughter-in-law to bring you some different clothes? Wouldn't you like to get out of that housecoat? I'm sure you have something at home that looks less like Pepto-Bismol."

They laughed.

Way back when, before she'd become a bride and a housewife and a mother, Boop had wanted to share her passion and knowledge of clothes and makeup with others. In her younger imagination, she'd heard the click of high heels and the ping of a typewriter. In reality she heard shuffling slippers and institutional televisions with volumes turned up.

Fashion had always been a source of camaraderie and happiness for Boop, and she'd always believed it would bring others joy as well.

Better here and now than never.

The next day was manicure day.

Boop stepped out of Georgia's room and looked down the hall. She saw no one except Mr. Marco with the walker he called Lucille.

"I hope nothing happened to Natalie," Boop whispered. She sat on the chair she'd come to think of as "hers," where she'd left a cardigan hanging over the back in case of a chill. "She's always on time."

"I'm here!" Natalie barreled into the room and strode right to the edge of Georgia's bed. "I'm sorry I'm late. It's not professional. It's just that Piper came home a day early, which is great because I get to see her, but I'm finalizing the program for the pageant and working on the schedule for that day, which is taking more time than I'd thought."

"How can I help?" Boop asked. "Stuff envelopes? Yell at someone?"

Natalie chuckled, then blushed the color of pink peonies. "Would you consider being onstage to crown the new Miss South Haven?"

Boop stared at Natalie, and Georgia stared at Boop. Onstage at a Miss South Haven pageant? Boop wasn't sure she could do that.

"There must be someone better than me. A local celebrity? The mayor?"

"I think you're the local celebrity," Georgia said. "If you want to be."

"Think about it," Natalie said. "The last Miss South Haven crowning the current one. I think it would be perfect. And selfishly I could go out with a splash."

"What does that mean?" Boop asked.

"I just had another meeting with my accountant. It looks like this will be the last summer for the salon." Natalie pushed her wavy black hair away from her round face, eyes glimmering with tears.

Boop unzipped Natalie's case and pulled out a shimmery champagne nail polish for Georgia. She shook the bottle and then handed it to Natalie. "What happened?"

"I don't really have enough business to pay rent on the shop and the apartment between October and May. And the projections for the rest of the summer won't be enough to make up for it. Last year it was close, but I made it. I really don't want to uproot Piper before her sophomore year, but kids are resilient, right?"

"Are there any other options? It can't be so black and white," Georgia said.

She was right. The problem was green.

"I'll have to get a job but after I sell the furniture and equipment, I should be okay for a few months, and my parents will help a little. The most important thing is that Piper have stability. If it was just me I could live anywhere. On a friend's couch, in the back of the salon, but not with Piper. She needs a home."

"You're her home," Boop said. "But I have an idea." She whispered to Georgia. Georgia whispered back.

"Move in with us," they said in unison.

"What?" Natalie screeched.

"Move. In. With. Us," Georgia said, as if Natalie hadn't understood the words.

"I have plenty of room," Boop said.

"Have you seen that rambling old house?" Georgia asked. "You'd be doing Boop a favor. Both of us, actually. I'm moving in with her for a while."

"You barely know me. And I have a *teenager*." Natalie gulped. "Why would you do this?"

Boop had wanted a full house again; now she would have it. "I like you. I always have. You're kind and generous; you're a single mom who needs a break, and teenagers don't scare me."

San Diego would have to wait.

Natalie's eyes welled with tears as she filed Georgia's nails. "You're a lifesaver." She coughed as her voice cracked with sadness and gratitude. "But are you sure you don't mind helping us out?"

"Will you mind helping us?" Boop asked. "We're two old ladies who are pretty feisty."

Natalie laughed as she wiped away tears and streaks of mascara. "Of course not," she said. "That's what friends are for."

Chapter 24

BETTY

The lightweight bedspread pressed on Betty's legs as if she'd had her limbs buried under sand. She folded back the pink blanket and saw that her shoes and hose had been removed. She sat upright. How did she get here? Why did her head hurt? "I'm fine."

She knew she wasn't fine but that was what you said.

Nannie pushed gently on her shoulder, and Betty lay down again. "Forget about the fact that you knocked over half the girls and ran off the stage; you vomited, and you fainted. Heatstroke maybe. Exhaustion, definitely." Nannie fancied herself a superlative diagnostician. "Dr. Silver's on his way."

"I don't need a doctor; I need Abe." *Please don't send a doctor.* Nancy Green's words reverberated in her head. If Nancy was right—no. Nancy just wanted to believe that. But why wish that on anyone? "Please, just get Abe. I need to talk to him."

Nannie shook her head.

"What do you mean, no? Where's Abe? Didn't he follow us back to the house?"

"He's not here, dear, he was never here."

"I don't believe you. I heard his voice when I was running to the beach."

"He's back home with his family, in Detroit, remember?"

"He didn't come back?" What had Betty heard? Had his voice materialized from wishful thinking?

Nannie wiped strands of hair from Betty's forehead. "He didn't come back."

Betty turned her head away, tears dripping onto her pillow and into her nostrils.

"Summer romances end, sweetheart. That's just the nature of things like this. You'll meet a boy when you're at Barnard and this will all be a nice memory, I promise."

"A nice memory?" Betty turned her head to look at Nannie. "This wasn't just a summer romance! Abe has to take care of his mother. His brother just died. We're going to marry one day."

Betty thought that would shock Nannie, but she didn't look surprised. "I know you think that." Nannie patted Betty's hand. "But it never would have worked."

"You're wrong." Betty turned her face into the pillow. The same pillow she had once shared with Abe. She wished it still smelled like him. Did she have anything that smelled like him? Betty closed her eyes to conjure the talcum powder, hair cream, and sandalwood aftershave.

They had to let her talk to Abe.

Betty pulled her hand out from under her pillow and laid it atop her head. She opened her eyes and spotted her Miss South Haven sash folded on her vanity. She had wanted that so badly—but now it meant nothing. She'd ruined the day and the pageant for herself and everyone else. But that silly sash was now all she had of sweet, simple dreams come true. "I need to talk to Abe."

Nannie shook her head. "That's not going to happen, Betty. Even if he had come back, this thing between you would have to end."

"It wasn't going to end. He's moving to New York when he graduates so we can be together."

"Zaide and I never would have approved."

Betty didn't want to say she didn't care, but Nannie's stare said that she knew. "No matter how smitten you are, Betty, it was never going to happen. He's a *shegetz*."

She had never heard Nannie use that nasty word for a gentile boy. "How did you know that?"

"You don't think we know everything about our staff?"

Too bad you don't know everything about your granddaughter.

"But you couldn't have known. You hired him."

"Zaide hired him. I didn't stop him."

"Why did you let me go out with him?"

"I wanted you to be happy. And if I'd said no, what reason would I have given? Not that he wasn't Jewish. Zaide promised me it wouldn't cause a problem."

"Abe was raised Jewish. His father is Jewish."

"You know he's not Jewish in the eyes of God unless his mother is Jewish."

"You're not even religious. Why do you even care?"

"It's the way it is. Maybe Zaide and I have been too relaxed this summer, but we wanted you to feel grown-up while we could still keep an eye on you. My mother wouldn't have even let me date a boy who wasn't Jewish. She'd have sat shiva for me just for suggesting it."

"That's horrible."

Nannie set her hands on her hips. "What's not horrible is that we own a kosher resort and our customers are Jewish families. Good Jewish families who want to be with their own people. Those people trusting us and looking up to us is why you have everything you have."

"What would people say if my granddaughter had a *goyish* boyfriend, or worse—God forbid? Your heart will heal, and you'll find a nice Jewish boy at Columbia who wants a modern, pretty girl like you.

You'll earn your degree—the first in the family—have your career, and start a family." Nannie patted Betty's arm. "I'll tell you what—because you're upset, we won't even discuss what happened to the blue dress I found all in pieces, or how you invited your parents here without telling anyone."

Betty was stunned silent. In public she had always honored and obeyed her grandparents. But her bedroom wasn't public. What would Nannie say if she knew what had happened right on that bed? What might be happening inside Betty?

"Knock, knock," Tillie said.

Betty had forgotten about her parents. As much as she had wanted them there, she wished even more that they'd leave. She had wanted to impress them, not humiliate herself.

Tillie stood at the door, holding a tray of food at her waist. The one time Betty had asked her to come to South Haven, and there she was, feigning maternal affection. Or maybe attending the pageant was maternal, though Betty reasoned that Tillie and Joe figured it would be time for their annual visit anyway. Standing with the tray, Tillie looked like a cigarette girl, but with a longer skirt. Betty had never seen her mother do anything domestic, yet she looked too much like Tillie for her to seem a stranger. Would Betty look like her as she grew older? Gain that slight definition in her cheeks that were still plump and somewhat girlish? Betty didn't mind looking like her mother. It had won her a beauty pageant, after all. But Betty would grow out of her frivolity. She would never place her own dreams ahead of the fundamental needs of her child.

Her child.

Betty saw Nancy's face again. She was wrong. Nancy didn't know Betty. Any fullness of Betty's was from too many cheese Danish. She wasn't one of those girls who needed "a trip to Europe." Plus, she and Abe had been careful.

"Nourishment for the beauty queen," Tillie said.

As Betty flipped to her back, the odor of scrambled eggs churned her stomach.

"I'm not hungry."

Tillie set the tray on top of the dresser. At Betty's bedside, her mother bowed and placed her hands on her knees. "There's plenty of fish in the sea." She gently pushed hair off Betty's face.

Fish.

A tightness crept up into Betty's throat. She wanted to scream. Cry. No—

Betty escaped from her bed, shoved Tillie aside, and ran down the hall into the bathroom, where she vomited into the toilet.

Alone, Betty sweated and shivered and purged the worst day of her life.

Soda crackers.

Betty changed into her blue terry-cloth robe that hung on the back of the bathroom door. Back in her room, someone had set a bucket by her bed. She had nothing left to give it.

She climbed into bed and under the cover without speaking to Nannie or Tillie, but she felt Tillie staring. Betty glanced at her mother and Tillie averted her gaze.

"I'll go down and wait for the doctor," Tillie said. "Unless you want me to stay."

Betty shook her head and Tillie left, her footsteps out of the bedroom followed by her footsteps down the stairs.

"I know you're disappointed," Nannie said. "And I know it's hard to believe, but you'll get over him."

Disappointed? Was Nannie serious? Betty was heartbroken. Bereft. Confused. Nauseated. Terrified.

"Once you're feeling better . . ."

"You'll let me phone him? I promise not to stay on too long."

"No, that's not what I was going to say. Before you leave, you're going to apologize to Mrs. Bookbinder for your behavior." Nannie spit her words as if she couldn't get them out fast enough.

Betty had fainted and gotten sick and this was what Nannie cared about?

Dr. Silver stepped into the room. Joe walked to Betty and kissed her on the forehead. Betty turned her head away.

Why did her parents even bother?

Dr. Silver pulled Betty's vanity stool next to her bed and sat. "I heard you had a little fainting spell. And some nausea."

Betty nodded. "I didn't eat breakfast."

"Let's just make sure there's no infection." He pulled a tongue depressor out of his shirt pocket. "Say *aah*."

Betty opened her mouth and stuck out her tongue, though she was becoming more certain that that was not how he'd find out what they needed to know.

Dr. Silver turned to her family. "Betty's eighteen now; we'll need some privacy. I'll let you know what I find."

The doctor wasn't rushing to any diagnosis; neither should Betty. The ambiguous nature of his black medical bag and the stethoscope around his neck eased her worries.

Nannie shooed the others out the door.

"You too, Yetta," Dr. Silver said. "No exceptions."

Nannie argued, but the doctor did not relent. Nannie closed the door behind her, and Betty hoped she wasn't right outside eavesdropping.

Dr. Silver looked, listened, tapped, and pressed. Did her heart sound different now that it had been stomped on by her grandmother and possibly abandoned by Abe?

The doctor leaned toward Betty and furrowed his brows. It looked like he wore a giant caterpillar across his forehead.

"Tell me," Dr. Silver said. "When was your last cycle?"

Betty felt sobs gathering inside her. He knew. *He couldn't know.* "I don't really keep track. June, maybe? The end of May?" She fanned through the weeks in her head, needing to figure this out. "Maybe the middle of June?"

"Betty, could you be pregnant?"

"No!" She covered her face with her hands as her empty stomach turned somersaults.

"I don't mean to upset you. I'm going to ask you another personal and very specific question and it's important that you answer honestly. Even if it's embarrassing. Do you understand?"

Betty nodded. What could be more embarrassing than asking about the timing of her monthlies?

"Have you had sexual relations in the past few months?"

Betty uncovered her face and bolted upright. She wanted to say no, preserving her reputation, and she wanted to say yes, validating her and Abe's love—but in that moment she knew her words didn't matter. If it were true, she wouldn't be able to deny it for long.

Betty had heard whispers about what happened to girls who got into trouble. She had paid little mind except to roll her eyes and giggle. Illegitimate babies were more of a concept than a reality. One day a girl was in school, the next she wasn't. No one asked questions.

Then the girl was back in school six months later or the next term. No one mentioned a baby.

This shanda had never touched her circle of family or friends. Well, not that she knew of. Not until now. But as soon as Abe knew, he would come.

Dr. Silver cleared his throat. "We'll confirm with a blood test, of course."

"I can't tell my grandparents."

"They have to be told. Keeping this kind of secret won't be good for you or the baby."

Betty had never even told Nannie she'd kissed a boy; now she had to tell her *this*? Could anything be worse? "Will you tell them, Dr. Silver?"

He nodded without any hesitation, and Betty realized he'd likely done this before. At least now Nannie would have no choice but to let her telephone Abe.

Someone tapped on the door. Betty's heart pounded and she shuddered. She wasn't ready—not for any of this but certainly not to face Nannie.

"Betty, it's us. We can come back if you'd rather." Georgia's voice was light and summery, as if she hadn't a care in the world. Which she hadn't.

"Don't leave!"

The door opened and it was as if Betty's personal fairy godmothers had appeared by magic. The light in the hall shrouded Georgia and Doris in the shimmery glow of dancing dust particles.

"We passed Dr. Silver on the stairs. He says you need your rest. Your grandmother said you're suffering from exhaustion and sunstroke. Is that true?" Georgia said. She grabbed Betty's arm and lay fingers on her wrist to take her pulse, not that it would mean anything. Betty knew one day, it would.

"It's not exactly exhaustion," Betty said, wiggling her arm from Georgia's hold.

"You're scaring us," Doris said.

"That makes three of us." Or was that four? Betty needed to say it aloud. Her heart thumped so loudly she couldn't hear her own voice inside her head. "I think I'm having a baby."

Georgia and Doris gasped. "No!"

"Yes."

"You had sex?" Doris asked.

"Obviously," Georgia said. She reached her arms around Betty and held on tight. "What do you need me to do?"

Exactly that, Betty thought. She leaned into Georgia, who rocked her. Back and forth, back and forth.

"What are you going to do?" Doris clasped her hands in front of her as if to blockade herself, then she opened her arms and leaned onto Georgia for a group hug.

"I'm going to tell Abe," Betty said.

They broke apart the hug.

"And do you think you'll get married?" Georgia asked.

Betty nodded. There was no other option.

"But you said he wasn't Jewish," Doris said.

"You sound like Nannie. She'll change her mind. She'll have to."

Georgia opened her mouth wide enough to let out a scream, but she stayed silent.

Betty knew Irish married Irish. Italian married Italian. Catholics married Catholics (as long as their grandparents came from the same country). And Jews married Jews.

"I don't care," Betty said. "It doesn't feel wrong, even though it goes against everything I was raised to think is right."

Georgia set her hands on her knees and inhaled a deep breath. "I understand completely. Sometimes the connection is stronger than any logic or good sense."

"Yes!"

"You're bonkers!" Doris said.

"Just wait till you fall in love," Georgia said. "It doesn't always happen according to plan."

At that moment Georgia's ease dissolved into a wistful sadness— which was not at all like the Georgia Betty knew.

Doris hugged Betty. "I have to get back, but I'll visit tomorrow."

Betty nodded.

"And if anyone asks—I know—you're suffering from exhaustion," Doris said.

She scampered down the steps, and Betty knew she had rattled her friend but that Doris would guard the secret with her life. She turned to look at Georgia.

"Please tell me what's going on with you," Betty said.

Georgia shook her head in a perpetual no. "You have enough going on."

"I have a feeling it's going to be all about me as soon as my grandparents know about my situation. Distract me. Tell me about your guy. I know there is one, Georgia. He's making you sad. Who is he?"

"I can't tell you. It's too awful. You'll hate me."

"I just told you I'm having a baby. You can tell me anything. Nothing will ever make me hate you."

"You're not going to like what I say."

"Let me decide for myself. Do you love him?"

Georgia nodded. "Oh yes."

"Does he love you back?"

"I think so."

I think so was never the right answer.

"Did you go all the way?"

Georgia's faced flushed crimson.

"And you didn't tell me?"

"I thought you knew and didn't say anything because you didn't approve."

"How would I know?"

"Because you saw us together."

"What are you talking about?"

"It wasn't Marv and Eleanor on the dunes that night. I couldn't believe you didn't recognize the sweater."

254

It had been aquamarine, with pearl buttons, folded neatly. The way someone trained in a department store would fold a sweater. Georgia's family's department store. A tingle skittered across Betty's shoulders and up her neck.

"Oh my God. That was *you*. It was *you* we saw on the ground having . . . You're in love with Marv Peck?"

Georgia slapped Betty's arm. "It wasn't Marv." Georgia glanced side to side and behind her. "It was Sam Bloomfield," she whispered.

"Sam Bloomfield?" Betty whisper-yelled, trying to match the name with a face. "You mean MISTER Bloomfield? Oh my God, he's old!"

"He's not old, he's thirty-two. He's mature and sophisticated. I love him."

"He's married! He has children. And one on the way. Oh, Georgia. You're too smart to do that."

"Apparently not."

"The Bloomfields left," Betty said. "They're not coming back until next year. How did you leave it?"

"He told me he cared for me, and it was fun, but it was over." Georgia laid her head on Betty's lap, and Betty stroked her hair.

A few months earlier, Betty might have silently held up Georgia to a traditional standard, but that measure was no longer relevant. Disparaging thoughts about Sam Bloomfield ran through her mind, but her friend didn't need to hear them. Betty just wrapped her arms around Georgia and rocked.

"I guess we both lost our first loves," Georgia said.

Betty released Georgia. "I did not lose Abe. He doesn't know." For the first time since that morning, adrenaline rushed through her. "Georgia, take me to see him. Drive me to Detroit. Or drive me to a bus and I'll take a bus to Detroit. As soon as he sees me and he knows about the baby, everything will be fine."

"Betty, you haven't had a telephone call or letter in two weeks."

"Two weeks isn't so long."

"Two weeks is *too* long."

"But everything has changed."

"Has it? Abe doesn't know that. But he knew how important Miss South Haven was to you and he didn't show up."

"So, he was busy."

"Too busy to send a postcard or a telegram to wish you good luck?"

"But he loves me—he wouldn't just stop."

"Betty, he did stop. He might care for you but he's not showing it, he's not here. That's a choice. It doesn't take long to jot off a postcard, even if he can't call."

Betty's stomach churned—from fear or from the baby, she didn't know. What she did know was this baby would never have to wonder about love, or wish for it. Betty loved him or her already.

But maybe Abe's love was like her parents' love, contingent on convenience, conditional and logistical.

Or, for some reason she had yet to understand, perhaps Betty was the kind of girl who was easy to leave behind.

Chapter 25

BETTY

Georgia skedaddled out of Betty's house as soon as they heard rumblings downstairs. She promised to return the next day.

Betty huddled on her bed with pillows and blankets and a lifetime of stuffed animals. Precisely where the baby lay inside her, she didn't know. Instead of patting her stomach, she rubbed wide circles, to cover all her bases.

What was her family doing downstairs? How long were they going to keep her waiting? Were they expecting her to present herself? Who willingly walks into a fire?

Maybe her grandparents were contacting Abe. The act of marrying a non-Jewish boy was something they'd overlook, come to accept in time, but having a baby without a husband just wasn't done. She had heard about married college students. They could set up house in Ann Arbor while Abe finished school, and then it would be Betty's turn. They could even marry in Detroit, if that was easier for Abe's mother. She had just lost a son, but now she'd gain a daughter-in-law, a grandchild. Betty knew she and the baby wouldn't be a substitute for Aaron, but the woman deserved some happiness.

A few minutes later Nannie walked into the room, pulled out the vanity stool, and sat with a thud instead of her usual grace. Betty steeled herself for a verbal thrashing.

Nannie's face was long and drawn, making her look worn, beleaguered, even a little sloppy, as if she'd just dressed and hadn't yet smoothed her dress or tamed and pinned her hair.

"I'm sorry," Betty said.

Nannie shook her head and clicked her tongue. "Zaide and I are so disappointed, Betty. Our dreams for you were so big, but that hasn't changed. You'll go to Barnard, as planned. This is just a delay."

They'd found a way for her to have everything!

"Zaide has gone to tell the staff you're suffering from exhaustion, and that no one is to bother you. That buys us some time."

"Time for what?"

"Mother to the rescue." Tillie, now in a crisp white linen skirt suit, stood in the doorway. Her mother looked sterile and cold, sounded sharp and flippant. She didn't look forlorn at all; the maternal woman carrying scrambled eggs had vanished.

And since when did she refer to herself as *Mother*? Tillie's short toffee-colored curls tamed every hair in place. Her red lipstick had been reapplied with precision. Attention to fashion detail was the only thing Betty liked that she had inherited from her mother. Tillie sat at the edge of the bed, barely indenting the bedspread. "I'm ready, Betty. *We're* ready."

"Ready for what?"

"Joe and I—your father and I—we got it wrong with you, but we're ready to be parents now."

"You're having a baby?"

"No, darling."

An army of invisible ants stretched across her back, a warning. "Then what?" Betty lurched back and away. The touches, the gentleness, the motherly words. They crystallized. "You want my baby?"

"Yes. We want him, or her, to be *our* baby. Mine and Joe's, I mean, mine and your father's. We would move back here for good." Tillie looked at Nannie. "Just like your grandparents have always wanted. And the best part is *you* would be the baby's *sister*. No one would ever have to know."

Vomit rose in her throat. This was not the time for evening morning sickness, but throwing up on Tillie seemed what she deserved. Betty turned away, the ache in her chest threatening to split it open.

Tillie scooted closer, like an advancing army on the attack. Betty stood and retreated until she was against the open window. She breathed deep to settle her stomach and held the sill so tight she could have sworn splinters were working their way into her palms.

Tillie stretched out her arms, as if measuring the space between them. "You'd get to go to college next year, Betty. Right to Barnard as planned. Your grandparents would have me and Joe here helping with the business, and I'd get to be a mother. Everybody wins."

Betty released the sill, forcing her hands to her sides. "You wouldn't know how to mother a rag doll. You couldn't raise a pet, let alone a baby. Isn't that right, Nannie?"

Nannie stared at the floor and didn't lift her head or her eyes to look at Betty. This was the grandmother who had sewn her clothes and bandaged her knees and sung her to sleep. The grandmother who had convinced Betty she could be best dressed *and* most likely to succeed. The grandmother who had helped Betty apply to Barnard, who said she could be anything from a beauty queen to a fashion editor. Betty crossed her wrists low in front of her belly. At that moment, she knew with unwavering certainty where her baby was growing, and the bile in her throat turned to fire.

Tillie glanced at Nannie, then back at Betty. "Would you rather the baby be raised by a stranger?"

Betty tipped back her head, forced herself to guffaw, then looked at Tillie. "You are a stranger. You're also a lunatic. Stark raving mad! Nannie would never agree to this."

"Oh, darling," Tillie whispered.

"Stop arguing," Nannie yelled. "Betty, it's the only way."

The words hit her like someone had pelleted her stomach with rock-hard snowballs. It couldn't be. There was no way her grandmother thought Betty would give away her baby to Tillie or to anyone. How had Tillie convinced her?

"Nannie, what did she do to get you to think this was a good idea?"

Nannie looked away and then back at Betty. "She didn't do anything. It was my idea."

"No!" Betty screamed. She folded over, crushed by pain. How much more could she take? "Get out," she shouted. She lifted the night-table lamp, yanking the electrical plug from its outlet.

Tillie leaped toward her and grabbed her arm, twisting the lamp from Betty's grip. "Sit."

Betty sank to the edge of the bed, less out of compliance than of fatigue. She heaved and sobbed her words. "I need to tell Abe."

"You'll do no such thing," Nannie said. "If he were a Jewish boy, it might be different."

"Why do you care what people think? I'm your granddaughter. This baby will be your great-grandchild."

"And I'm doing this so he or she doesn't grow up a bastard. I'm doing it because I love you. This is the way it works; we marry our own. No matter what."

"Abe's parents didn't think so."

"And look at the mess that's made of things."

"This baby isn't a mess. It doesn't have to be. I know Abe will do the right thing when he knows." Betty needed to find a way to talk to Abe.

"There is no right thing," Nannie said.

"Says who?"

"I say." Zaide stood at the door without entering the room.

"Ira, I have it under control."

"I could hear her downstairs. Voices carry. I will not have anyone thinking my granddaughter is having a nervous breakdown."

She couldn't have a breakdown, she couldn't have a baby, she couldn't have Abe.

"You do have choices," Zaide said. "We just hope you make the right one, Betty."

She wasn't his bubbeleh anymore. But he said she had choices.

"Now keep your voices down." Zaide left the doorway.

Tillie sat next to her. "Here are your options. And you'd be wise to count your lucky stars, because most girls don't get choices. There's a home for Jewish unwed mothers on Staten Island in New York. It's the best place for girls in your situation. You can go there and have the baby and either this child can stay in the family, or a stranger can adopt it. Or . . ." Tillie locked the latch on the bedroom door and then stood against it. Betty didn't know if her mother was keeping Betty in or keeping others out.

"Or what?" Betty asked.

"Or we can get rid of it. There are real doctors who will do it."

"That's illegal!"

Nannie turned away and said nothing. For the first time in her life, Betty thought Nannie a coward, or worse.

"That's your answer if I don't want you to have it? Some mother you'd be."

"Your grandparents aren't going to allow you to have a baby and live here. And they aren't going to support you in a life somewhere else. What kind of life would you have unless you're married to a Jewish man? We'll make it like this never happened."

Betty hadn't felt the tears until that moment. They streamed down her face in anguish that transformed into resolve.

Betty pushed Tillie aside—in every way. She unlocked her bedroom door, sprang from the room, and ran downstairs.

Zaide was sitting in the kitchen, not looking up at Betty. "You have until the end of the week. Tillie will take the train with you to New York on Saturday. Until then, you will stay at home and recover from your bout with exhaustion and pretend everything is the same. Everyone will think you're going off to Barnard."

"I'm calling Georgia." Betty wasn't asking permission. The boldness surprised her more so than her grandfather.

"No need to tell your friends about your predicament. The fewer people who know, the better."

But the girls already knew, thank goodness. They were the only ones who would help her.

That evening, with her bedroom door open, Betty lay in bed, recovering from actual exhaustion and shock. Georgia rustled through childhood keepsakes at the back of the cedar closet in the corner of the room.

"Found it," she said.

Betty's child-size tackle box would transform into the perfect makeshift treasure chest. It had once served as a symbol of tomboyish fun and her bond with Zaide. On the banks of the Black River he'd taught her to bait a hook, to jiggle a lure, and to cast a fishing line. He'd taught her silence and patience and how to reel in a big one.

As Betty unlatched and opened the metal lid, she was accosted not by nostalgia but by indifference. The box still held a few hooks and lures, but they might as well have been bottle caps or broken pencils.

"I can't believe they want you to give away your baby, but I guess that's what girls do." Georgia rolled the Miss South Haven sash into as tight a coil as possible and placed it inside, wedging it into the main compartment, then shutting the lid.

"Not this girl," Betty said.

"They're putting you on a train."

"Not if Abe comes here first."

"And how are you going to make that happen?"

"I'm not," Betty said. "You are. Just go to Western Union and send a telegram that says I'm unwell. Then Abe will come."

"I can't, Betty. You know that. Your grandparents know *everyone*. And whoever they don't know, knows them. The telegraph operators read the telegrams in order to type them. Someone will tell just to get on your Nannie's good side."

"But if you send it, at least he'll know something is wrong."

"You shouldn't have to do this."

"Of course I shouldn't have to. They should let me go to him."

"That's not what I mean."

"You shouldn't have to chase Abe down to be with him. Or beg."

"Wouldn't you do anything to be with Mr.—I mean—Sam?"

"Anything? No."

"Then it's not love."

"I'm not going to fight with you, Betty, but I want what's best for you and it's not him. And it has nothing to do with not being Jewish or even that he got you into trouble. It's because he didn't come back. If Abe shows up because he thinks you're sick, is that really what you want? And then you'll tell him about the baby? Do you want him if he's only 'doing the right thing'?"

"Yes, I do!" Betty huffed. The person she had been—unfettered, joyous, hopeful, most likely to succeed, Miss South Haven—flashed before her eyes. She lay on her stomach, buried her face in her pillow that smelled like Cheer, and screamed all of her dreams away, except the one about her baby.

Finally she sat up, her throat raw, her voice quiet. Georgia was watching her, waiting. "I know you don't want to," Betty said, "but will you do it anyway?"

"Do what?" Nannie asked from the doorway.

Georgia clamped her lips. Betty stammered. "I asked Georgia to send my regards to Marv. Apparently, people are concerned about my well-being."

"And I'm not nuts about him, but I'll do it, because Betty is my best friend."

The next morning Betty waited for Georgia. She didn't show up. Betty sat by the window in her bedroom, avoiding her parents until she couldn't wait any longer. She trudged downstairs and telephoned the resort, hoping her grandfather didn't answer the phone. As Betty relayed her nonchalant message to Anita at the front desk, Georgia knocked on the front door and Joe let her in.

The girls walked upstairs in silence. This time Betty shut her door.

"I think your grandmother followed me," Georgia said. "She was at the Western Union office when I arrived and interrogated me about the telegram I was there to send, so I left. You're going to have to find another way."

Betty took meals in her room when she could stomach them. Her parents and grandparents wanted to send her away and then steal her baby. She couldn't bear to be in their presence; it was hard enough to be in the same house.

As her anger snowballed, it gathered fear and sadness. She was an adult and they thought they could make decisions for her; they thought she'd hand over her and Abe's baby and go to college a carefree coed. Betty knew that was an impossibility for her heart, but could they force her? Not if she had Abe by her side.

Not if they were married.

That night Betty forced herself to stay awake well past midnight. It wasn't ideal, but it was the only way, and once Abe knew he'd be glad she'd awakened him. She crept down the stairs in her bare feet in the dark, padded to Zaide's office, and shut the door behind her without making more than a faint click. She would have to whisper, but the switchboard wouldn't be crowded with voices. Nor would she likely know the overnight operator.

Betty carried the phone behind the desk, where she sat on the floor, guarded by bookcases. She lifted the receiver to her ear and placed her index finger into zero.

The office light turned on, blinding her.

"Go to bed, Betty." It was Tillie, unglamorous with her hair in a kerchief and no makeup. "Just hang up and I won't tell your grandparents."

Betty stood in defeat, but just for the moment. "You couldn't be a good mother so you don't want me to be one? Is that why you're stopping me? You say you love my father. Well, I love Abe. I don't care if it's not perfect, or expected, or right."

"You should care. It won't be good for the baby to be raised under those conditions."

Betty seethed. This woman who had ostensibly dumped her was suddenly concerned with propriety and conditions? How did Tillie know what was right for Betty or a baby?

"I know you won't find this hard to believe, but when we had you, Joe and I weren't ready to be parents. That's why you grew up here. It was best for you. Don't you think it was hard for us? That it's still hard?"

"No, I don't." Even if it were true, it was too late for Betty to ever believe it.

"That just shows you how little you know about being a mother," Tillie said.

Was Tillie claiming to love Betty? That made her feel as nauseated as morning sickness. "You don't really believe you're fit to be anyone's mother, do you?"

Tillie snatched the phone from Betty. "You should have gotten knocked up by a Jewish boy. At least then we'd be planning a wedding."

The next morning Betty faced facts. Nannie stopped Georgia from sending a telegram. Tillie thwarted her telephone call. A letter to Abe would arrive after she'd left for Staten Island, but at least he would know about the baby. Abe could come and rescue them both. Staten Island was all the way out east. He'd have to drive or take the train, leave his mother, miss classes.

But what if weeks or months passed and he didn't come? What if it wasn't just the distance that stood between them but the fact that he didn't love her anymore? Had he ever?

Didn't he wonder where her letters were? The last letter she'd written was a few days before the pageant. Wasn't he worried? Even curious?

Sadness washed over Betty. She wanted to climb into bed and never get out again. But this wasn't only about her anymore. There was a baby inside her who needed a father—and to make that happen, she'd need a husband.

Betty walked to her desk and pulled out a sheet of paper.

She clomped down the stairs and through the living room, folded paper in her hand. As she glared at her mother, swear words tickled Betty's lips. But that would accomplish nothing. Maybe Tillie and Joe were the ones suffering from exhaustion, since they'd been charged as her guards, or maybe it was Betty's self-assuredness, but neither of them rose from their seats, asked where she was going, or tried to stop her. She pushed through the front door and allowed it to slam behind her.

A minute later she sat on a beach bench and slowed her breathing.

Betty smoothed her green polka-dot dress, glad she'd chosen something feminine and cheerful, yet modest. Glad it still fit. She combed her fingers through her hair and rested her hand on her stomach.

I'm doing this for you.

Betty tapped on the door of Stern's Summer Resort cabin 7A. It was one of the most premium cabins on the property, its wood siding painted to match the sand, with two small bedrooms, and a sitting room that faced the lake. She noticed the movement of the panel curtains and remembered when her worst days were washing and pinning the lace.

A moment later the door opened.

"Hey, Betty Boop. I was hoping I'd get to see you before we left."

No matter what happened next, everything would be different from now on, even what she called him. "Hi, Marvin. Are you alone?"

"Yes. My mother's playing cards."

"I guessed she might be."

"I've been asking about you, but your grandparents won't let anyone see you. Are you feeling better?"

"No." Betty held out her hand and looked into his eyes. They were light brown rimmed in amber.

Marvin pressed his palm against Betty's and wove his fingers through hers. "Tell me what happened."

The grasp did not resemble Abe's but was strong just the same. Betty held on tight and stepped inside the cabin she'd cleaned beside Zaide, just a few months earlier. She sat on the edge of the settee, hands on her knees to keep them from knocking.

Marvin didn't wait for her to speak. "Fall semester must be starting soon."

"Don't play along with the charade, please. You've always been honest with me."

"I wasn't sure you liked that about me."

"I think it's what I like best."

"You're not going to Barnard, I take it."

"You know I'm not. There must be gossip."

"I don't listen to gossip, not when it comes to you. If you tell me you're going to Barnard, well then, you're going to Barnard."

"I wish I were. They're sending me to a home."

"What kind of home?"

"Are you going to make me say it?"

Marvin moved next to her. "Nah," he said. He draped his arm around her. It was the closest he'd gotten to her since the night of the bonfire. Some girls might think he was trying to take advantage, knowing that she wasn't innocent, but Betty felt compassion, not a come-on. She scooted closer, and Marvin held on to her a little tighter. She didn't ask him to stop.

"Please don't think less of me," she said.

"Don't be ridiculous. It's Barsky who's the louse. Do you want me to take him out? I know someone . . ."

Betty gasped. "No!"

"Good," Marvin said. "I was half-kidding. Anyway, I'm more of a lover than a fighter."

"That's what I was hoping."

Abe wasn't coming back. Whatever happened to him, wherever he was, Betty didn't figure into his plan.

It was time for a new plan, one where there was no train, no horrid home for wayward mothers, no Tillie.

"I made a list," Betty said. She handed Marvin the paper. "Read it out loud."

Marvin swallowed. "'Why I should marry Betty Stern.'" He lowered the paper, his hands trembling. "What does this mean?"

Betty looked at Marvin and counted to three inside her head. "It means I want to marry you. If you'll raise this baby as your own. I'll be a good wife; you know I will. I need you, Marvin. They're going to take this baby away from me. You can stop that from happening. I'll never mention Abe, I promise, or anything about this summer. We can pretend we were planning this all along, just making sure by seeing other people. I know your father wants you married. We both win."

"You don't love me," Marvin said.

Betty couldn't lie. "I will learn to love you."

Marvin kissed Betty with an enthusiasm she then imagined had been building all summer. She placed her arms around his neck and forced herself to kiss him back.

Nannie pulled Betty out of the cardroom, where she and Marvin were talking to his mother. "You cannot marry Marv Peck." Nannie scowled.

"I can't please you, it seems. Well, I'm eighteen, and he's a nice Jewish boy. I can do what I want." Betty lowered her voice to a hush. "And he is going to raise this baby as his own. Problem solved."

Nannie was silent. Betty had stunned her speechless.

"Your parents are going to be very disappointed," she said at last.

"That will make three of us then."

Coming to this agreement with Marvin had emboldened Betty. She was going to be a married woman, a mother. She'd have a family of her own whom she would never betray.

"I never thought you could be taken advantage of so easily," Nannie said. "First Abe, and well—you know." Nannie waved her index finger in circles. "Now Marv and marriage!"

"No one has taken advantage of me, Nannie." Her grandmother's doubtful stare dared Betty to continue. "It was one hundred percent my idea to get married, not Marvin's."

"Don't be naive, Betty. He's already in love with you." Nannie's sharpness surprised her. "It's what he's wanted all along. Otherwise he'd never go along with this."

Betty supposed she had already known. "I thought you would be happy."

"I would have been happy if you were a nice girl going off to college and then fell in love with a nice Jewish boy."

Now Nannie cared about love? Betty wasn't having it. "Don't worry about us, Nannie. You don't have to do a thing. We'll elope and then go to Skokie."

College and a New York City career as a fashion editor seemed like they had been part of a dream, and now Betty had woken up.

"You'll do no such thing." Nannie started back to the cardroom. "I suppose I'll get used to the idea. We wanted so much more for you, Betty."

Where was the grandmother that had defended Betty's rights and bolstered her confidence? She missed that Nannie. Maybe more than she missed Abe.

"Nannie, for the record, Abe didn't take advantage of me either."

Chapter 26

BOOP

Filled rooms filled Boop. When Natalie and Piper moved into their bedrooms upstairs, and a bed and dresser transformed the downstairs TV room into recovery central for Georgia, the house hummed with conversation, footsteps, laughter. It sounded like a home.

While Boop's nuclear families had always numbered three, in the off-season often her grandparents' cousins and friends visited for weekends and holidays. During the summer, her house may have been emptier, but her life had been jam-packed—like now.

Boop thought of Hannah. No news meant that she and Clark were talking—that they were communicating.

Things were falling into place.

Now Boop just had to get through the pageant.

The next day, Natalie rehearsed her welcome speech and reviewed the schedule. Georgia planned her day with Charlotte and Poppy (the Lighthouse girls, Boop called them) so they could sit together in the auditorium. Maureen was still a patient; they'd promised to show her pictures.

The last time the house was abuzz with this much Miss South Haven chatter, Boop boasted a twenty-four-inch waist and walked from room to room with a book on her head. The sights and sounds set Boop's heart alight, especially Piper, who was pleasant and polite and not just for a teenager. Boop knew she was happy to stay in South Haven, and to have her own room. Boop had given her a key, though she never locked the door. She hoped the gesture conveyed that this was Piper's home now.

She and Georgia set the table for a Delightful Buddha dinner.

Boop leaned against the kitchen counter. She was blessed. When was the last time the house had thumped with the heartbeat present during her childhood? She closed her eyes and leaned back, as if doing so would allow her to record not only the voices, but the humanity, and to safeguard it all for later.

"Are you ready for tomorrow?" Natalie asked as she poured water into tumblers.

Boop opened her eyes. "That depends," she said. "I don't have to say anything, right?"

"No, but I'd like to introduce you as Miss South Haven 1951. And I thought you might want to wear your sash so we could get a good picture."

"You can introduce me, but I'm not sure about the sash. It's not really my style anymore. My pageant days are far behind me."

"Not anymore," Piper said.

Out of the mouths of teens.

Later, Boop stepped onto the porch to watch the sunset and found Piper sitting alone, as teens were apt to do. Boop didn't ask where Natalie was, lest Piper think her presence wasn't enough. She didn't ask if anything was wrong, or what was "up." Boop just smiled and Piper smiled back.

They each sat in a chair without talking. Words weren't necessary to keep someone company. That was a good thing, since words were clattering around in Boop's brain. She had won a beauty pageant. What would a present-day audience think of that? There were no photos to show how she looked that day—would they believe it?

"Mrs. Peck," Piper said. "Can I ask you a question?"

"I'd love it if you called me Boop; everyone does."

Piper shrugged.

"Whenever you're comfortable, you just switch to Boop, okay? And if you're not, that's fine. I'm sorry, me with my instructions. What were you going to ask?"

"Can I see your Miss South Haven sash? I'm really into vintage."

Boop smiled at the trendy term for *old*. She hadn't unwrapped the sash. The fabric had her lost dreams woven right into it. What could happen if she looked at it or even tried it on?

"Come upstairs."

Boop handed Piper the sash, still wrapped in tissue. With the abandon of a child with a birthday gift, Piper opened the paper and lifted the end of the sash. It cascaded toward the floor.

Hannah had been right: it looked like new—iridescent pink with soft black lettering and white satin trim.

"Try it on," Piper said.

Piper needn't bear witness to Boop's baggage. All the girl knew was that a long time ago, and not so far away, Boop had won a beauty pageant. This beauty pageant. She lowered her head and Piper placed the sash over it, resting the fabric on her right shoulder and over her chest, still as pliable as it was all those years ago, falling at and hugging her left hip.

Piper stepped back. "That must bring back a lot of good memories."

Boop shoved aside that day's aftermath. "I guess it should," she said. "Do you know they read our measurements aloud?"

"No, they didn't," Piper said.

"They did. It was a beauty contest—a tradition in town."

"Then why did they stop having it?"

"Because I ruined it."

"How could one girl ruin a beauty pageant for an entire town?"

Boop had never considered the power Nannie and Zaide had wielded over a South Haven institution. They hadn't just taken the pageant from her, but from everyone.

"My grandparents didn't want a reminder of how I'd embarrassed them. I kind of made a mess of things that day. I ran out and got sick."

"No offense," Piper said. "Sounds kind of selfish of them. I bet it was worse for you than for them, right?"

Boop smiled at Piper's kind and easy insight. "Has anyone told you you're very wise?"

"I keep trying to tell my mom that."

Boop guffawed as she smoothed the sash and the embroidered letters tickled beneath her fingers. She had never seen herself as Miss South Haven. Not in a mirror, nor in a photograph, until the one Natalie had shown her. She walked to the corner of her room and looked into the cheval mirror.

An old lady with a beauty queen's sash. That's what Boop saw. Then she startled at a glimpse of Betty behind her, toffee-colored curls, red lips, bright eyes, and a smile revealing hopes and dreams unmarred by disappointment, heartache, or grief. Boop swirled around to get a closer look—but Betty was gone.

Though maybe she didn't have to be.

Chapter 27

BOOP

Boop stared into the audience. What had she been thinking? How could she have allowed Natalie to talk her into this? The auditorium was filled with pageant parents who wanted to see their daughters win a trophy, a tiara, and a check. Who the heck was she to be sitting on the stage, let alone thinking she should be wearing her ancient, short-lived title across her chest? Who cared that she had been Miss South Haven?

Then she saw them. Natalie, Piper, Georgia, Charlotte, Poppy, Hannah—and Clark. Hannah and Clark. Boop didn't need to know how or what, though she reasoned Hannah would tell her. Even without details, relief flooded through her. Hannah would get her chance.

Piper had helped Boop choose her robin's-egg-colored suit with the tulip sleeves she'd last worn for High Holidays three years ago. Natalie and Georgia had had coffee and warm blueberry muffins waiting on the kitchen table when she'd walked downstairs at seven o'clock this morning. Sitting on this stage, reclaiming a piece of herself, was the kind of thing Betty would have done—if she could have.

Natalie stepped to the microphone. Boop closed and opened her eyes, an attempt to remain present. She didn't want to remember Mrs.

Bookbinder tapping on the microphone, but the sound resonated in her ears.

Boop focused on Natalie, and the past faded—dear Natalie, who'd followed her dream to own a nail salon and her heart to raise her daughter in a place they both loved. Boop believed it was a privilege to help her and Piper have a home and fewer worries, like she believed it had been her duty to tell Hannah her story.

"I'd like to introduce Boop Peck," Natalie said after welcoming everyone to the pageant. "She will be crowning our new Miss South Haven because she was the last Miss South Haven in 1951."

Applause rumbled through the auditorium as Boop leaned into her cane and rose. Some people slow-clapped, some fast-clapped. Her friends and family stood, followed by everyone in the room.

Boop clasped her hands and bowed her head. Her throat tightened in a way it hadn't since Marvin's funeral. She swallowed the viscous pride along with an equal mass of sadness as she allowed her past to rest in peace.

There were no flashbulbs, just smartphones held in the air, lenses pointed in her direction. Boop stared straight ahead. This time she didn't run.

"It's time," Natalie whispered.

Wasn't it over?

"The pageant, it's time." Natalie led Boop back to her chair.

Time trickled forward as twenty teenage girls marched across the stage. They were both more mature and more naive than Boop had been at the same age. They turned and twirled, answered questions about their goals and education, and noted their connections to South Haven as they posed in front of the judges, wearing modest summer dresses.

After computer calculations, Boop was handed a card with the winner's name.

"Miss South Haven 2017 is . . ." Boop cleared her throat and double-checked the card. "Ms. Jennifer Morgan."

As clapping thundered, the petite, green-eyed, blond, Michigan State trumpet-playing agri-business major gasped, covered her face with her hands, and then lowered them to reveal a wide smile. Boop outstretched her hand and Jennifer stepped next to her.

Boop placed the sash over Jennifer's head and laid it on one shoulder. It was time someone else wore this title. "A little advice from an old lady?" Boop asked.

"Of course."

"Save all this. Even when you don't think it's important anymore." Boop tugged lightly on the sash and glanced at the tiara. "A long time from now, you might be very glad you have them."

Jennifer nodded as she turned toward the crowd. Then she looked back at Boop. "I will! I promise! This is the best day of my life."

Boop smiled but hoped that wouldn't end up being true. God willing, Jennifer's best was yet to come.

Was it possible that the best—or something close to it—was yet to come for Boop as well?

Hannah walked up onto the stage, hugged Boop, and helped her down the steps. "You did great."

"Thank you for coming," Boop said. "And I'm glad you brought Clark. Does this mean what I think it means?"

"It means we're together," Hannah said. "The rest is to be determined."

"Sometimes it takes a long time to get things right," Boop said.

Hannah looped her arm through Boop's. "I was thinking the same thing."

Boop and Hannah sat at the back of the auditorium, watching Piper and Natalie collect discarded programs and carry recycling bins outside. Clark and Georgia had driven the Lighthouse girls home.

"I don't know how to say this," Hannah said.

Boop's thoughts flitted from tragedy to tragedy. She knew Hannah wouldn't keep a secret if her dad or sister were sick, or in trouble. She'd just said she and Clark were together, although tenuously. Georgia was healing. Was this about Doris?

There was no way Georgia would have kept something from Boop about their friend. Not now.

That left Abe.

She'd ignored that she'd asked Hannah to look for news about Abe. Boop chose to believe Hannah was looking and hadn't found anything. But that was presumptuous—with a heaping helping of a rosy outlook on the side. It was something Betty would have done.

Boop's heart hammered against her chest. That couldn't be a good thing. "You found Abe."

Hannah nodded.

"And he's dead."

"No!" Hannah shouted, her voice echoing through the room. "He's nearby."

"Nearby where?" Boop's voice faltered.

"He's spent the past fifty years or so in South Bend. I found his granddaughter. Her name is Becca and she lives near him and sees him all the time. I told her you were an old friend who was looking for him."

Boop's heart fluttered in a way it hadn't in ages. It was not a medical episode, but affection and warmth, tinged with nervousness. She'd felt it the first time Abe had looked at her from across the lawn. "Did she tell him?"

"Yes."

"Does he remember me?"

"Do you really have to ask?"

"We're in our eighties, yes, I have to ask."

"Of course he remembers you."

Tears sprang to her eyes. She hadn't expected that. Not after so long. "How is he?" Boop asked.

Hannah kissed her cheek, stood, gazed behind Boop, and nodded. "You can see for yourself." She walked away, and Boop shivered, despite the midsummer temperatures.

A sob collected in her throat. She couldn't turn around. This was what Betty had longed for, what Boop had packed away. Mourning Marvin had been sad and arduous. Boop was too old to turn and face more heartache.

But she had to turn around. For Betty's sake. For her own. For what was, and wasn't, and what might have been.

Boop shuddered, then turned.

And after all this time, he still looked like William Holden.

Even from a distance Abe's blue eyes pierced her. They weren't ordinary blue—nothing about Abe had ever been ordinary—but a special blue that matched the lake in the early morning. She shivered and her heart pounded from fear and excitement. She recognized the patter of her youth. That was Betty's heart pounding, though decades earlier she'd painstakingly detached it from her consciousness. Now it thumped loud and strong. Betty's heart had been part of her all along. And now it beat freely. Abe had *been* Betty's heart, and his proximity enlivened her beyond the words stuck in her throat, beyond the sadness that lingered in her thoughts.

Abe pushed aviator glasses up on the bridge of his nose. The style was both outdated and on-trend. Either way, they magnified his eyes, and Boop's insides prickled. His circle of hair was as white as if it had been bleached. He moved toward her. He smiled and dimples emerged, deeply cushioned in his skin.

"I'd recognize you anywhere, Betty."

She warmed with a flush. His voice was the same. No, it was better—deep and familiar but with the tenor of a life well lived. "No one has called me Betty in a long time."

"What should I call you?"

With Abe she would always be Betty. "Betty is fine."

"May I sit?"

Boop nodded.

Abe sat, leaving a chair between them. "Where shall we begin?" he asked.

Boop had always considered a conversation with the Abe she had known—not an old-man Abe. She had pictured him as she'd last seen him, driving away. He was not that boy anymore. But he knew what that boy had done.

"Perhaps you can tell me why you didn't call or write or come back to Stern's that summer. Even to say goodbye."

"You never answered my letters."

Letters? What letters? There were never any letters. Boop began to shake.

"You never wrote me any letters. All I got from you were a few postcards."

Abe shook his head as he spoke. "Betty, I wrote to you almost every day for a month, asking for your forgiveness, explaining everything. My mother lost her marbles after Aaron died; I couldn't leave her. I didn't go back to school, but I wanted you to go to Barnard." Abe looked down at his hands as if examining a lifetime of wondering.

He hadn't abandoned her.

"No one gave me any letters. What did they say?" Fury simmered beneath her words—what had her grandparents done?

"They said that I loved you. That I wanted you to write to me from Barnard and tell me everything. I asked you to wait for me."

Boop felt woozy, as if realizing her loss for the first time. "I couldn't go to Barnard."

"Because you decided to marry Marv Peck, which your grandfather was only too happy to tell me."

"I didn't know you were here that day."

280

"I knew they wouldn't tell you. I thought Georgia might, but she didn't know about the letters. When I drove away, I knew I'd lost you. I didn't understand why you got married so quickly. Though I remember Marv had a thing for you."

Boop rested her left hand on Abe's right. "I married Marvin because—" She couldn't say it.

"Why, Betty? To hurt me because you thought I left you?"

"No," she said. "Because I was pregnant."

Abe swayed and grabbed the seat of his chair as if he was about to fall. "Excuse me?"

"I married Marvin because I needed a husband. I was going to have a baby. Our baby."

Abe glanced at Boop's midsection as if trying to imagine it, as if he wished to lay a hand there, innocently and tenderly, and feel a kick. "A baby? Why didn't you tell me?"

Fire and forgotten fears burned inside her. "I tried. They wouldn't let me. They convinced me you didn't care. And they were going to send me away. And take the baby." Boop recoiled at the memory of her own mother wanting to raise the baby. What if she had agreed?

"I would have asked you to marry me."

Boop gasped. Her instincts had been right. "I so wanted to believe that." She looked away, ashamed that in that moment she was wishing away the life she'd known for the one she hadn't.

Abe touched Boop's face and turned it toward him. "What happened to the baby?" He gulped, cleared his throat, and looked into her eyes. "I haven't met Hannah, but I talked to her briefly. Is she my granddaughter?"

Boop saw tears mixed with hope. A longing sparkle had replaced the mischievous glint of long ago. "No." She patted Abe's hands as a way to soften a blow he didn't know was coming. And to soften it for herself, even though she did. "I lost our baby."

Boop had never said it aloud. Back then it was an incident, not a hardship. She knew her grandparents, and even Marvin, had been relieved. Her grief had been swept away like sand from the porch.

"Oh, Betty." Abe looked away and sniffed. "I'm sorry."

She allowed him a few moments to grieve a child he never even knew had been a possibility. Boop understood the instantaneous and unexpected hole that a child created in your heart. She felt it now. After all this time.

"But you were okay?" he asked.

"Not at first," she said. "But a year later I had my son, Stuart. I can't imagine my life without him."

"I understand," Abe said. "But still. That would have been something, huh? If things had been different."

"Indeed."

Abe cleared his throat. "Maybe this is none of my business, after so many years, but was he good to you? Were you happy?"

Boop gulped away unexpected reticence. "Yes. I was happy." Boop smiled at Abe, looking right into his eyes. "I'm blessed. One son, two granddaughters, two great-grandsons, and another great-grandchild on the way." She hesitated. "But I missed you for a long time. I wondered what we might have been." Then Boop lowered her voice to a whisper as if she wasn't sure anyone should hear her. "I also wondered who *I* might have been if I hadn't gotten pregnant. But I did." She composed her barrage of thoughts and plucked out two. "Did you marry? Have children?"

"I married a few years later. Nora and I were happy together for almost fifty years before she died of lung cancer. We had a good life and a lot of fun together. And I loved her. We had three daughters, seven grandchildren, and I have eight greats so far. Becca is our youngest granddaughter—she's the one who spoke to Hannah."

Boop smiled at the thought of Abe's large family. "Nora must have been a lovely woman for you to love her for so long."

"She was. You might remember her. She worked for your grandparents a few summers. Her maiden name was Rosen. Back then she went by Eleanor."

Boop smiled wide, knowing that Eleanor had gotten whom she'd wanted all along. Marvin would've gotten a strange kick out of that story. Boop placed her hands on her knees and braced to stand.

"Would you like to meet Hannah and my dear friends Natalie and Piper? They're probably in the parking lot, waiting to see if we ever come out."

Abe chuckled. "Becca is out there too."

"I hope you'll come back to the house. We're just ordering Chinese but you and Becca are more than welcome."

"I'd like that," Abe said. "If you're sure."

Boop had never been surer of anything.

After dinner, Boop and Abe sat on the porch alone. They stared into the indigo sky, which, as always, promised a resplendent wash of color to come.

It was time for Boop to embrace her inner Betty again, to pursue happiness without regret or guilt, as if she expected only good things to happen.

"I don't want to leave," Abe said. "I got a hotel room."

Boop blushed.

"No, no." Abe laughed a deep, sweet laugh. "Just so I can see you in the morning. And maybe the morning after that? Or is it too much?"

Boop gulped away her wishes as they became a reality. "It's just right."

Hannah knocked on the door and then opened it, poking her head outside. "Cake and ice cream are ready. We also have blueberry pie, shnecken, and there might be a Manhattan or two in here. It's time to party like it's 1951."

Boop laughed. "We have a lot to celebrate."

Reconnecting with Abe after almost seventy years had been the final puzzle piece to Boop's life. This did not disparage the years in between; it simply made the picture whole.

If that wasn't bashert, what was? Would Nannie agree it was meant to be? Why did Boop wonder when the answer no longer mattered?

What mattered was that Doris had been right all along: you're never too old to find love and throw a good party.

EPILOGUE

HANNAH

A few months later

Dusk fluttered over South Haven like a sheer curtain dangling from the sky. A white frame tent, with the sides rolled down to mimic walls with windows, draped the back patio of the Stern family home. A dozen or so guests mingled under the tent beneath the sky, all swathed in fading sunlight and illuminated by flickering candles.

Hannah turned the front doorknob. Unlocked as usual. She tapped open the front door with her hip, and once inside, she pushed it closed with her foot. She set the box of burgundy dahlia corsages and thistle boutonnieres onto the arm of the sofa before lifting them again, eager to deliver each to its recipient. These flowers best matched fall sunsets.

Natalie walked in from the kitchen, her ankle-length dress with a handkerchief hem made her look like a princess, the way its soft skirt sashayed when she walked.

"How are things going here?" Hannah asked.

"A little hectic, but now that the heaters are set up it'll all be fine. Everything is under control. You just get upstairs."

"And Boop?"

"Your grandmother is amazing. You know that."

Natalie spun and her skirt spun with her, which was the best part.

Hannah waddled through the living room and up the steps to the landing, where she stood and caught her breath. She held out her left hand, as she was prone to do, and the diamond sparkled. Marriage wouldn't make Hannah complacent; it would make her even more determined to get it right. She had trouble believing there was ever a time she doubted Clark—or herself.

She'd relearn that lesson every day of her life if she had to.

Hannah couldn't believe they'd planned a wedding in three months, but Peck persistence had paid off.

"Ready or not, here I come." Hannah stepped inside her grandmother's bedroom. Doris and Georgia were seated at the window.

Boop swiveled side to side and smiled as if she held the secret to life. Hannah supposed she did.

"Boop, you're the most beautiful bride I've ever seen," Hannah said.

"We agree," Doris said.

Georgia nodded.

Her grandmother's skirt was the color of a ripe peach and fell to the middle of her calves in a cascade of silk chiffon. The matching shell reflected color onto Boop's cheeks, not that she needed it. There was a natural glow to brides, even at eighty-five. Of course, that didn't prevent Boop's use of a shimmery lipstick. She was still Boop, after all. A rose-gold watch she had worn as a girl shifted and settled onto her wrist.

Something old.

Hannah held out the iridescent bugle-beaded jacket made to match Boop's skirt and blouse. Boop had purchased her ensemble at Kleinfeld during their girls' trip to New York. She'd slipped her arms into the sleeves. "It's like *buttah*," they'd said at the store, where they were crowded among shoppers with their entourages and tourists with their smartphones. But they were right. Like butter.

Something new.

Hannah removed her dress from the closet, slipped off her simple rose-colored maternity dress over her head, then reached into her bag and withdrew a strand of pearls.

"They're beautiful," Doris said.

Hannah dangled them in front of Boop. "Dad gave these to me when I turned eighteen. Will you wear them?" How many girls got to help their grandmothers on their wedding day and offer to loan them pearls? Like the necklace, Boop was a treasure.

Boop nodded. "I'd be honored."

Hannah walked behind her grandmother and placed the strand over her head.

Something borrowed.

Someone knocked on the door. "We're ready," Stuart said.

How had Hannah even doubted for a moment that he was Pop's son? He looked just like him. Everyone said so.

"Be down in a minute." Hannah rifled through her purse, then motioned to the bubbes. "She still needs something—"

"No, I don't." Boop strolled to the window and opened her arms. Hannah walked to her and melted into her embrace. Georgia and Doris turned, and they all looked out the window.

And there it was.

The lake.

Something blue.

Hannah's family's South Haven roots entangled with the dunes' spiky brambles, glistened in pieces of smooth beach glass, and surged from between the layers of the violet-, strawberry-, and saffron-colored sky. The stories—most accurate, some embellished, others lovingly invented—dwelt safely within her. She would share the stories with her children, who would share the stories with their children.

Hannah tugged away. Georgia and Doris stepped to the side, allowing Boop a moment alone with her lake. Then Hannah whispered, "It's time to marry Abe."

The sunset radiated around Boop, forming an aura of beauty and hope. She smirked like a girl anticipating a magic trick, but her eyes sparkled with generations of wisdom. Boop smoothed her dress from her waist to her hips, something Hannah had seen her do many times, something, perhaps, that reminded Boop of the curves beneath, how they had changed—but maybe how they felt somewhat the same.

Georgia and Doris headed downstairs. Hannah stood in the doorway holding Boop's bouquet, the combination of flowers her grandmother had selected to evoke her favorite time of day. The small bundle was wrapped with silk ribbon the color of sherbet, replete with purple, red, and orange blooms, filled in with berries and vines.

Boop possessed a spirit more beautiful than all the sunsets and bouquets mixed together. Her heart as brave as any warrior's. What lessons she'd taught Hannah—taught everyone—about family, about love, about being true to oneself while honoring those around you. There was more than a house in the legacy she'd leave behind. Hannah gulped away rising emotion and tipped the flowers toward her grandmother.

Boop accepted the bouquet and closed her eyes as she lowered her nose to the blooms. Hannah imagined her grandmother savoring not only the fragrance in that moment, but the promise of all the splendid moments to come.

Boop lifted her head and opened her eyes.

"How do you feel?" Hannah asked.

"I feel like a very lucky girl."

ACKNOWLEDGMENTS AND AUTHOR'S NOTE

The Last Bathing Beauty is a work of fiction, but it wouldn't have come to fruition without some very real people, especially Charlene Klein. I met Charlene in South Haven in 2016, when I'd already written nuggets of a novel about the beauty queen granddaughter of a Jewish resort owner in 1950s South Haven, and her present-day counterpart. This is where it gets weird and wonderful. Charlene grew up in South Haven during that era and was the granddaughter of Eva and David Mendelson, owners of Mendelson's Atlantic Hotel, a Jewish lakefront resort.

Charlene's generous spirit, friendship, and stories about her teenage years, as well as her present-day life, helped me craft *The Last Bathing Beauty* with deep insight and a profound sense of place. Every time I visited South Haven or talked to Charlene, I learned things I felt I already knew. I was, and remain, connected to this Midwestern lakeside community and its history. This is a bit odd considering 1) I am a native Philadelphian, and 2) I discovered South Haven "by accident" after falling into an online research hole.

I no longer believe in accidents.

I do believe in serendipity.

My literary agent, Danielle Egan-Miller, agrees with this sentiment. She championed this story through all its iterations, and trust me, there have been many. Ellie Roth's attention to detail provided thoughtful questions and necessary corrections. Jodi Warshaw, my Lake Union editor, saw in *The Last Bathing Beauty* pages what we saw—a story about friendship, love, and second chances in a unique setting—and I'm grateful for a trusting and intuitive advocate. Tiffany Yates Martin, my developmental editor, supported and guided me (even on weekends) as I polished this novel to a shine. Danielle Marshall, Lake Union's editorial director, expressed confidence in me and in this story when I needed it most.

Novel writing is both solitary and collaborative. Dawn Ius and Pamela Toler were the best critique partners a writer could ask for, reading many pages at a time, or sometimes one or two, and always telling me what I needed to hear. But it doesn't stop there. Friends and colleagues always stepped up with support, brainstorming, answers, opinions, or company if I asked. Thanks to Kelly Levinson, Sheila Athens, Larry Blumenthal, Elaine Bookbinder and Jim Smith, Alice Davis, Kimberly Brock, Fern and Manny Katz, Lynda Cohen Loigman, Jamie Ford, Ann Garvin, Kelly Harms, Melanie Hooyenga, Susan Meissner, Katie Moretti, Jennie Nash, Kate Pickford, Renée Rosen, Renee San Giacomo, and Judith and Lou Soslowsky. A group hug for Carole Farley, Heidi Gold, Sheryl Love, and Rachel Resnick, for showing me (again and again) the restorative power of old friends. And I mean *old* in the very best way.

Online reader and writer groups are at least partially responsible for preserving my (relative) sanity through the writing and publishing process. Cheers to Bloom, Bloom Bloggers, Readers Coffeehouse, A Novel Bee, Women's Fiction Writers blog readers, Book Pregnant, WFWA, Lake Union Book Club, and all the talented #bookstagrammers. Last but never least, I wouldn't want to do any of this without my trailblazing and loyal Tall Poppy Writers.

This was the first book I've written since moving back to Philadelphia and it often kept me sequestered. My parents, Sarah and

Mike Nathan, were enthusiastic and understanding even when I cut our visits short to continue writing. Hugs to my children (the best adults I know)—Zachary, Chloe, and Taylor—for always asking about the book (and listening when I answered), for being proud, and for tolerating my Bitmoji habit. I love you all.

For historical insight and accuracy, I relied heavily on local newspapers, clothing catalogs, magazine covers, interviews, advertisements, menus, and cookbooks. I used great care to remain true to 1951 South Haven when, for the sake of the story and character development, I took creative license with details, as novelists are prone to do.

I built the fictional Stern's Summer Resort on a foundation of facts from the time, along with my vision for the story, and two overnight visits to the Victoria Resort (formerly Glassman's Resort, popular in South Haven's heyday). Jan Leksich, the owner at the time of my first visit, was kind enough to allow me to stay in a cabin typically reserved for her family, and to give me a tour of the property, while sharing its facts and folklore.

Stern's Summer Resort's fictional location on North Beach is the approximate site of the original Mendelson's Atlantic Hotel, to where Charlene would walk from her childhood home, just like Betty. Unlike Betty, Charlene lived not only with her grandparents, but also with a twin sister, an older sister, and her parents, who owned a local restaurant. While Mendelson's no longer exists, Charlene spends every summer in the house where she grew up. I'm fortunate to have visited her there, spent time on her porch, and soaked in the beach, lake, and lighthouse views. It's my privilege to call Charlene a friend.

If you'd like to read more about the history of Jewish South Haven and the resort era, or South Haven in general, I recommend the following books: *A Time to Remember: A History of the Jewish Community in South Haven* by Bea Kraus; *Jewish Resort Era in South Haven Driving Tour: Catskills of the Midwest* by J. Ollgaard; *Cottages and Resorts on the North Beach: Historic L. S. Monroe Park, South Haven, Michigan,*

1890–1960 by Helen B. O'Rourke, Ken Hogan, and Lynda Hogan; and *A Place to Remember: South Haven—A Success from the Beginning* by Bea Kraus. While writing, I also referred to *Betty Cornell's Teen-Age Popularity Guide* by Betty Cornell.

Essential to the writing of this novel were the countless contributions of the Historical Association of South Haven, namely its director, Sue Hale. When I couldn't find a fact in a book or a newspaper, or online, she was always helpful. Sue had welcomed me to the reopened *Catskills of the Midwest: The Jewish Resort Era in South Haven* exhibit in June 2016. I stepped into the room and back in time, as it had been filled with murals, photos, interviews, memorabilia, and stories. I pulled out my laptop and sat on the floor to take notes and write. After that, Sue introduced me to Charlene.

The rest, as they say, is history.

ABOUT THE AUTHOR

Photo © 2019 Zach Gropper

Amy Sue Nathan is the author of four novels and the founder of the award-winning Women's Fiction Writers blog, named a Best Website for Writers by *Writer's Digest*. She is a frequent speaker and workshop leader, a member of Tall Poppy Writers, and a writing coach for aspiring authors. Amy lives near Philadelphia and is the mom of two grown children and a willing servant to one geriatric dog. For more information, visit www.amysuenathan.com.